THE GATHERING

"A novel so intense and horrific that the spell of evil lingers after the last page has been read."
—*Joan Lowery Nixon*

"I was impressed by the strong control Ms. Carmody has over her style and the way that, like Susan Cooper, she combines actuality with a sense of mysterious threat and impending catastrophe."   —*Joan Aiken*

"The suspense never slackens, and the resolutions of the many conflicts are powerfully wrought. Utterly riveting."   — *Publishers Weekly,* starred review

"Includes enough suspense and unsettling violence to satisfy any horror fan. . . . Contains first-rate prose, intriguing characterizations, and an emotional depth lacking in most of the currently popular teenage horror novels."   —*The Horn Book*

OTHER PUFFIN BOOKS YOU MAY ENJOY

The Gathering

ISOBELLE CARMODY

PUFFIN BOOKS

For Danny and the Regulators

In memory of Bruss

PUFFIN BOOKS
Published by the Penguin Group
Penguin Books USA Inc., 375 Hudson Street, New York, New York 10014, U.S.A.
Penguin Books Ltd, 27 Wrights Lane, London W8 5TZ, England
Penguin Books Australia Ltd, Ringwood, Victoria, Australia
Penguin Books Canada Ltd, 10 Alcorn Avenue, Toronto, Ontario, Canada M4V 3B2
Penguin Books (N.Z.) Ltd, 182-190 Wairau Road, Auckland 10, New Zealand
Penguin Books Ltd, Registered Offices: Harmondsworth, Middlesex, England

First published in Australia by Penguin Books Australia Ltd., 1993
First published in the United States of America by Dial Books for Young Readers,
a division of Penguin Books USA Inc., 1994
Published in Puffin Books, 1996

1 3 5 7 9 10 8 6 4 2

Copyright © Isobelle Carmody, 1993
All rights reserved

This work was assisted by a writer's fellowship from the Australia Council,
the Federal Government's arts funding and advisory body.

THE LIBRARY OF CONGRESS HAS CATALOGED THE DIAL EDITION AS FOLLOWS:
Carmody, Isobelle.
The Gathering / Isobelle Carmody—1st ed.
p. cm.
Summary: When fifteen-year-old Nathaniel moves to a sinister town that
has been bruised by an ancient evil, he finds himself one of those
Chosen to fight the cycle of darkness.
ISBN 0-8037-1716-4
[1. Supernatural—Fiction.] I. Title.
PZ7.C2176Gat 1994 93–31844 [Fic]—dc20 CIP AC

Puffin Books ISBN 0-14-038538-X

Printed in the United States of America

Contents

Evil comes in many shades: fire-red, uniform-blue;
but love comes in white, and transcends the Dark

———

Prelude

• • •

Sometimes you get a feeling about a thing that you can't explain; a premonition of wrongness. Mostly you ignore it the way you would a little kid tugging at your sleeve. You think, What do kids know anyhow?

We drove into the outskirts of Cheshunt at the tail end of an early autumn day, cold and crisp and fading to gold. Sunshine slanting through the car window rested in my lap, warm and heavy as a cat.

I was sleepy and a bit woozy from reading my way through a stack of Phantom comics. As a rule I am not the kind of guy who goes for stories about superheroes from Krypton or talking ducks and dogs. I like *National Geographic*, but I was reading these comics because the lawyer had sent them in a box along with a lot of my father's things that had not sold at auction.

My mother thought comics were rubbish. She only read factual books and medical journals. I had just been a little kid when my parents were divorced and they had not kept contact, but I always had a clear picture of my father in my mind as a big, serious man. The comics were a surprise and made me wonder what else there was about him that I did not know. Naturally I had tried asking my mother, but as usual she said she couldn't remember what he used to read, and that it was A Long Time Ago. She drives me crazy the way she acts so secretive about him, especially now.

Suddenly she coughed in the dry, fussy way she has of getting my attention before she says something. I waited for her to go on again with her usual speech of us making a new start, but she just nodded sideways.

"That's your new school, Nathaniel."

Your school, I thought, because she chose it, just like she chose all the others. Her face had a closed look and she was staring straight ahead, concentrating on the road.

So I looked.

The school was a square slab-gray complex set on an asphalt island in the middle of the grounds, running away to dry, bare-looking flatlands. She had told me Cheshunt was close to the sea. You can go to the beach on weekends, she had said, as if it were across the road from our new house. Except there was no sign of the sea and the skyline bristled with pipes belching smoke into the sky.

Closer to the school I noticed there were no trees or shrubs around the buildings. In fact, Three North looked a lot like a concentration camp. The few bushes along the roadside were stunted and shriveled, empty branches on the side that bore the brunt of the gritty wind flowing across the low hills and over the school. Cold air blew through the window, a bitter blast straight from the Arctic.

I lifted my hand to close the window, but it was shut. I looked around, but all of the windows were rolled up. Even the vents were closed. There was no way that wind could get into the car, yet I could see the fine, downy hairs on my arm flattened under its force.

I looked at my mother, who wore only a light, sleeveless shirt. She did not seem to notice the wind, though her hair was whipping into her face and eyes.

Fear crept through skin and bone and folded itself in my chest as I looked back at the school and felt that wind; the same kind of shapeless terror I felt when she took me to look at my father in his coffin before they closed it and put him in the ground.

"You don't have to," she had said nervously, after doing a song and dance to get me there. It bothered her that I asked so many questions about him. Her wanting me to see the body was so bizarre that I guessed she had this stupid idea that I would forget about him once I saw that he was really dead and gone. But when it came right down to it, she seemed jittery and uneasy. Maybe she was a little scared herself, of what we would see. I went forward, drawn by dread and morbid curiosity.

He had been much thinner than I remembered. It seemed as if death had shrunken him, sucked the bigness out of him. His hair had gone straight and his limbs were stiff as a dried-flower arrangement.

"He's so small," my mother had said in a shocked whisper, as if he were sick instead of dead; as if loud voices would disturb him.

Looking down at that strange, still face, I had barely been able to control the watery horror in my gut. I was suddenly terrified of being so close to a dead body; terrified that by staying there I might somehow catch death.

That's how I felt, staring out of the car window at Three North: like I was looking at something wrong and unnatural, something dead, something bad that might be catching. Might get up and come after me.

And the old nightmare seemed to hover about me, almost real, one stage from visible. The nightmare of running through a dark, wild forest with a monster after me. A shambling, leering thing with a shark's smile, whose reeking breath filled the air around me. The monster that was, since the funeral, sometimes my father; and above, a bloody, full moon rode high in the black night.

But I just sat, still as a bone, tongue glued to the roof of my mouth, eyes watering from the force of the wind.

The car glided around the corner and I let the memory of what had happened slip through the fingers of my mind like fine sand.

Because a feeling like that has no more business being in my life than a dead father.

ONE

The Choosing

The Choosing

1

"Why can't I just board and go back to Nelson High?" I said, trying to keep my voice even in the living-room quiet. She stops listening the minute you raise your voice.

"You know why. There isn't enough money."

"But I could board with Gran. She said I could."

Her expression froze up. "You wrote and discussed this with your grandmother?"

I realized I had made a tactical mistake. She had a real chip on her shoulder about taking charity, especially from her mother. "She suggested it," I lied.

"I won't have you going to her behind my back."

"I didn't go behind your back. She asked me. She's my grandmother."

"She's my mother and she doesn't need the worry of a teenager at her age. You'll make new friends at Three North. You haven't given it a chance."

New friends? I never had any old ones. We never stayed anywhere long enough. In fact, my grandmother was the closest thing I had to a best friend. Besides, I couldn't relate to kids my own age.

"Why bother?" I asked bitterly. "You'll just up and move us in another year like you always do. Why should I keep having to move just because you do?"

"Don't take that tone with me, Nathaniel," she said coldly.

"You think I enjoy moving so often? I do what's best for us both."

I could feel my temper rising because yes, I did think she enjoyed moving. Otherwise why would she do it? Another second and I would start yelling, and that would mean the silent treatment. She is good at silence, a real grand master. I have tried the same tactic, but I always end up talking before she notices I'm being silent, so why bother?

I stared past her at the photographs huddled on the end of the bookshelf. Right at the back was the only one we have of my father. He is holding me, a bald baby in a lemon bunny-sleeper. My mother is beside him in a pale dress, her hands folded in front of her like a praying mantis.

I noticed something I had not noticed before. The baby me had its tiny bone-white fingers wrapped around my father's thumb. Maybe he looks so troubled because of the strength of that baby grip; as if in that second it struck him that I would not be a baby forever, that I would grow up, stretch out into a man, die.

The photograph came in the box with the comics. My mother had none of my father and seemed shocked to see this one. She had kept all the wedding photos except the ones showing him, and the lack of a groom made it look as if she'd married a ghost. I don't know what she did with the others. She might have burned them, or more likely she'd put them in a neat pile in the trash. I guess she must have hated him. Maybe she had wished he was dead.

Sometimes wishes come true.

"This is a good, safe neighborhood."

"I don't know anyone," I said. *I hate it*, I thought.

"You've only been here two weeks. Why don't you join the school youth club? Or the football team."

"I don't want to join any groups. I want to go to Nelson. I liked the teachers and I got good marks."

She frowned slightly, studying me as if I was one of her patients. "What are you trying to prove?"

I just looked at her.

"Nathaniel, exactly what is it that you don't like about Three North?" Now she had her reasonable judge face on. *Give me some evidence*, her eyes said.

"It stinks," I said defiantly. I meant that literally. It did stink. There was a slaughterhouse up in the low hills behind the school, and when the wind blew the wrong way it smelled as if the whole place was rotting. I couldn't believe that sick, smoky stench came from killing cows. She said I would get used to it, but it's not the kind of thing you get used to. Even when the wind doesn't blow at all you can smell it because the cafeteria hamburgers taste of it.

"Don't be ridiculous," she snapped.

I shook my head, knowing I did not have the kind of proof it would take to change her mind about staying in Cheshunt. I hardly knew myself why I disliked the place so much.

I turned away. "I'm going out," I said dully. For a split second I had the old longing for my father to come bursting through the door, telling me that he wanted me to come live with him, that he was taking me.

"Dinner will be ready in half an hour, so don't go far." She sounded satisfied, as if something had been resolved.

I closed the door quietly behind me and went around the back, whistling up The Tod. He is a Chihuahua crossed with some other small dog, but he looks more like a tiny fox. He came up to me, wagging his feathery tail and tilting his head quizzically.

"Walk?" I said.

He responded with a flip of excitement, jumping up and down on his hind legs and generally telling me in dog body language what a great idea he thought this was.

"Good Tod," I murmured, closing the gate behind us.

I looked both ways along the street. It was just about twilight and everything had an unfocused look. The dairy bar and a video shop were in one direction. The park was in the other.

The old lady who ran the dairy bar down the road told me a boy disappeared from the park a few years back. Some nut took him away, dressed him in pajamas, shaved his head, then left him in the mall. They never got the man. Somehow it didn't surprise me that this sort of thing had happened in Cheshunt. I decided to tell my mother that story the next time she started telling me how law-abiding it was. She really flipped out over stories about abducted or murdered kids.

Without really deciding where to walk, I started to head for the park, still thinking about what had happened there. The park was so bland, I found it hard to believe the old woman's story. It was just a neat, mown block with a couple of swings, a monkey bar, and a public restroom. There were only about ten trees in the whole place. It was like a thousand parks you find in any small suburb anywhere in the country.

Hardly anything ever happened there, though the two neighboring suburbs were always in the paper because this gang beat up a man or that kid robbed a 7-Eleven store.

But what could I say to my mother? Cheshunt is too perfect? She would say I was being ridiculous and she would be right.

I sighed.

The Tod was sniffing his way industriously along the fence line, stopping every few minutes to pee, marking the way home like Hansel and Gretel. I had taught the dog to be a homing dog, and I guess he used his own scent to guide him. It had been part of a school project on conditioning.

The Nelson High teacher had told us about these experiments based on research by this guy called Pavlov. They had trained dogs by putting them in boxes with food dispensers and levers. If the dogs ate or drank from the wrong dispenser, they would get an electric shock. Aversion therapy it was called. It means that if you hurt a dog every time it does a thing, it soon stops doing that thing. And if you ring a bell every time you hurt the dog, after a while it will react to the bell as if it was the pain.

That Pavlov was clever, but he was cruel too. An animal would never think of hurting you just to see what happens. Rather than using aversion therapy, I had shown that you could train a dog just as well with pats and dog biscuits.

The Nelson teacher said I should try to keep more detached in an experiment.

By the time we reached the park it was dark and the streetlights had flicked on. Two women were walking a fat dachshund on the other side of the street. They walked close together, taking quick, careful steps, as if they thought the ground might open up and swallow them.

The Tod noticed them and barked a challenge. The women looked over in startled fright and the dachshund gave a hoarse cough as the woman holding its leash tugged on it so hard that she nearly throttled the poor thing.

That was Cheshunt for you. Everybody acted like they were afraid they were being watched. You would see people look behind themselves, as if they feared they were being followed.

The Tod dragged at the leash and we crossed the street to the park. He stopped suddenly and bent to sniff the grass, then whined urgently, as if he wanted me to get down there and have a smell too.

Dogs have a very acute sense of smell, like bears. And each smell must be a little like a story to a dog. But they can only see in black and white. I guess as far as The Tod was concerned, humans *smell* in black and white.

I decided to stick to the streets and jogged past the park to the end of the block and around the corner to Ende Crescent. From there I could see the school in the distance, and I slowed to a walk again. The security lights were on, showing disjointed angles and corners of buildings and asphalt in pools of grainy light.

The Tod gave up sniffing the fence and sampled the air blowing from the school in an interested sort of way. I stopped beside a big, ornate fence post to tip some grit from my sneaker, wrestling with a temptation to go over to the school.

"Hullo," said a voice right next to my ear.

"*Eya!*" I yelped, jumping sideways. Then I realized the ornate fence post was just an ordinary post with a little kid sitting cross-legged on top.

"Is that a dog?" the kid asked softly.

This was not as stupid a question as it seems. A lot of people think The Tod is a strange-looking cat or a pet fox.

"Did you get a stone in your shoe?"

I realized I was standing there like an idiot with my shoe in my hand. I put it back on and laced it up.

"I'm keeping watch," the kid went on in a confiding voice.

"What for?" I asked curiously.

"For the monsters," he whispered. "They come out at night."

I grinned. "Out of where?"

He pointed wordlessly to the school and I felt the hair on my neck stand up.

"It's late," he said, a warning note in his voice.

"So?" I demanded, because I felt stupid letting him spook me. I pushed myself off the fence and jogged back along the street, whistling The Tod after me.

"What about the curfew?" the kid called, his voice swallowed up by the night.

2

That night in bed I remembered something else.

A girl in my science class had told me Cheshunt Park used to be a meeting place for a group of witches years back. A coven, she called it. At first I thought she said an *oven*; an oven of witches. These witches were supposed to have stolen people's pets and sacrificed them to the devil.

Somehow in my mind I must have gotten the park and the school muddled up with the slaughterhouse because when I went to sleep I dreamed the slaughterhouse was actually at the school and was a front for witches; a makeshift coven where they sacrificed people's pets, and the awful smell was not the smell of burning waste, but the smell of death. I had gone to investigate and found them sacrificing The Tod. It was one of those terrible nightmares where no matter what happens you can't move or speak. I had woken the next morning aching all over with tension, the death smell of the dream lingering in the bedclothes.

Walking to the school later I was relieved to find the wind was blowing away from it.

Coming into Ende Crescent I noticed a couple of girls going into one of the houses, carrying clipboards. All the signs of a survey. Houses around schools must get so sick of surveys and walkathons and sponsorships and raffles. There was a lineup at the school gate, with two eleventh-grade boys from the school patrol checking that kids had their grade level badges on. There was a different color for each year.

As I went toward the line, a girl from one of the lower grades came up to me, her hair as white blond and fine as dandelion fluff. There was a vacant look in her face that told me there was something wrong with her, and pity stopped me from shying away when she reached out to touch me.

Her hand was icy cold and the contact gave me a tiny static shock.

The air-raid siren went off and I started. Actually it was the school bell, but it sounded exactly like the sirens out of the film of *The Time Machine* with Rod Taylor. In the film the sirens were the signals for the cannibal Morlocks to come out and feed.

A police car glided up to the curb and a policeman got out of the driver's seat. All the kids in the line stopped talking at the sight of the uniform. Maybe they thought they were going to be arrested.

The passenger door opened and Seth Paul, head captain of the school patrol, climbed out.

"What did *he* do?" asked a girl behind me in a stage whisper. I wondered too. Seth Paul was one of those golden boys who could do no wrong. He was a brain, he looked like one of those perfect guys off Coke ads, and both kids and teachers liked him.

"Dumbo," sneered a wild-haired kid called Danny Odin. "That's his father: the Pig Man." He made an oinking noise loud enough for both Seth Paul and his policeman father to hear.

I stifled the urge to groan aloud and tried to make myself invisible.

Danny Odin was the school's pet mad dog. He was one of those legendary bad kids you know about from the first day in a new school. His name was forever being called over the PA system. He was like some sort of wild kid that had lived with the wolves all his life and was not sure how humans were supposed to act.

Every now and then he reverted to wolf. I had actually seen him bare his teeth at a teacher.

"What are you looking at?" he snarled now, pushing his face at me. His eyes were so pale, they looked transparent.

Fortunately he was distracted as the policeman swept through the gate with his son. He was dark and handsome like Seth, but older and harder. His eyes looked like bits of stone, and he passed us as if we were a clump of toadstools.

"Come on," said one of the boys at the gate, and the line started moving again. Danny Odin pushed through the pair and ran off laughing.

When it was my turn to be inspected, the biggest of the boys, a beefy kid with flat green eyes, looked me up and down. His name was Buddha, and like all of the school patrol kids, he was aggressive and bossy.

I tried to go through the gate, but he put his hand up to stop me.

"Did I give you permission to go through yet?"

The line behind me fell silent and my heart started to speed up.

"What do you think, Jacko? Do we pass this kid?" Buddha asked his gap-toothed comrade.

I made to push past him, but Buddha shoved me back in the chest so that I trod on the toe of the kid behind me. "You wait until I'm ready," he hissed.

"Let him through," said someone behind me. I looked over my shoulder to see a big guy with long, dark hair drawn back into a ponytail.

"What's with you, Bear? Are you his bodyguard?" Buddha's mouth twisted up into a sneering smirk.

There was no answer and his smile faded. After a long minute he took his hand away and I went through, half expecting him to grab me from behind. I felt churned up inside, thinking I should have said this or that.

"You okay?" Ponytail asked gently, falling into step beside me.

I nodded, wondering why he had bothered standing up for me.

"I'm Bear Mahoney. You're new, aren't you?"

I nodded. "I'm Nathaniel Delaney."

"You have to bluff people like Buddha. That's all it is. Bluff." He seemed to be talking to himself as much as to me, but I looked at him and thought it was a lot easier to bluff when you were six feet tall and built like the Terminator.

"Hey. Where are you going?" he called.

I looked back at him. "Class."

He shook his head. "First up every second Monday is general assembly in the hall."

The hall was the newest part of the school, built with money raised by the local community committee. It was a big utilitarian rectangle, with a pine floor that had overlapping circles and lines needed for different sports painted on it, and a stage up at one end. The walls were white and clean, and there were windows all along both sides of the building. One side looked out onto the football field, the other onto the parking area—which was off limits to students—behind the school cafeteria.

Kids were jostling and milling around, arranging themselves by grade level and facing the stage.

Bear took his place beside me and I realized that he must be in my grade. He was wearing a sweater instead of his blazer with the color badge. He was big enough to be a senior. Probably he had failed a couple of years.

There was a low hum of talk as we waited for the teachers to take their places along the sides, and I thought how different it was from the ear-splitting racket at Nelson High. Here no one yelled. They all murmured in quiet, polite voices so it sounded like the wind rustling through the leaves rather than seven hundred or so school kids.

"Where did you live before?" Bear asked in a low voice.

"Lots of places," I said.

The hall settled down as the vice principal, Mr. Karle, came to stand behind the microphone. I had met him the first day my mother brought me up to enroll. I had been surprised to learn he was also the head coach. He had impressed my mother with his talk of the school policy of noncompetitiveness and community spirit.

He had said the purpose of sports was to help people be better coordinated, fitter, and to teach them to work together. Without a competitive element no one was ever left out or humiliated, and he never let the class go beyond the capability of the least able in the group.

I guess he said that because I was kind of compact for my age.

Mr. Karle was quite a small man himself. He was bald too, and his head was tanned and shiny like polished wood, but there was an aura of physical strength about him.

He tapped on the microphone and raised his hand. I was close enough to see the flash of green as the hall lights caught the tiny greenish metal ring he wore on his little finger.

He smiled down at us and instructed us to sit.

"Welcome to assembly . . ."

I sensed Bear stir alongside me and looked at him out of the corner of my eye. His face was impassive, but he seemed tense.

Mr. Karle started out reminding twelfth-grade students to see him after assembly if they had not yet paid their money for some excursion. Then he flicked over a page of his notes and read out some schedule changes. He told students to tell their parents that a special meeting of the community committee had been called for Wednesday night, and that the youth club would meet the following week.

17

"That concludes school messages." His voice became serious. "Now Chief Paul wishes to speak to you. Give him your full attention."

He stepped back from the microphone and Seth Paul's father strode up the steps onto the stage and positioned himself behind the microphone, his legs planted one on each side as if he meant to frisk it.

"Good morning, students."

There was a mumbled response, and I saw Mr. Karle frown. I knew from gym classes that he liked answers to be snappy, the whole group speaking with a single, clear voice.

"You may have heard on the radio or read in the *Examiner* that someone broke into the Willington Maritime Museum last Friday," the policeman said. "There were two witnesses whose statements suggest the person may have been a student from this school."

His eyes ran back and forth along the rows as if he were reading a giant book. I guessed he was searching for a spasm of guilt in someone's face.

"The description of clothing worn by the intruder indicates the person wore a yellow Three North sweater."

I felt immediately guilty, the way you do.

"We have reason to believe this break-in may be connected to the recent vandalism of a monument at Cheshunt cemetery." Chief Paul glanced around at Mr. Karle, then back at us.

"Now, we are sure someone here knows who broke into the museum, and we are asking that person or persons to come forward. I am sure you are as proud of the reputation young people have in this area and will want to protect it as much as I do. Cheshunt is a model neighborhood, and we want to keep it that way. Thank you."

He stomped off the stage, and Mr. Karle came back to the microphone. "I expect the person who broke into the museum to own up to his deed." He stopped and I realized he actually expected whoever it was to get up and announce himself. Fat chance, even at a weird school like Cheshunt, where kids were polite to teachers.

No one spoke and Mr. Karle frowned. "Very well. I am very disappointed. Assembly is over."

No one moved for a minute, it was such an abrupt dismissal.

"I wonder if something is missing," I said to Bear as we filed out.

"Who knows." He seemed bored by the thought of the robbery.

"It must have been something pretty valuable if the police came to the school about it."

He gave me a peculiar look. "You don't know this school. If a thimble disappeared, there'd be an investigation."

"What do you mean?"

"Forget it," he said, and moved away into the crowd.

I stared after him for a minute, puzzled, then I looked over my shoulder. Mr. Karle had come down from the stage and was talking to a girl with buckteeth. I thought she might be confessing to the break-in from the look on her face, but she just handed a sheaf of pink pages to him.

"Watch it!"

I had walked onto the heels of the girl in front of me. She scowled and turned back to her friend.

"I say we should take it to the Gathering. Find out who did it ourselves."

"Yeah." The friend nodded fervently and they wriggled their way through the bottleneck at the door to the hall.

That was the name of the school youth club, I remembered. The Gathering.

3

First period of the day was science, which was a disaster.

Second period was math. Three North was about five steps ahead of Nelson, which meant I had some catching up to do. Miss Santini gave me extra stuff to fill in the blanks. Bear was in the class, but he sat at the side of the room on his own. Maybe he was regretting starting up a conversation with me.

"I don't care what the dog did to it," Miss Santini told another kid who failed to hand in his homework.

Last two periods were free so I retreated to the library. You looked like less of a loser if you sat in the library alone, rather than outside. I hated new schools, though changing school so often had taught me how to blend in fast. But I had never managed to figure out how you made friends with total strangers. Maybe that was why I did well academically. I had no social life to distract me.

The library was the only part of the school that wasn't ugly. It was a big bluestone building with stained-glass windows and a barrel-vaulted ceiling that birds nested in. According to the school librarian it was once all there was of Three North when Cheshunt was just a one-horse town in the middle of nowhere. There was even an old sepia photograph of students from about sixty years back, the names written underneath in neat lettering. A bronze plaque on the wall beside the photograph said the whole building was listed by the National Register of Historic Places, which was probably why whoever designed the rest of the school had not managed to ruin the library too.

I plugged away at the math until the bell rang, then sat back and stretched, glad the day was over. The other kids in study hall must have sneaked out early, because the library was empty except for me and a girl on the far side with odd, spiky red hair sticking up in all directions.

She looked like she was doing homework too, bent over a notebook writing furiously. She was wearing a sweater about ten sizes too big for her, and a green badge that said she must be in my grade.

The library door swung open and a teacher came in. She looked across at me, then went over to the girl.

"That will do, Nissa. You can go now."

The red-haired girl gave the teacher a cool look, then she handed over the notes she had been writing, gathered her blazer and bag, and walked out without saying a word. The teacher shook her head and stalked across to the librarian.

"Problem?" the librarian asked softly.

"That girl is the bane of my life."

The librarian looked surprised. "I thought she was a bright student."

The teacher scowled. "Students like Nissa Jerome should not be in ordinary schools. I don't have the time to keep setting special assignments for her because she finishes other work too quickly. She should be made to work at the pace of other students." She glared down at the pages the girl had given her. "And now I am supposed to go home and spend my time reading through this. I can't even make sense of half of it."

The librarian's eyes flicked to where I was sitting and they dropped their voices so I couldn't hear any more.

Later that night, walking The Tod after my mother had gone off to work, I found myself thinking how it must feel to have teachers mad at you because you were smarter than they were.

Not that it was something I was ever likely to experience.

I had decided to jog and I did a circuit of the whole neighborhood to get in shape for track training. Despite his short legs The Tod ran circles around me. But by the time I reached the outer perimeter of the school, it was dark again and we were both panting hard.

I stopped to catch my breath and stared across at the school buildings with a strong sense of déjà vu because of the previous night.

The Tod whined and twitched his nose, and I wondered what he could smell. He took a step toward the fence, then looked back at me.

I was thinking about jumping the fence, when a security car came around the corner and pulled up under the streetlight.

I sighed and straightened up, expecting a lecture about trespassing. The Tod started barking frantically as the security guard got out. His face was shadowed by the brim of his hat, and for one second I wondered if he actually had a face. Then he tipped his head back and the light fell on a thin, lined face folded around sharp brown eyes. He looked about sixty.

"Shut up!! Shh!" I told The Tod, but he went on yapping hysterically.

The old security guard grinned. "Game little critter, isn't he?" He looked up at me. "Sister's got one of those yappy dogs. Heart of a lion. Good as an alarm." He rattled his keys and looked around in that characteristic Cheshunt way. I realized it was probably a nervous mannerism, but I couldn't figure out why he would be nervous with a heavy-looking gun hung visibly in a holster attached to his belt.

"You new around here?"

I nodded.

"Thought so. Local youngsters don't come here after dark."

"I was just walking my dog," I said.

He nodded. "I'm from over Willington myself. Live there

with the wife. My territory covers Willington West and all of Cheshunt."

"Lot of ground to cover in a night," I said, because it seemed like I should say something. "I guess you must have had some adventures. Burglars . . ."

He grinned. "People always think that we spend our nights scaring off burglars. Truth is it's more often youngsters with spray cans. Not in Cheshunt though, leastways not now. Wasn't always such a quiet spot." He looked faintly troubled.

"My mother said it's practically crime-free."

He nodded, but not as if he really agreed. "These days it's the quietest section on my rounds." He rattled his keys again. "Listen, I wouldn't hang around here at night. Seems there's a pack of feral dogs that roam around sometimes. Not surprising they'd choose the school. Some places are made for trouble. Years ago, some bad things happened here."

"Bad things?" Our voices had dropped nearly to a whisper. I had the feeling someone was watching us. But what would they have seen? An elderly security man in a whispered conversation with a nondescript brown-haired kid. So what?

The security man had a faraway look in his eyes, like he was seeing something on the inside of his eyelids. "An old caretaker was murdered by a young fellow from the school. Burned him to death. Terrible thing, but lots of bad things happened back then. Cheshunt was a dangerous place. Trouble. They say it's changed, but I don't know." He shuddered and the movement seemed to bring him back to the present. He gave me a startled look, as if he had forgotten whom he was talking to.

"Why did the boy burn the caretaker?"

He frowned. "How should I know? I wasn't even born then." His voice was oddly aggressive, so I stopped asking questions. He looked as if he might say something else. But he coughed and put the keys purposefully in his pocket.

"I'd get on home if I was you," he said briskly. "Don't forget curfew." He nodded and strode away, disappearing into the shadows.

I watched him go, thinking about the curfew.

The pamphlet stuck under the door the day we arrived had welcomed us to the neighborhood and urged my mother to join the community committee. It had a lot of bylaw information, and the bit about the curfew was last. It said no one was to be out in the streets after ten at night without a specific reason. If you were under eighteen, you weren't allowed to be in the street after nine without your parents' permission, except in an emergency.

Naturally my mother had thought it a good idea and claimed it was one of the main reasons Cheshunt was such a quiet, law-abiding neighborhood. I thought it was fascist, but she told me I was being childish. I asked her what happened to anyone who broke the curfew, but she hadn't known.

I looked at the luminous dial of my watch.

It was getting near to nine, and it was half in my mind that I would flout the curfew and see what happened.

Then I remembered the security man's words and thought better of it.

I must have had the heebie-jeebies because when I jogged past the park, it looked bigger and darker than usual, and I could have sworn I saw two sets of yellow eyes staring at me from the monkey bars.

4

My mother had not come home by morning, which meant she was working a double shift, and outside, the wind was blowing the wrong way and the world was filled with the death smell.

I could hardly concentrate at school, the stench was that bad, but maybe it was true that you could get used to it since no one else seemed to be bothered by it.

First period was American studies, and the only interesting thing about it was that the red-haired girl from the library was in it.

She sat by the window and stared out. No one spoke to her or sat next to her, but she seemed not to care. She looked as if her thoughts were a million miles away. In spite of the weird haircut and sloppy uniform, she had the sort of face that you couldn't help looking at. She reminded me of a cat, but not a house cat. Some kind of exotic wild cat with bright blue eyes that would scratch yours out if you went near it.

The teacher had a nervous tic in one eye that made him look like a mad professor. His name was Mr. Dodds, and he started out by saying history was about facts, not truth, which seemed very profound to me.

I wrote it in the margin of my book and stared at it for a minute.

"Most often when students think of studying history, they think of looking in books written by historians," Mr. Dodds said. "Can anyone think of any other ways of getting information about the past?"

No one put their hand up. It took a better teacher than Mr. Dodds to get kids volunteering answers right off. He seemed to slump a little, then his brows raised in surprise.

I turned to see that the red-haired girl had her hand up.

"Nissa?" he said doubtfully.

"Primary sources," she said with faint impatience, then she went back to staring out the window.

"Er. Yes. Primary sources. That's correct."

There was a knock at the door, and Bear came in. He was wearing a leather thong around his head, his hair scraped back in a ponytail.

"Sorry I'm late."

Mr. Dodds frowned at him. "Not a good way to start the day."

Bear gave him a mild, confused look, as if he was not sure what language Mr. Dodds was speaking. It was the best technique for passive aggression I had ever seen, and I reminded myself to try it on my mother some time.

Mr. Dodds sighed. "Sit down and take off the headband."

Bear obeyed, choosing to sit by himself at the back. I felt slightly offended since there was an empty seat next to me.

"The sort of history you read in history books is secondary information," Mr. Dodds went on. "That is, someone has looked at primary sources and produced a book based on facts that are composed according to their own attitudes to history and the subject at hand, as well as straight conjecture."

"You mean, they made it up?" someone asked.

Mr. Dodds beamed. "In a sense that's exactly what historians do. The study of history is a bit like a jigsaw puzzle. A lot of the pieces are missing and a historian tries to work out what the missing bits are, based on what he or she has. Now primary information is what a historian uses. Can anyone name some types of primary information?"

It was kind of interesting and the class was warming up like a sluggish car. I thought if it were true that history was made up like that, how could you ever trust a history book? How could you know what really happened unless the historian had seen what happened. Even then you couldn't be sure. In an accident, witnesses' stories were always different.

"Letters?" someone offered.

"Good, Peter. What else?"

"Newspapers?" a girl suggested uncertainly.

Mr. Dodds nodded. "Of course. And farm records and court reports and government documents and ticket stubs. Then, there are people's memories. Living history."

"How do you mean?" someone piped up.

"I mean, you can actually talk to people about events in history that they lived through. The problem with those sources is that when older people die, their memories die too. More and more, historians are looking at ways to preserve those living memories. This is called 'oral history.' "

There was a slight rustle of interest.

"This semester we are going to be doing individual projects based on living primary sources. That is, an oral history project. Now, the easiest source available to you will be your own grandparents."

"What if you don't have grandparents?" a boy called out.

"Then you will just have to find some other elderly person who will talk to you, Phillip."

The class laughed.

"Obviously, you won't be able to go back more than about a hundred years, so that cuts out settlement, but you might be able to find someone who can remember World War I, or certainly the Depression."

"But what's the topic?" someone called.

"That's for you to define," Mr. Dodds said.

Everyone groaned.

"I know. It's a terrible thing for me to ask you to think for yourselves." There was a titter of laughter. "As I said, you might decide to cover World War I, or the Depression. But those subjects are still too big. You have to narrow them down a bit. That's where your source comes in. If you're interviewing someone who was a politician in the Depression, he or she will have different things to say than a mother with three kids. Or you could choose a subject closer to home. You might like to research how one of the factories came to be established. That would mean talking to someone who remembered the early days. An employee."

"Can you use books as well?"

Mr. Dodds nodded. "Books, newspapers, photographs. But the focus of the assignment is the interview. Now this project will be worth forty percent of your final mark, and I want to see some ideas by next class."

There was a muted groan at the mention of marks.

At lunchtime I went into the library to check out some books, racking my brains for a topic for the assignment.

I was debating calling my grandmother to see if she could suggest something, when the old school photograph on the wall caught my eye. I went over for a closer look. Nineteen kids of varying ages dressed in old-fashioned, baggy clothes stood in front of the library. No houses or streets. The picture was blurred and faded at the edges, but the faces were clear enough.

Working it out, I guessed the eldest students would have been about fifteen or sixteen when it was taken. Maybe a little older. That would make them in their seventies now. And maybe a couple of them still lived in Cheshunt. If I could find one of them I could do an interview about the early days of the school for the oral history assignment.

I went up to the librarian's assistant. "That old photo on the wall. How would you find out what happened to the people in it?"

She looked startled. "You mean the students? I guess they'd all be dead by now. Wait. No, maybe not." She frowned, pushing John Lennon glasses back up her nose. "Is this for school?"

"An oral history project."

"All right. Let me think. You could go through old school records. We have those, but you'd need permission from Mr. Karle. Or you could simply look up the last names in the phone book and try to track them down that way. And I'd try some old age homes."

That really made me interested because my mother was a nurse in an old age home. It was like a sign.

Before long I was armed with a list of names from under the photo and a whole lot of possible avenues to try tracking down the former students.

When the bell rang for the end of lunchtime, I was astonished because it had gone so fast. I thanked the librarian's assistant.

"Makes me feel a bit like a detective." She laughed, then her smile faded.

Buddha and another of the school patrol guys had come up behind me. Buddha grabbed my arm in a bruising grip. "You Nathaniel Delaney?"

I was startled, then I realized he must have had my picture pointed out in the enrollment book. Getting one taken had been an enrollment requirement.

"Mr. Karle wants to see you."

"What for?"

Buddha scowled. "Just move it. You're supposed to report to his office right after lunch."

5

The front office receptionist let me stew a full three minutes before noticing I was there. The placard on her desk said her name was Miss Bliss.

"I'm supposed to report to Mr. Karle."

She lifted her plucked eyebrows, as if I were an idiot who had asked her something incredibly stupid. Then she nodded at the orange plastic seats against the wall.

A door with Mr. Karle's name on it was firmly closed and there was no way of knowing if he was in there or not. Two boys walked past and stared at me, as if I were on death row.

I heard some heavy footsteps, but it was Bear Mahoney. He bypassed the receptionist and sat down on one of the orange chairs. There was a mark on his forehead that said he had just taken his headband off. He nodded in a friendly way that puzzled me after the way he had ignored me in class.

"What are you up for?"

"Who knows?" I said glumly.

"Karle's in charge of school discipline, so you must have done something wrong."

I grinned at him and was startled to see how serious he looked.

"What do you mean?" I asked uneasily.

I must have talked louder than I meant to because the receptionist stopped typing and looked across at us. Bear didn't answer until she was typing again.

He hesitated, then leaned nearer. "Be careful of what you say in there. Don't look in his eyes too much."

The door to Mr. Karle's office opened and he ushered an older girl out, her eyes red from crying. "You did the right thing, Amy. The necessary thing," he told her soothingly.

His smile faded as he turned to face us. "Bear," he summoned, and went back into his office.

Bear followed without a backward glance, and the door closed. I sat there trying to figure out what he had been trying to tell me. It was twenty minutes before he came out, and the red band mark on his head was beginning to fade. He winked and I felt like a sucker.

"I think you should give some thought to what I have said, young man," Mr. Karle said heavily. "You are building a reputation for yourself, which is exactly why it was suggested that you might be responsible for the break-in. And get your hair cut to regulation length. It is untidy and shows a bad attitude."

Bear gave Mr. Karle his politely uncomprehending stare.

"And make sure you get to school on time tomorrow. I am aware you are in the habit of arriving late."

Bear sloped away, then Mr. Karle was turning to me. "Nathaniel, come in."

His office was square and pale, like everything else in the school, the desk set exactly in the center of the room, one chair behind and one facing it. It reminded me of the kind of room in jail where a prisoner goes to talk to a lawyer, except for a stack of pink pages on the desk held down by a silver paperweight.

Mr. Karle sat himself on the edge of the desk and waved me to the chair. "I'm sure your last school was excellent, Nathaniel," he said pleasantly, giving me a level look.

He had eyes the indefinite shade of the sea before a storm. Not quite green or blue or gray, but a mixture of all those colors. I thought of what Bear had said about not looking in them, and wondered if Mr. Karle were one of those teachers who regarded it as a sign of disrespect.

"Three North, however, is a new school with different priorities and different rules, and you must learn to abide by them."

"I haven't broken any rules."

He held up his hand. It was big and sun-browned, hairless, like his head. There were almost no lines on his palm. His eyes looked at me over the tips of his fingers, and I felt a strange falling sensation. For a second it seemed as if the whole universe were shifting and the only safe, steady things were Mr. Karle's eyes. They were not like stormy seas after all. They were still, safe pools.

It was hard to think, staring at him like that, so I looked past him and fastened my eyes on the paperweight. It was not the shapeless blob I had first thought, but one of those collections of metal shapes heaped up artistically on a magnetized base.

"Nathaniel," Mr. Karle said. "In this community, in this school, respect for your elders is paramount. Particularly for figures of authority such as policemen and teachers. Now, Mr. Ellis mentioned to me that you were having trouble accepting some of the concepts in a class. Would you call that a fair summation of your attitude in science yesterday morning?"

I looked up and instantly his eyes bored into mine.

"I asked you a question, Nathaniel. Would you call that a fair summation?" His voice was much richer and more compelling when I was looking at him. But more importantly, he sounded as if my answer really mattered. He made it seem like he would listen to me even if I did yell or get mad.

I nodded.

Mr. Karle's habitual smile deepened. "Nathaniel, disagreeing in class is not the problem. What is a problem is the way you chose to express your disagreement. Your lack of respect for your teacher. Now, it was Mr. Ellis's recommendation that you see the school counselor, Mrs. Vellan."

I had no idea what to say. The last thing I wanted was to go to a shrink. My mother would have a fit.

"I think we can sort this out between the two of us. I want us to be friends, Nathaniel, but we must be able to be honest with one another. There must be trust. Now let's just examine your dispute with Mr. Ellis. He said you had been discussing the social habits of the ant world."

The memory of the argument in science was like a splash of cold water, and I dragged my eyes away from his.

"He said you found the ant society . . . disturbing." Now his voice sounded distant. Cold.

I shrugged, remembering how angry Ellis had been when I said I thought ants were no more than genetically programmed robots. Normally I would have kept that kind of thought to myself, but the whole lesson had been so weird.

"Mr. Ellis is a brilliant researcher," Mr. Karle went on. "His specialty is the insect world, and he has had studies published all over the world. You understand, I'm sure, how he must have felt, having you contradict him. You must allow that he would know more about ants than a schoolboy."

"I wasn't arguing with his knowledge of ants," I said indignantly. "It was just that he started talking about how humans could take a lesson from the way they act. He talked like they were a higher life-form or something."

The truth was, Mr. Ellis had gone a little crazy, but I stopped short of saying that.

"All I did was answer his questions," I mumbled.

Mr. Karle chuckled. "Mr. Ellis asked you to name positive characteristics of ant colonies that humans would do well to emulate. You told him ants would make good slaves, because they obey orders and work till they drop. But that they could never be artists or poets or great writers because really great people were nonconformists. Is that the gist of it?"

I nodded, thinking Mr. Ellis must have taken notes because it was not just the gist of what I had said; it was exactly what I had said.

I looked up as a grin spread over Mr. Karle's face. There was something unpleasant about the smile. I thought a maniac who killed people for fun might smile like that. Then it disappeared and I wondered if I had imagined it, because Mr. Karle just looked concerned and sympathetic.

"I think Mr. Ellis was simply trying to impress on you the cooperative nature of ants. You find it difficult to cooperate with others? You think cooperation pointless?"

"Ants have wars."

"Not against their own nest. They do not have internal wars," Mr. Karle corrected gently. "And their ability to submerge themselves and become a single mind enables them to do things an individual ant could not achieve. As a team can do in sports. One player cannot work alone."

He stood up suddenly and crossed to look out the window over the football field, to watch two people walking across it. I recognized the loping walk and wondered if he realized one of them was Bear. On the other side a window opened out onto the cafeteria cul-de-sac and a big blue garbage truck was backing into the yard.

"Nathaniel, here at Three North we set great store by harmony and cooperation." Mr. Karle paced across the room and around behind me.

"Cheshunt is a special place," he said almost dreamily. "Because of what it has become, people are drawn here. People like your mother who are seeking refuge." He paused to let that sink in, and I stared at the desk sculpture, wondering if the pieces would be heavy.

"Cheshunt is not the place for people who want to stand out, because loners are troublemakers. Those individualists you seem so fond of are the ones who make life hard for everyone else." Mr. Karle's voice suddenly had an edge.

"Don't swim upstream, Nathaniel. There is no room for salmon at Three North."

A buzzer sounded and he excused himself. I wondered why he couldn't take the call in his office. "Chief Paul asked if you . . ." Miss Bliss's voice drifted through the door opening.

I sat forward in the chair and looked over my shoulder. Mr. Karle had his back to the door. All of a sudden I felt like I was going to pass out. I swayed in the seat, grabbing at the edge of the desk to support myself, and knocked my arm against the paperweight. Shapes spilled across the desk. I scooped them back onto the stand hurriedly.

The last piece was a flat metal circle with the center cut out. I was startled to find it was hot when I picked it up. Hearing Mr. Karle hang up, I thrust the circle back in place.

"Have you joined the school youth club yet, Nathaniel?" he asked in a friendly voice, coming to sit behind the desk. "We like all of our students to belong, and I think it would help you to have a better understanding of the way we operate at Three North."

My student advisor had mentioned the club, and a couple of the school patrol kids came around to the class, asking everyone who wasn't a member to join. I had even considered it, but I didn't like the way he was putting the pressure on. It woke a stubborn streak in me.

"Do I have to join?"

"You don't have to," Mr. Karle responded after a long moment, his voice distinctly cooler.

I said nothing, determined not to be railroaded. I felt his eyes boring into me. He was trying to stare me into doing what he wanted, but I looked down at my knees.

"Perhaps you need some time to think it over," he said at last. "Detention here at school all day Saturday."

Mr. Karle rose, crossed to the door and opened it. "You think about it, Nathaniel."

6

The Hanging Judge was waiting for me when I got home. My mother had never heard of being innocent until proven guilty, and Mr. Karle had gotten in first.

"He gave me the detention for not joining the club," I tried to tell her.

"Are you saying you didn't shout at your science teacher?" This was the first time I had ever gotten detention, and having the school call her about it had freaked my mother right out.

"It was a disagreement! But that's not why he gave me the detention!"

"I see," she said softly, her eyes reproachful. "Nathaniel, I don't know what has gotten into you since we came to Cheshunt, but you needn't think you can manipulate me into leaving by misbehaving at school."

My mouth fell open. "I wasn't trying to do anything. I told you. I had an argument with the science teacher, and whatever he told you, Mr. Karle gave me the detention because I refused to join the school youth club."

"Mr. Karle was very kind on the phone. He is worried about you being such a loner, but I doubt he would punish you for it."

"If you'd just let me tell you what happened."

"I won't have you behaving like an irresponsible hooligan. You will respect your teachers and control yourself."

I gaped at her. "I can't believe this!"

37

"And now you are shouting at me," she warned softly.

I tried to calm myself, but I was boiling mad inside. All she cared about was that I kept my voice down. I could have just murdered someone, but that was fine so long as I didn't talk too loudly!

"Does that mean I'm supposed to respect my teachers even when they lie, like Mr. Karle?"

"Oh, for heaven's sake, Nathaniel. Don't be ridiculous. A teacher doesn't give a detention for not joining a voluntary club. You must have gotten it wrong."

For a minute I felt confused. Maybe I *had* gotten it wrong. Surely it couldn't have been the way I remembered. Why would Mr. Karle care whether or not I was in the youth club?

My mother calmed down. "I'm sure that's it, Nat. It's all just a misunderstanding. Mr. Karle will accept an apology. He was very kind on the phone."

That word again. I thought about telling her a lot of mass murderers are kind to their mothers and their dogs. Her idea of calling Mr. Karle "kind" made me angry all over again. He had lied to my mother and I was supposed to apologize?

"I didn't make a mistake and I'm not apologizing or joining his stupid youth club no matter how many detentions I get." It felt good to shout and I stood up abruptly. She drew back and for a minute she actually looked frightened, as if she thought I was going to hit her.

That stunned me, and all the anger drained out of me. I felt suddenly empty and depressed.

"I'm taking The Tod for a walk."

She just turned away without saying a word.

Outside the night was dark and cold. I tried to dismiss the whole stupid business about the youth club and the detention from my mind, whistling up The Tod. He rushed at me, wagging his tail and barking in a frenzy of welcome. Instantly I felt better. Dogs are good at that.

"Hey, buddy," I said, picking him up and cuddling him. He

licked me in the eye and I felt like howling, more because of my mother and me than over what had happened at school. He cocked his head anxiously, sensing my turmoil. I set him down, clipped on the leash, and closed the gate behind us.

I let him lead the way. I walked because I was too depressed to jog. If only I could talk to her properly, get through to her.

I thought of the man my mother had gone out with for a while who had gotten me into running. I had liked him a lot. He had been quiet like her, but silence with him was not a weapon. It was not a shutting out. I used to jog with him some mornings. He always set the pace, throwing instructions over his shoulder: "Lean into the hill," or "Fill your lungs," or "Push into the pain barrier."

He told me the pain barrier was a threshold sports people reached. When he said that the first time, I thought he was trying to tell me about some kind of sports academy you could go to. But it turned out this barrier was a mental thing that tried to fool your body into thinking it had run out of energy. You had to resist the pain telling you to stop; you had to keep on going and suddenly the pain barrier would dissolve, and you could go on for a lot longer. Defeating the pain barrier meant your mind had control of your body rather than the other way around. That, he explained, was the difference between an amateur and a true athlete.

Back then I would hit the pain barrier pretty fast with a cramp or shortness of breath. "Tough it out," he would say. I always ended up stopping, panting and clutching at my side, with him shaking his head and giving me sorrowful looks.

He stopped coming around after a while and my mother never said why, but I kept on jogging, trying to beat the pain barrier. Sometimes I felt there was a kind of pain barrier in my mother that I kept coming up against.

I made myself jog and The Tod ran ahead, pulling at the leash like a bloodhound on the scent. We slowed to a walk along the edge of the park because it was muddy in patches, the ground soft and treacherous underfoot. The Tod waded through a puddle and I realized I would have to bathe him when we got back.

He hates baths. He always stands in the water rigid and shuddering with loathing, no matter how little water I use. I never worked out the difference between the puddles he happily plunges through and the dreaded bath.

He knows the word too. Bath. As soon as I say it, he cringes and puts his ears down. My science-project partner, Lewis, had wanted us to use baths as aversion therapy when we trained The Tod to find his way home.

"He'll be just like Lassie," he had said.

I told him it was a stupid idea. I also told him Lassie was about a dozen dogs with a couple of tricks each. "You think too much, Nathaniel," he had said, disgusted when I offered my idea for a positive conditioning project. "Pain works better."

I broke into a jog as soon as we left the park street. I paid no attention to where we were going, giving myself to the physical sensation. I didn't want to think anymore.

Then The Tod stopped and I did too.

Somehow we had wound up at the school again. The hair on my neck prickled because it was the third night in a row we had come there without meaning to.

The Tod whined and tugged at the leash and I let him draw me forward and across the road.

At the fence line I looked around, but tonight there was no sign of the security guard or the kid keeping watch for monsters. I unclipped The Tod, dropped him over the fence and vaulted after him, giving myself no chance for second thoughts.

It was very dark and a foul, constant wind blew across the football field. Out in the middle, with the streetlights behind me, I had the feeling I was on a vast plain. I turned to look back at the line of houses on the other side of a sea of inky blackness, their windows squares of light. Reminders of warmth.

I shook my head, thinking how things could seem so distorted at night. Because it was so dark, the stars were super-bright in contrast. I noticed one bigger than the rest and close to the horizon.

"Look, Tod. It's the Dog Star."

He growled.

I let my eyes drop to the school. It seemed surrealistic and alien in the patches of security light. I jammed cold hands in my pockets, wishing I had grabbed a coat. I thought about turning back, but when I looked for The Tod, he had disappeared. My heart sank as I noticed a slight movement right at the edge of the asphalt—The Tod disappearing around the side of a building.

It wasn't until I was on the edge of the light that I remembered what the old security guard had said about feral dogs. My heartbeat sped up.

I walked past the science building, too uneasy to call out. Suddenly I had a powerful urge to be inside. I came to a steel door, but didn't bother to try it. There was no way it would open.

Sidling around the corner, I was startled to find myself beside the outdoor restroom attached to the end of the building. I don't know where else I had expected to find myself. But everything felt strange and unfamiliar.

Hearing another sound closer than before, my heart started to pump. Very carefully I tried the wire security door to the restroom, but it was bolted. A faint urine smell drifted out. I wrinkled my nose, thinking fleetingly that my memories of Cheshunt would always be of the smells.

I froze at a rasping sound somewhere close. When I was younger, I used to sleep with a towel pinned around my neck to stop Dracula from sinking his fangs into me. Even after I grew out of that, I always felt fear in my neck first. Hearing that noise, I had an overwhelming urge to turn my collar up.

What I did, though, was to step back into the narrow gap between the boys' and girls' restrooms.

For a long moment I stood completely still, listening to a piece of loose tin grind and rattle in the rising wind, and wondered if The Tod had gone home.

"Shh," a voice hissed.

"I can't hold it any longer," said a second voice. Both voices seemed to be coming nearer, but there was no one in sight.

"Shut up, stupid." The first voice was fierce and urgent.

"Don't call me stupid. The security guard left an hour ago. I'm getting out." The scraping sound went on for a minute and I realized with horror that it was coming from the steel grating underneath my feet. *They were in the storm drain!*

"It's not the security man I'm worried about. It's the dogs," said the first voice. There was a bit more scuffling and grunting. I stepped back off the steel grate just as two sets of fingers poked up through the gap.

The grate tilted and I saw a pale blob of a face a split second before I backed deeper into the gap, pressing myself into the shadows. One of the figures that appeared switched on a flashlight, and for a moment the other was illuminated clearly in its beam. I stifled a gasp of recognition. It was Bear, and the boy holding the flashlight was quite a bit smaller. I nearly groaned aloud when I saw his face.

Danny Odin.

"You're imagining things again."

"Smart ass," Danny snapped. "Wait until one of them chases you in the dark."

"There's nothing here and we better go. It's almost curfew."

"Shut up, stupid. I'm trying to listen."

"Don't call me stupid. Come on. Give me a hand with this."

"Carry it yourself. Serves you right for getting something so big."

They went off wrangling around the other side of the building.

I leaned weakly against the wall. My legs felt like lumps of jelly and my heart was still galloping, but I was curious too.

When I was certain they were gone, I came out from between the restrooms. By the sound of their voices, they had gone toward the cafeteria. The only building past that was the library and that was a dead end.

I headed that way too, sticking to the shadows and stopping to listen at every turn. I felt a stitch beginning in my side, the pain barrier out to rein me in. Ignoring it, I stepped around the corner into the shadowy cafeteria courtyard, only to be spotlighted in a fierce white flashlight beam.

"Well, if it isn't Sherlock Holmes," sneered Danny Odin.

7

"I wasn't following you," I said. "I was walking my dog."

"Oh yeah? So where is it?" Danny demanded, thrusting his face toward me like a closed fist. I prayed the security man would come back and see the flashlight.

"I don't know. He must have gone home."

Danny snorted in disbelief. "Without you?"

"I trained him." I wondered if there was any hope of talking myself out of the mess I had walked into. If it were anyone but Danny, I might have stood a chance. I looked at Bear. Surely he hadn't saved me from Buddha to let Danny Odin maul me?

"You came here just by chance?" Bear said slowly.

Danny elbowed him in the stomach. "Idiot! He was snooping. Spying on us! No one comes here to walk a dog."

"But he's new," Bear said, frowning.

"He was spying," Danny snarled.

"I wasn't."

"You were!" He glared at Bear. "You saw how he sneaked around the corner. Did that look to you like he was walking his dog?"

Bear gave me a speculative look, verging on suspicion.

"Who sent you?" Danny demanded of me triumphantly.

I sighed. "No one."

Danny lowered his head to his chest so that he was staring at me from under the blunt cliff of his forehead. It made him look like a mad troll. "We can't let him go. We'll have to get rid of him."

Up until then I had been worried about getting a beating, but something in Danny's face reminded me of what the security man had said about the guy burning the old caretaker.

"He didn't see anything," Bear pointed out.

"He saw us take stuff from the cafeteria," Danny retorted. "We can't let him give us away. We have to make sure he can't tell anyone about us."

"I think we better wait and ask the others."

"Can't you decide anything on your own?" Danny taunted Bear.

The others? I wondered what I had stumbled on. Was there a whole gang of them robbing the school? Without meaning to, I took a step backward, wild thoughts of making a run for it in my head.

Danny reached up his sleeve with horrifying ease and slid out a switchblade knife. It was homemade and that made it seem more dangerous than a store-bought knife with a pearl handle. His knife looked lethal and businesslike; not a knife for show.

I stood very still, my mouth slimy with fear.

"Danny," Bear said urgently. "Danny, don't stab him."

They both froze at the sound of a car passing the school.

"My bike!" Danny hissed, pale eyes flaring with panic.

But the car did not stop.

"That was lucky," Bear said. "You better hide it."

Danny nodded, handed him the knife and the flashlight, and sprinted away, leaving Bear and me staring at one another.

"What is this?" I asked at last. It didn't make sense that they would be stealing food from the school cafeteria when there were computers and electronic gear worth thousands in the rest of the school.

Bear collapsed the blade, dropped the knife into his pocket, and pointed to the package he had brought with him. "You take that and I'll take this."

Bewildered, I did as he said. It weighed a ton. "What's in here?"

Bear kicked the door shut with his heel, ignoring my question. "This way."

Since he was a lot bigger than me, it seemed safest to do what he wanted. I followed him around the corner onto the walkway leading to the library, then at his instruction put the package down on the steps.

The neon Exit sign inside the lobby gave off a weird glow that made him look sick. He squinted out into the black night, reminding me of his namesake.

"That Danny—" I began, then stopped.

"You scared of him?" Bear asked, as if he read that in my smell. I heard animals can smell the change in sweat that comes with fear. Maybe Bear could too.

"He was really going to stab me. He's crazy."

Bear nodded. I was unsure of whether this meant he agreed Danny was crazy or whether he would have stabbed me.

"Are you going to tell me what's going on?"

Bear only shook his head.

I looked out into the darkness. "Who are you waiting for anyway?"

He took so long to answer, I thought of asking if he needed thinking music. Before he could speak, Danny reappeared.

"Why the hell did you bring him here?"

"I had to get the stuff out of sight in case someone comes," Bear said calmly. He nodded at the package. "He carried that."

Danny's mouth fell open. "What if he had taken off with it?"

"He didn't try," Bear said in a way that made me fervently glad I hadn't.

"I was just . . ." I began. Danny whirled and snatched the flashlight out of Bear's hand, switching it on me again.

"You shut up . . ."

"*Switch that off!*"

All three of us jumped about three feet in the air at the sound of that low, angry voice coming out of the dark.

The flashlight beam wavered and flicked off, and Nissa Jerome stepped into the neon light, white to the lips with fury.

"Are you crazy waving that light around? Why don't you take out an ad in the newspapers. Then we can let the few people you missed know we're here?" She sounded furious.

She spotted me and her eyes widened. "Who the hell is this?"

"Bear brought him!" Danny announced.

"Danny wanted to kill him," Bear said.

"He was spying!" Danny shrilled. Nissa's pasty face shone unhealthily, the neon glow turning her cobalt blue eyes into stainless steel.

"You were hanging around the library last night," she said with dawning suspicion.

I was surprised she had even noticed me.

"See? He was spying on you!"

"Calm down, Danny-O," Nissa snapped, and to my astonishment he did, glaring at me malevolently. She threw Bear a questioning look.

"I don't think he was spying. Snooping maybe." Bear shrugged.

Another car passed, but this time it slowed down and we could hear it pull in the driveway.

"Shit," Nissa said. "Quick."

They dragged the box and package into the shadows, and Bear pushed me into the corner. My heart pounded as I saw a police car roll slowly past the cafeteria and out of sight. We could hear it drive right around the whole school, then out of the gate and away.

Nissa was the first to relax and move away from the wall. She propped her hands on her hips and faced Bear and

---

47

Danny. "You two are idiots bringing him here. You should have just chased him off. Even if he reported it, it would have just been your word against his."

"Bear brought him here!" Danny protested. "I was going to silence him."

Nissa shook her head exasperatedly. "Were you born this stupid or did you take lessons? You think that's what we're supposed to do? Kill people?"

A defiant, sheepish look flashed over Danny's face.

"He chose to answer the Call," said a new voice.

"*Lallie*," Nissa said, whirling around and sounding relieved. "I went looking for you."

The pale girl with the flyaway mop of white-blond hair who had touched me in the school yard stepped out of the shadows onto the step beside Nissa. I gaped to see The Tod trotting alongside her.

Nissa dropped to her knees so that she was looking up into Lallie's face. "What do you mean he answered the Call?" Her voice was as soft and low as a cat purring. There was a kind of nakedness in her voice when all the toughness was stripped away.

I looked at Lallie and found her watching me, a faint mischievous smile on her lips, as if she knew exactly what I was thinking. This was impossible, but I felt my face heat up anyway. Her lips twitched and she looked back at Nissa.

"He is the fifth and last of the Chosen," she said in a windy little voice that spoke of asthma or hay fever.

"Wha-at!" Danny moaned. "Jesus H. Christ!"

8

Nissa gave Danny an unfriendly look. "You heard what Lallie said, Danny-O. He's with us."

"Just like that?" Danny demanded. "We don't know anything about him. What if Lallie made a mistake?"

"The Choosing is over," Lallie said dreamily.

A picture came into my mind of the way she had come up to me just outside the school ground and tagged me. Maybe it was some kind of game.

"What do you mean, the Choosing? Who chose me?"

"No one," she answered, looking momentarily less vague in her surprise. "You chose to answer the Call."

"I didn't choose anything," I said. My mother did all the choosing in my life for me, I thought bitterly.

"We'd better get inside," Nissa said briskly. She reached in her pocket and took out a set of keys, holding them up to the neon glow. For a moment her eyes caught mine, the keys dangling between us.

Then she turned and slid the key into the library door, pushing it open.

I gaped. How did Nissa come to have the library keys? And what the hell had I gotten myself into?

Bear winked at me and nodded at the package. "Bring that, but be careful."

"I'm not vandalizing anything," I warned him.

Bear grinned and picked up the box. "You have it all wrong."

I lifted the package, grunting at the weight of it and trying to figure out how to get away without inciting the wolf boy into more murderous plans to dispose of me. The Tod went in the door behind Lallie, which gave me the creeps because usually he acted like every stranger was an ax murderer.

Nissa said coolly, "We're not planning to mess up the library or anything."

Inside the lobby The Tod was sitting near Lallie's foot, and as I watched, she dropped her fingers down and let him gnaw softly at the ends. The hair on my neck prickled because how did she know he liked to do that?

There was a click and Nissa locked the doors behind us. I expected her to come across and unlock the doors leading into the main part of the library, but instead she went to a big trophy case set against the side wall. Bear put the box down and he hooked his fingers together to boost Nissa up on top of the case.

She opened out a stepladder that had been stored flat up there and climbed up, pushing open a section of the crumbling plaster scrolling. Then she heaved herself into the attic and disappeared.

Danny went up on the case next and Bear passed the box up to him. Groaning and swearing, he heaved it to Nissa and between them they manhandled it into the attic. The whole thing happened with a minimum of words.

"I'll take him," Lallie said, scooping up The Tod. He blinked at me from her arms, sleepy and relaxed, and I knew I was dreaming. He barely tolerated being picked up by my mother, let alone a complete stranger.

Bear hefted them both up to Danny who helped them into the attic and went up after them.

A faint orange glow showed through the opening, but there was no clue as to what was up there. I knew just getting inside the lobby was breaking and entering, but I was too curious to take off now that I had the chance. Besides, maybe they were testing me to see if I'd take the chance to run.

"Hurry up," Nissa snapped from above.

I let Bear hoist me up. He pulled himself up behind me, then followed me into the attic, hauling the ladder up behind him.

I stared around, amazed. The attic was huge and that meant the fancy barrel-vaulted ceiling of the library was mostly a facade. The real roof was the roof of the attic, with massive exposed beams jutting out and down to the floor, sloped at the edges. Two old-fashioned hurricane lamps hung from nails, illuminating the whole area in overlapping pools of flickering light. There was a mattress bed made up against one wall, and beside it an upside-down crate stacked with books. On the other side of the space was a kitchen area, with pots and pans, a portable gas stove, and a table fashioned from a large storage crate. Next to this were two old car seats with ripped upholstery. There were books on all the beams and some piled on the floor.

I looked at Bear. "Who lives here?"

"I do," Nissa said calmly. "Help Bear unpack the box and we'll have something to eat. We'll talk when we're all here."

Lallie came over and took Nissa by the hand. "He will not come tonight."

Nissa frowned. "What do you mean? He promised."

Lallie shook her head solemnly. Bear elbowed me gently and I helped him drag the box he had been carrying across to the kitchen area. He unpacked it while Nissa poured some of the jug water into a dented kettle and lit one of the burners, her face grim.

"Who won't come?" I asked Bear softly.

Before he could answer, we heard a car pull into the school ground. The others were instantly alert, like deer scenting a lion. Nissa moved first, going to a dormer window shaded by dark cloth down near the end of the attic. The others moved toward her in a restless little tide, and I let myself be carried with them. I had no earthly idea what was going on, but their air of apprehension was infectious.

Nissa relaxed as the car went by without stopping, shaking

her head and pulling the shade cloth back. She looked at Lallie. "It's dangerous meeting tonight if he's not going to come." There was an angry edge to her voice.

Lallie said nothing, but her eyes flickered my way. Nissa gave me a hard look. "What's your name then?"

"Nathaniel," I said.

"Well, Nathaniel, I hope you're worth the risk," she said.

Dressed in jeans splitting at the seams and another shapeless sweater that could have doubled as a tepee, Nissa was all sharp edges. Even her face seemed to be made up of feline angles— her pointed jaw, the perfectly straight nose, and the heavy arching brows. Her blue-black eyes . . .

"I think you've stared long enough," she said haughtily. My face burned.

"What if the dog barks and someone hears?" Danny demanded. He was sprawled on one of the car seats, glaring over at me.

Nissa gave him a weary look. "Can it, Danny-O." She went over and began to arrange the tins and packets Bear had unpacked on a beam. On the other car seat Lallie patted her lap and The Tod jumped up in a springy bound.

"What did you do with the package?" Bear asked me. I pointed to the floor near the trapdoor, and he told me to bring it over. I set it down with a thump and watched as he untied the strings, unpeeling layers of crumpled newspaper. At first I thought he had wrapped up a rock, then I saw it was a big, rough stone bowl like a Neanderthal housewife might have used for mammoth stew.

There was a sticker on the side of the bowl that read "*Maritime Museum.*"

I looked at Bear incredulously. "*You* were the one that they were talking about at assembly!"

He nodded, blowing dust out of the bowl. "Luckily they didn't get a good look at me."

"Are you sure of that?" Nissa asked worriedly.

"I was called up to the office, but it seems the witnesses thought I had blond hair." He grinned.

Nissa ran her hands over the stone, then looked over her shoulder. "Lallie, come and see what Bear came up with."

"The bowl of healing," the little girl said softly, her hair floating like a pale halo around her head.

Bear and Nissa exchanged a startled look. I must have looked the same way, only more so, because Lallie couldn't even see the table from where she was, let alone the bowl.

"Did you know what he would bring?" Nissa demanded, looking annoyed.

Lallie ignored the question, setting The Tod down and coming over. "Let me see the other things."

Nissa went to the bed and reached under the mattress, withdrawing a long, rigid object wrapped in a blanket. She put this beside the stone bowl and folded back the cloth. Inside was a rusted sword.

My mind did a sidestep. "You broke that off the monument at the cemetery."

"Pretty quick," Nissa said, giving me a surprised look. She held it up, her lips curving into a triumphant smile. The first I had seen. If anything, the smile made her look harder. "An avenging angel lent me her sword."

"The sword of strength," Lallie wheezed.

Danny brought out a stout, cone-shaped package. Unwrapped, it turned out to be a wire and papier-mâché version of the Olympic torch. "The torch of justice," Lallie said.

"Is this a witchcraft thing?" I said.

"Oh, boy," Danny said, rolling his eyes back in his head.

Just then the water in the kettle began to bubble noisily, overflowing onto the stove.

Nissa hurried to switch off the gas, and Lallie reached over and touched my hand with a single cold finger. "The symbol shows the secret truth of the one who chose it." She lay back against the chair and closed her eyes as if she were exhausted.

"Give us a hand clearing these off the table for tea," Bear said, as if nothing out of the ordinary had happened. They all just assumed I would stay. I wanted to. The mystery unfolding in the attic was infinitely more exciting than going home to a dark, empty house. I helped lift the collection off the table, stacking them on the floor.

"What are they for?" I asked curiously. "Is it some kind of initiation ceremony?"

Bear shrugged. "Kind of. You'll understand when you get yours."

"Mine?"

"Each of us has to have one."

"Then it is a game?"

He gave me a somber look. "It's no game." He turned away.

"Who wants a drink?" Nissa asked.

"I'll just have hot water," Bear said.

"Hot water?" Danny echoed. "How come?"

Bear crossed to stand beside Nissa. "Tea's bad for you. So's coffee."

"What about hot chocolate? That's okay," Danny retorted, following him.

"No, it isn't. That's bad too. If you ever gave too much of it to a dog, the dog would die. There's some sort of chemical."

"Bull! You made that up."

"It's true," Bear said. "It's lethal to dogs."

"Well, what's that got to do with anything?"

"I'm just saying."

"Well, I'm human," Danny said triumphantly.

"You sure about that?" Bear demanded.

I drifted over to where The Tod was curled up on Lallie's lap again. He opened his eyes and flapped his tail. Lallie stroked his silky butterfly ears, and I couldn't help smiling at the dopey, swooning look on his face.

"He loves you," Lallie said. She gave me a long unfathomable look. "Animals hear the Call too. Did you know that? But few

54

answer it." She frowned, her cloudy eyes intent. "Now that you have come, you have to find your symbol."

"Why?" I asked, humoring her.

"It will help hide you."

A coldness came over me. "Hide me from what?"

Lallie's eyes widened until it seemed they might overcome her whole face. "Don't you understand? Can't you feel?" She looked really insane for a second, then she leaned nearer, dragging me closer so that her lips touched my ear. "He's looking for you. The symbol will hide you from him."

Suddenly Nissa was kneeling beside us, and gently she unfastened Lallie's fingers from my sweater. "Tell *Nathaniel* how to find his symbol," she said.

Lallie stared at her with frightened intensity, but slowly the vagueness seeped out of her eyes. "Yes." She looked back at me, her eyes wide. "You have to look inside your own mind. It's there, waiting for you to find it. When you know, you must get it and bring it here."

"Why?"

The fear came back into her face. "No more. Don't ask me any more."

Suddenly The Tod sat up and licked her chin. Lallie laughed in delight and hugged him. The spell was broken and at once she was just a girl with vague eyes.

I looked past her at Nissa, but she only shook her head warningly and moved away.

"I'm starving. What's to eat?" Danny demanded.

"Beans," Bear offered, looking at the label of the can in his hand.

"Ugh!" Danny stuck his fingers down his throat and made vomiting noises. "Wouldn't mind a burger with ketchup."

"Burgers are ninety percent blood plasma," Bear announced.

9

Nissa would not let us leave the attic after we had eaten because of the community committee meeting due to take place that night. Luckily my mother was on night shift so she wouldn't know when I got home.

As we waited, Danny wandered up and down the attic restlessly, a wolf on the prowl. Lallie and The Tod curled up together on the bed and slept, and Bear read.

Nissa sat opposite me at the card table, nursing a cup of tea, a faraway look in her eyes.

"How come you live up here?" I asked impulsively.

She shrugged. "The old lady I lived with died one day when I was at school, and her house was sold to cover her debts. I had nowhere else to go."

"How did you find out about this place?"

She smiled grimly. "You might say it found me. I was doing a modeling project of the library and the measurements showed the building was a lot higher outside than inside. I guessed there was a lot of space up here, so when the old lady died, I decided to take a look. I stole the keys and got them copied. It was close to the school, the rent was right, and I can take as many books out as I want."

I wondered what had happened to her mother and father. Maybe they were dead. I had a sudden vision of my father in his coffin and shivered.

"What are you thinking? You look like someone died."

I was startled into telling her.

"Oh," she said, taken aback.

"It's okay. I thought you might have known . . . like Lallie knows things."

She was no fool. She knew right away that I was probing and a guarded look came over her face. "No, I'm not like Lallie. I don't think anyone is. She's . . . special."

People often use the word *special* to describe people who have something wrong with them. There was something wrong with Lallie all right. But there was more to it than that. There was some mystery here.

"What happened to your father?" Nissa asked, changing the subject.

Usually I hated to talk about it, but up there in the attic felt like time out of the real world.

"He was killed in a car crash, but we were already divorced. I mean, he and my mother were, so I didn't see much of him anyway."

"Did you like him?" Nissa asked, which was a strange question.

"I was pretty young when he left, and he never came to see me after that. We moved around a lot too."

"Why did they split up?"

I shrugged. "I don't know. My mother never talks about it."

"My father left when my mother got pregnant," Nissa said. "When I was born she was living with the old woman who died. Mrs. Kennett was mad as a meat ax." She grinned and I was startled because this smile made her look completely different, softened the edges.

"The old bat always thought men were out to get her," she went on, half laughing. "You'd get on a bus with her and she'd start screeching at some poor guy who just happened to look at her a second too long."

"What happened to her? Your mom, I mean?"

The smile faded and I was sorry I asked. "Sometimes I think

the whole parent thing is a con job, you know. I read that kids from a single-parent family are better adjusted. I figure I'm even better off with none."

"How did you get mixed up with someone like Lallie?"

A shutter fell over her face then and I knew I had blown it. I expected her to go quiet and cold, but she leaned forward angrily. "Listen, buster. I don't know why Lallie thinks we need you, but that's the only reason I didn't let Danny punch your head in."

I took a deep breath. "I'm sorry, but those things she said about symbols and someone looking for me . . ."

She glared at me and sipped at her tea in jerky controlled movements. Then she seemed to calm down. "Okay. Look. Lallie is not like ordinary kids. She sees things no one else does. I know she's strange but . . ."

"Car!" Danny hissed urgently from the window.

"The lights!" Nissa rapped. She pinched the flame out in one lamp and Bear extinguished the other, plunging the attic into a blue-tinged darkness that lightened as our eyes grew accustomed to it.

Bear, Danny, and Nissa were huddled at the window.

"Who is it?" I whispered.

Nissa stepped back. "The head of the community committee, who else? Take a look," she invited.

Apprehensively I peered out into the night. At first I could see nothing. Then I spotted a man walking across the asphalt from the parking lot. Loping along beside him were two huge hairy dogs. Just before he went out of my sight he passed under a security light. I couldn't see his face, but the top of his head gleamed and I knew at once who it was.

Mr. Karle.

"That's who's looking for you," Nissa whispered. She looked at me, her eyes full of shadows. "And for us."

A trickle of icy premonition ran down my spine.

It was well after five in the morning before Nissa would let us leave the attic, though everyone who had come to the meeting had long gone.

I was amazed they let Lallie go first and alone, but no one else found it odd. The rest of us left together, detouring to collect Danny's bike from a clump of bushes.

He coasted along beside us, trying to do wheelies and bumping up and down off the curb. I asked Bear outright about Lallie.

"I guess you better ask Lallie those kind of questions," he said, giving me Nissa's warning look. Then he began telling me how his mother thought he and Danny were out hunting rabbits. If spotted, he said we could say we had all been hunting.

"Without a gun?" Danny asked skeptically.

Bear grinned. "Sure. We were spying out the land. Seeing if it was worth coming back with guns."

"What was that business about symbols and Lallie?" I persisted.

Bear chewed on his top lip. "Lallie told you. You have to get a symbol."

"But why? She said it would hide me. Hide me from Mr. K—"

"Don't say his name!" Bear cried.

I was shaken by the fear in his eyes. They really believed what Lallie had told them.

"We call him the Kraken," Bear explained. "He can feel it if you say his name. We can't talk about him until the symbols are forged."

"I don't understand. How could he possibly hear us say his name?"

Bear looked uneasy. "We're not supposed to talk about this until we all have the symbols."

He plodded on, a closed, stubborn look on his face.

I took a deep breath, recognizing a good silence when I saw one.

A dog barked and Danny barked back. Then The Tod barked.

"Shut up," Danny snapped.

"You started it," I said indignantly.

"Someone will call the cops if you two keep on bellowing," Bear said pacifically.

"Not the cops!" Danny hooted in a cartoon voice and rode ahead.

"It's after curfew," Bear explained.

"What happens if we get caught? Do you get arrested?"

"You can't be charged because it's not an actual law. You'd be sent to Velcro—Mrs. Vellan. She's the school counselor. She makes like a headshrinker, but the common opinion is that she's the one whose head needs shrinking. She believes there are no bad children . . ."

"Dere are only des-turbed children." Danny finished the sentence in a weird accent I presumed must be Mrs. Vellan's. *You'd know*, I thought, watching Danny slalom along the broken white line.

"Why is there a curfew anyway?"

"It's supposed to keep the street free of delinquents."

"If that's all that happens, why was Nissa so worried about us being caught?"

Bear gave me a slanting sideways look. "It would draw attention to us and he might wonder about us."

Mr. Karle again. "Wonder what?"

Bear ran his big hands over his head. "Lallie said not to talk about this yet."

I gave up. "All right, then who else was supposed to come tonight?"

Bear hesitated, then shrugged. "Seth Paul."

"*Seth Paul*! You've got to be kidding!"

"He ain't so perfect," Danny sneered, pedaling backward.

I stared blindly ahead. If Seth Paul wasn't perfect, he was pretty damn close. "His father is a policeman," I added.

Bear nodded bleakly. "Yeah, and not just any policeman. He's a good friend of the Kraken. Most likely he came tonight too. They set up the community committee together."

"The police," I muttered, shaking my head.

"Yeah. Hard to believe, isn't it? Everyone knows teachers and cops are the good guys," Danny sneered, appearing suddenly on the footpath ahead, riding straight at us. At the last second he veered, clipping The Tod who yelped in pain.

"You idiot!" I yelled, enraged.

The Tod whimpered as I fingered his paw. I felt like killing Danny.

"He won't be back," Bear said. "He lives down that way. Is the dog all right?"

I put him on the ground and he trotted off favoring his front paw.

"Damned idiot," I fumed. I looked at Bear. "How come you hang around with such a jerk?"

Bear stuffed his hands in his pockets with a sigh. "This is as far as I go. You said you lived past the park?"

I nodded, still mad.

"See you in school then." He turned to go, then he said over his shoulder, "Listen. We've made it a rule not to be too friendly at school, so if the Kraken does suspect one of us, he won't immediately guess who the rest of us are."

"And who are we?" I asked, frustrated.

"All I'm saying is when I said 'see you,' I meant that was about all I'd do. Okay? And you better keep a low profile too."

I stood watching him stride away down an overgrown side lane until he was swallowed up by the shadows, my mind in turmoil. As I walked the rest of the way home, The Tod trotted along at my heels contentedly, no longer limping.

I sucked in deep, faintly salty breaths of air, glad the wind was blowing in from the sea instead of from the slaughterhouse. The Tod glanced at me, then raced on ahead to the park.

It was dark and deserted at that hour, and wind hissed through the trees making them sway, dim silhouettes in the gray pre-dawn. Again, in the dark it seemed as if the park was much bigger and deeper, just the edge of a great wilderness. I squinted across the road, thinking it really did look like there were a lot more trees. The Tod looked over too, and growled. I shivered, then thought about Nissa living in the attic on her own. I tried to imagine myself living as she did and knew I would never have stuck it out. No wonder she was so different from the other girls. And they knew it too.

Normally girls would torment a girl who was different, but they took no notice of Nissa. It was as if she was some other sex altogether and therefore none of their business.

I found myself picturing the way her eyes lost their tough wariness when she looked at Lallie. Nissa had said Lallie saw things other people didn't. That didn't surprise me. There was something wrong with her and they all knew it. But still they went along with all the things she had told them. What had she seen in Mr. Karle that made her so afraid of him? And how did the police fit in?

Did it have something to do with the things they had stolen?

I came around the elbow in my street. The gray sky was transformed gradually into a fiery red as the sun began to rise. I blinked, murmuring, "Red sky at night—shepherd's delight. Red sky in the morning—shepherd's warning."

I looked down the street at my house.

Parked outside was a police car.

My heart started to gallop. I bolted along the street and up the front path, almost squashing The Tod as I slammed the gate closed behind me and unlocked the door. All I could think of was how Nissa had come home one night to find the old woman she lived with had died.

I ran into the living room. Stopped.

My mother was sitting on the edge of the couch between two policemen. They all looked up.

Her face crumpled. "Nathaniel. How could you do this to me?"

10

"Where have you been all night? I was worried sick."

Even white to the lips, my mother kept her voice calm and that made me mad. If she had been genuinely frightened, she wouldn't worry about how loudly she talked. She wouldn't be so controlled.

A policeman, with a face like a bull terrier, said, "I presume this is the missing lad?"

The other policeman closed his notepad with a snap. He was very fat and reminded me of one of those big blubbery elephant seals, a dugong. Or maybe a rhino with mean squinty eyes. "Where have you been since last night, boy?"

"I . . . went for a walk," I mumbled, trying to figure out how come my mother was home. Her shift must have gotten out early.

"Are you aware the community here has set a curfew?" the first policeman asked.

I nodded.

"Do you have a good reason for breaking that curfew?"

"I forgot about it," I said, startled at how aggressive I sounded. It was just the way the police were talking to me, as if I were a criminal. They were interrogating me, and my mother was just sitting there with her white face and her knees pressed together, letting them.

"I wouldn't take that tone of voice, son. We don't get much call to deal with delinquents in Cheshunt. But we'll be happy

64

to make an exception, if you force it," Dugong said in a tough voice. "Young people need to be kept in order."

"I haven't done anything," I muttered. From what Bear had said, I was pretty sure they couldn't arrest me for breaking a community curfew, but I didn't have the guts to say that to them because maybe they would arrest me for something else.

Dugong gave me a disbelieving stare. "I suppose you know about the break-in at the Maritime Museum? We have been warned by the school that there may be a gang of young people operating in this area. I don't suppose you know anything about that?"

My heart was thudding so loudly, it was a miracle he couldn't hear it.

"I told you, I went for a walk. I forgot the time."

Dugong turned to give my mother a pointed look, and the other cop poked me hard in the chest with a stiff finger. "This is a good neighborhood. Not so long ago it was rough and it was unstable. It was as bad as Willington and Saltridge, but with the help of the school and the community committee we cleaned it up. We don't want it backsliding because of a couple of bad apple kids."

Bull Terrier grunted. "You better straighten yourself out, kid, or we'll do it for you." He patted my mother's arm. "You give us a call if you have any more trouble with him."

I stared at the ground as they left.

"Nathaniel, you were very rude to those policemen," my mother said when she came back. "They were just doing their jobs and they were very kind."

I looked at her, shaking with rage. "They acted like Nazis! How could you call the police on me like I was some kind of criminal!"

She gave me a shocked look. "Nathaniel, don't talk like that. When I came home early and you weren't here, I was worried, so I called the police. You think I liked doing that? I did it for you."

I shook my head and the words just busted out of me. "You did it for yourself, the same way you do everything."

She stared at me incredulously. "I don't know what has happened to you, Nathaniel. You used to be caring, thoughtful. Now . . . I don't know what you are. Where were you last night?"

She sounded really upset, and that got to me because she was always so controlled. "I went for a walk . . ." I began. I don't know how much I would have told her, but she drew herself up and gave me a disbelieving look.

"A walk?" Her voice was sarcastic, as if I had said I went to visit the fairies at the bottom of the garden.

I felt like smashing her in the face. "Yeah. A walk." I turned and went out of the living room and into my bedroom. She didn't want to listen to me any more than she ever had.

She followed me. "You weren't with that gang the policemen were talking about, were you?"

I ignored her. Gave her some of her own silence back.

"What are you doing?" she asked sharply as I threw my bag on the bed and started rummaging in my drawers. She probably thought I was running away from home.

"I'm getting ready for school," I said flatly, without looking around. "Is that all right?"

There was no answer, then I heard the car start up and realized she had been wearing her uniform. That meant she was doing a morning shift. It explained how she had been home to notice my absence. Just my luck.

It was too late to sleep but too early to go to school, so I had a bath instead. Lying in the tub, I felt the strange tensions of the long night melt out of my bones. I floated drowsily with my eyes closed, then rolled onto my stomach and let myself go limp, holding my breath for as long as I could. I practiced being a fish lying on the bottom of a stream. A salmon resting in the shadows.

After a while I lay back, drowsing on the edge of sleep, when I thought of what Lallie had said about getting my symbol. I had no intention of going back to the attic, but I wondered what my symbol would be.

Nissa's had been a sword, Bear's a bowl, and Danny's a torch.

I thought over what she had said about figuring it out and closed my eyes. I tried to clear my mind so that an image would come. Irrelevant thoughts kept drifting in. I thought of Seth Paul's father and the things I had said to my mother. I thought of writing a letter to my grandmother and I thought about my math homework.

I opened my eyes, exasperated. It was hopeless.

Try harder.

I sat bolt upright. Lallie's voice had been so vivid that for a second I thought she had really spoken. I lay back again, determined not to think of anything. Gradually the thoughts stopped intruding. My mind felt dark and warm, as if the bathwater had leaked into my head. I had a peculiar sensation of floating downward.

Then a picture of Mr. Karle came into my mind. He was smiling his happy murderer smile, but his eyes were dead and lifeless. His lips were moving, but though not a sound came from them I knew what he was saying. He was telling me not to be a salmon.

Then he slapped his hand down on his desk. The magnetized sculpture flew apart but in slow motion, pieces flying out in all directions.

One piece floated toward me, spiraling around and around until it seemed to hang right in front of my eyes.

It was the flat metal disc I had seen in Mr. Karle's office.

You must get your symbol, Lallie's voice urged.

I opened my eyes.

The bathwater was freezing cold. I had fallen asleep. I leapt up and checked my watch.

It was quarter to nine!

I saw Nissa in the school yard. She behaved exactly as she always had—as if I didn't exist. The whole night seemed more like a dream than ever.

On the way to class I noticed Seth Paul sitting with a group of other twelfth-grade kids. They were all laughing and talking about a mural they were going to paint. There was no way I could imagine him in the attic with Nissa and the others.

First period was science with Mr. Ellis. There were two classes in the room at once, as well as some kids doing individual projects. I noticed Danny among them. He looked at me but I turned away, still mad at him for running over The Tod.

I made for the back of the room, hoping not to be noticed. The last thing I wanted was a repeat of the previous science class.

The subject for the day, Mr. Ellis said, was arachnids. Spiders, he added in a sinister voice.

He had a couple of jars with dark, hairy tarantulas, and another jar containing a small deadly looking spider.

"Size matters less than the sort of spider and its venom," he said, and unscrewed lids to gasps from the kids in the front row, tipping one of the big spiders in with the small one. For a minute they sat crouched at opposite ends of the jar, then the little one ran forward and pounced. A moment later, the big spider folded its hairy legs and curled up in a ball, dead.

"Oh. That's cruel," said one of the girls.

A shadow fell over my desk, and I looked around to see Danny slide into the seat next to me. "That's life," he said softly. "Kill or be killed."

I ignored him, concentrating as Mr. Ellis outlined the spider world. He showed us some slides of a spider eating an ant, a spider eating another spider, and even one of a spider eating a bird.

"It's an arachnid feast," Danny murmured.

I thought the pictures were pretty good. Whoever had taken them must have had a lot of patience. You couldn't talk to insects and ask them to pose. You just had to wait.

Mr. Ellis saved the best till last. He showed a color poster of a big spider being eaten by a whole lot of ants. He must have gone through his collection to find it so that he could show it to me.

His eyes bored into me when he said ants were able to defeat animals many times their own size because they were able to submerge self-interest and work together as one.

"History shows us quite clearly that humans who behave as the ants do are capable of conquering the greatest single hero," he concluded triumphantly.

"History is lies," Danny said aggressively, fortunately in a low voice.

That was pretty much what Mr. Dodds had said the day before, and it reminded me I had to make some sort of start on the history assignment. Mr. Ellis passed out the spiders in their jars, and as they started to move around the room, the level of noise increased.

Danny leaned nearer to me. "Nissa said for me to tell you we're meeting tonight. She said make sure you bring your symbol."

"I can't!" I hissed, forgetting I had decided not to go there again. "I haven't gotten it yet."

"You better move it then. Do you know what it is?"

I told him.

His eyes lit up. "You're kidding! In the Kraken's office?"

"Unless I was hallucinating."

"What are you going to do?"

"I don't know," I said. I had meant to say I wasn't going to do anything, but a crazy bit of me wished I had the guts to get the circle and bring it back to the attic. Just to see what Nissa would say about it.

The spider jar arrived and I pretended to examine it. The little spider ran around the base of the jar looking for a way out. I sympathized with him.

Danny drummed his fingers on the desk for a minute, then he grinned.

"You know, the Kraken's not here today. He went to give a talk at a community center in Willington. Come on." He stood up, taking the spider jar out of my fingers.

Instantly I wished I had kept my mouth shut because there was absolutely no telling what Danny might do. He was a human wild card, and it was too late to stop him because he had marched straight up to Mr. Ellis.

"Excuse me, sir, but one of the spiders escaped."

He said this loudly enough for everyone in the room to hear, and there was immediate chaos as students made a rush for the exits. Danny grabbed me by the arm and dragged me through the staff door, leaving Mr. Ellis yelling at everyone to stay calm.

We were both laughing our heads off by the time we reached the carpeted corridors in the administrative part of the building. I stopped grinning when I realized where we were headed.

"We can't just barge into his office and take it!" I said, feeling like I had been sucked into a whirlwind. I couldn't believe I had even come this far, and with Danny Odin of all people!

Danny grinned at me over his shoulder, a wild excitement in his eyes. "Why not?"

"His secretary," I whispered, because we were almost there. "She'll stop us."

"Not if she's busy with something else."

He didn't explain. He just opened his mouth and started screaming at the top of his voice.

Then he launched himself around the corner at the receptionist's desk, screeching that there were poisonous spiders loose in the science lab, and that he had been bitten.

Miss Bliss gave a single ladylike shriek, and a second later staggered past, supporting an apparently hallucinating spider-bite victim. Danny had the gall to wink as they passed the niche where I was standing.

For a long second I just stood there paralyzed. Then the same mad instinct prodded me. I took a deep, shaky breath and walked around past the desk. I knocked on Mr. Karle's door, praying Danny was right about him being away. When there was no response, I tried the handle.

It was locked.

Recklessly I turned to the receptionist's desk. She had to have a spare key. I went around the back of the desk and began riffling through the drawers. My heart thudded against my ribs as I noticed a set of keys suspended from a small hook on the underside of the desk. I snagged the bunch and sprinted across to the Kraken's door, thinking insanity must be catching. What on earth was I doing, trying to steal something from a teacher's office because some weird kid told me to?

But I kept trying.

The third key on the set opened the door and I slid inside, breathing so hard I felt as if I were hyperventilating.

Muffled yells from the science lab were cut off when the door closed. In fact, the room was so utterly silent, it had to be soundproofed. The room was icy cold too, and I was amazed to see that a thin rim of frost had formed on the back of the door.

I sensed Mr. Karle's presence stamped on the room and tried to stop picturing him. I felt as if thinking about him too much would make him materialize. The lunacy of what I was doing finally got through to me and I realized I had to get out of the office before I was caught.

I opened the door to escape, peered out the crack, and almost fainted with fright.

Mr. Karle was standing about seven feet away, talking to the principal, Mrs. Severne.

I closed the door and turned to the window in panic, but they were the kind that didn't open. There was no escape.

Then my eyes fell to the desk and the magnetized paper-weight. My arms were covered in goosebumps as I crossed the floor. In spite of being suddenly scared out of my wits, or perhaps because of it, I thought of Lallie telling me my symbol would hide me from him. If ever I needed some magical protection, it was now.

There were about fifty different pieces in the pile of shapes. Which one was the one from my vision? Then I remembered the disc had felt warm the last time I touched it.

In seconds I had it. In spite of the cold it was still warm. In fact, it felt hot. I slid it into my pocket and crossed to the door, trying not to notice that the frost on the door had thickened.

Mr. Karle and Mrs. Severne were still outside.

"It will have to be entered into the boy's record, and that is a pity since he has only just joined us," Mrs. Severne was saying.

"We can have no exceptions," Mr. Karle said flatly. "He deliberately broke the community curfew. His mother is very concerned about him. I think we will need to keep an eye on him," he added thoughtfully.

I stared out of the crack disbelievingly. They were talking about me! That meant my mother had phoned the school and told them about my breaking the curfew! What would happen when the Kraken found me in his office?

I felt sick. I squeezed my hand into a fist around the metal shape, the nails biting into my palm.

In the distance someone screamed.

"What on earth is that?" Mr. Karle demanded.

Mrs. Severne sighed. "One of the students was bitten by a spider in the science lab. Mr. Ellis assures me it is nothing, but the boy is hysterical."

They moved away from the office, and when their voices

72

faded, I came out, relocked the door with shaking fingers, and replaced the keys.

A moment later the receptionist passed me without giving me a second glance. As I went out into a sunlit courtyard, I could hear Danny's yells subside.

11

I didn't see Danny in the afternoon, but someone said he had gone home early because he was so distressed. In spite of everything I laughed every time I thought of him faking the spider bite.

I arrived home to find a note from my mother telling me to come to the nursing home for dinner. It was a peace offering, and she must have dropped it off during her break. It didn't make sense that she would call the school about me if she wanted to patch things up.

Riding the bus across to Saltridge, I thought about the frost in Mr. Karle's office and wondered if I could have imagined it. I frowned and dug in my pocket. The metal circle felt cold now and looked perfectly ordinary. Had it protected me, hidden me from Mr. Karle, the way Lallie promised? Or was it all just a coincidence?

The bus creaked to a halt at a set of lights right next to a fire truck. The crew was trying to repair a burst hydrant spewing water across the intersection, while a group of small kids stood around staring solemnly at the torrent gushing out. I turned to watch them, thinking how serious they all looked. In any other neighborhood they would have been racing through the water, screeching and ignoring the firemen's instructions to stand back.

The nursing home was called Elderew. My mother said it used to be someone's house back in the days when everybody had a house that looked like a hotel. The lawns were smooth as green felt, and willow trees slumped forlorn and graceful over a pond filled with fat goldfish. Tall, neat poplars lined up along the crescent driveway, shading it in stripes.

According to my mother the job at Elderew was one of the main reasons we had come to Cheshunt. She had been a research nurse, but in the time she had been married to my father, she hadn't worked, and so she had gotten behind on the latest techniques, which meant taking whatever position she could get. I had been by a couple of times to eat so far.

One of the nurses was helping an old lady along the path in the fading light as I came down the drive.

I went around to the staff entrance and pushed the button. A short Asian nursing assistant in a lollypop-pink uniform opened the door.

"Hul-lo, Nat-an-yel," she said in a singsong voice. "I go get your mudder," she said carefully, watching me to see that I understood. Then she hurried off down the corridor. I sat in one of the chairs and opened my math homework, but I found myself reading the same formula over and over without taking anything in.

"Hullo, Nat," my mother said. One look at her face told me she didn't want to talk about the morning, but I found I was mad after all.

"Why did you call the school about my breaking the curfew last night?"

She looked taken aback. "I didn't."

It was my turn to be surprised.

She sat down beside me, the starch seeming to flow out of her. "Nathaniel, what made you think I had?" She sounded genuinely puzzled.

I couldn't very well tell her that I had overheard Mr. Karle talking about it. Besides, now I knew. If she hadn't called the school, it had to have been the police.

In a strange way it gave credence to the things Lallie had said in the attic.

I shivered superstitiously.

My mother sighed. "If only we had more time to talk, but it's just one thing after another. Maybe when the job eases up, we can take a vacation together. Sort some things out."

I stared at her wonderingly because for a minute she sounded like she wanted us to spend time together.

She stood and smoothed her hands over her hair, which was knotted at the back of her neck. Instead of making her look severe the way she thought, the knot made her look younger, like a girl dressing up and pretending to be grown up.

"I just came down to tell you I won't be able to join you for dinner tonight. We're short two nurses, so you just go down to the dining hall and help yourself. Come and see me later and I'll get someone to drive you to the bus stop."

The dining room was simply an old hall with a wooden floor, filled with tables and chairs that were mostly full. I went to the counter.

The girl behind it nodded in recognition. "Better have the chicken schnitzel. It's the only thing you need teeth to eat."

That was the biggest problem with nursing-home meals. Practically everything was mush because a lot of the patients had no teeth or couldn't wear their false teeth to eat. Actually it was pretty revolting because a lot of them just sat their teeth on the table beside them while they ate.

I took the chicken and sat down at a table where a single nurse was reading a book and eating her dinner. It occurred to me this would be a good time to see if any of the people at Elderew had been students at Three North.

"Hi," I said brightly.

The nurse looked up. She had a mop of short dark curls, silver-rimmed glasses, and red cheeks.

"I'm Nathaniel Delaney, Mrs. Delaney's son," I introduced myself.

She closed her book and took off the glasses. "Wow, for a minute I thought I was in the wrong place. You don't see too many young faces here. I'm Lilly Astaroth."

"What are you reading?" I asked, noticing she had taken the chicken too.

She turned the book to show me its cover.

"*Lord of the Rings*. I loved that."

She grinned, showing twin dimples. "A lot of people think it's a kid's book, but it's pretty complicated."

"I know; he invented a whole elf language for it."

She nodded enthusiastically. "I wouldn't want it to get around, but when I was applying for work, I saw the name of this place and decided that was it. Elderew. It sounded elfen to me."

I laughed, thinking how easy it usually was to talk to people older than me, and wishing I felt as comfortable around kids my own age.

"I was just thinking. Maybe you can help me with something. I've got this assignment in history, and I'm trying to find some of the people who used to go to my school about sixty years ago. I was thinking maybe some of the people here . . ."

She looked doubtful. "Well, I don't know how you could find that out unless you ask them all, and I don't think . . ."

I fumbled through my school pack. "I've got a list of the names of some old students. Could you just have a look?"

She pushed her plate aside and put on her glasses. "Sure. Though I expect most of them who still lived in the area would have gone to the home in Cheshunt; Mingen House, it's called." She ran her eye down the list. "Of course, the chances are all of them will have moved away from the whole area. Not many people end up living in the same town they grew up in. . . . Wait a minute. There's one name here I recognize. Anna Galway."

I felt like leaping up and hugging her. It was almost too good to be true. "Great!"

"It might not be the same one," she said. "You'll have to ask permission from the coordinator of the home before you speak to her though. And then Anna might just refuse to speak with you. She's not the world's friendliest person."

"Can you tell me anything about her?"

Lilly shook her head regretfully, but before she could speak, one of the windows blew open with a loud clatter.

"I'll get it," I said quickly, not wanting her distracted. But as I pulled the window closed, I felt my arms rise into goosebumps because it seemed to me I could smell the slaughterhouse very faintly.

"There was something," Lilly said as I sat back down. "Something about a court case." She frowned, as if riffling through her memory, then her face cleared. "That's it. Anna Galway saw a murder when she was just a kid. She was a police witness." Lilly stopped, suddenly pale. "For goodness' sake. What am I doing? Those records are absolutely confidential. I don't know what made me just babble on like that." She gave me an imploring look. "Please don't say any of this to anyone. I'd get fired if you did."

"I won't get you into trouble," I told her. "I promise."

She looked relieved. "I've got to go now. Good luck with the search."

It was still too early for my bus, so I went down to the recreation room where most of the patients spent the hours before bed. I had met a couple of them last time, and one old man called out a greeting.

"Hi, Mr. Pellman," I answered.

He beamed. "How about a game of thirty-one?"

He had taught me the game the week before. It was a simple variation of the game of twenty-one. "Okay. But only matches. No money." I had lost all of my pocket money to the old shark the last time.

I sat down and Mr. Pellman dealt the cards.

"Is Mrs. Galway in here today?" I asked casually.

"Miz," Mr. Pellman corrected, squinting at his cards. "Don't suppose so. She ain't the socializin' type. Matter of fact she's an old battle-ax." He gave me a mischievous slice of a smile. "That's the nicest thing about gettin' old. Yer stop lyin' for the sake of politeness."

I grinned back at him and swapped a card off the discard pile for one in my hand. He frowned at my discard.

"That's another flower! Yer building bridges already," he said accusingly. He called clubs, flowers; spades, shovels; and diamonds, jewels. Hearts were the only cards he called by their right name. It made the card games we played sort of exotic.

"I might be bluffing," I said.

"Aha," he said craftily, taking a card from the fresh pile and throwing a ten of diamonds. He stared at me intensely, waiting to see what I would do.

I took the ten.

"Aha! Yer *were* bluffing! Yer after the jools!"

"It might be a double bluff." I threw out a three of spades.

"Hmmph," he grunted. "Why are yer interested in the old dragon anyhow?"

It took me a second to switch from cards to Anna Galway.

"I just wanted to ask her about her old school," I said.

Mr. Pellman took a card from the fresh pile and discarded it. I swapped a club for a smaller club.

"I wouldn't." Mr. Pellman took up my discarded club and threw a heart. I took up the heart and swapped it for the ten of diamonds.

"Why not?"

"Painful memories," Mr. Pellman said. "Painful memories."

"I heard . . . I heard she witnessed a murder when she was a kid."

Mr. Pellman took a card and swapped it for one in his hand. "Yeah. Remember that myself. It was a big deal. All the papers had it on the front page. That kid over Cheshunt burned a caretaker to death."

I blinked. The security guard at the school had mentioned the death of a caretaker. It had to be the same one.

I took a card and discarded it without noticing what it was.

"Horrible way to die," Mr. Pellman said soberly, taking up my discard. "I saw men die that way in the war. That's why I'm not going for cremation. My wife was cremated, but I ain't going out in a blaze. Soon enough to burn after I die." He leered at me wickedly and lay his hand down with a flourish. "Thirty-one."

I looked at my own hand. I had a two of clubs, a three of hearts, and a ten of spades. A score of ten. I sighed and passed in one of my three matches.

"Come on. Deal," Mr. Pellman said gleefully.

"Do you know why that kid killed the caretaker?"

"Huh? Oh, dunno. I read he was friends with the old guy. Maybe they had a fight." He frowned at his cards.

"What about Anna Galway?" I took up a ten of spades, giving myself a respectable twenty score. I didn't want him to see how shaken I was.

Mr. Pellman eyed my discard, then took a card off the fresh pile, discarding a seven of spades. I took it up. Twenty-seven.

"Shovels! Yer after shovels. Yer'll get no more from me!" He took up another from the fresh pile and grinned. "Ahh. Now yer sunk." He threw a heart.

I knocked.

"What!" Mr. Pellman squarked.

"You get another card."

He snorted, taking one from the fresh pile. It brought him up to my score.

"Ha! Cooked yer own goose. We both lose a match. That means yer've got one left."

"Never say die," I said, passing the pile over to him.

"Anna Galway was a police witness," Mr. Pellman said, dealing.

"Then, she actually saw him kill the old guy?"

"I guess. She didn't testify in the end, but that's what the papers said. But who knows? Women's lie," he said in a confiding voice. "They lie a lot, and they're better at it than men."

"But why would she lie about a thing like that?"

"Not sayin' she did, only that she might have done."

I decided the crafty old devil was trying to distract me. "What happened to the kid who did it? Did he go to jail?"

"I guess. Or maybe one of them boys' homes. Detention centers."

I took another card, thinking I had come a long way from the school oral history project, and maybe I was letting some of the weird things that had happened in the last few days get to me. You often heard a strange name. Then, just by coincidence, you'd hear it again the very same day.

I decided it would be best if I just bumped into Anna Galway. If she was as bad-tempered as Lilly and Mr. Pellman said, she was sure to refuse to let me interview her for the assignment.

"What does she do then, if she doesn't come here? Does she just sit in her room?"

"Eh?"

"Anna Galway."

"Oh. Don't know why yer so interested in the old prune face. Why don't yer chat up some of these young nurses?" He worried a lot about me not having a girlfriend yet. The week before he even tried telling me about sex. For about ten minutes I thought he was describing a yoga exercise. It was kind of embarrassing, but he was a nice old guy. "She stays in her room of a night. Reads. Sometimes I seen her in the library, but mostly, if the weather's right, she goes in the garden." His eyes widened. "I got it. Yer after shovels, ain't yer!"

"Nathaniel?" It was one of the nurse assistants. "Your mother said you have to catch the bus now. I'll drive you to the bus stop."

I stood up. "I guess you win by default."

Mr. Pellman glared at the nurse. "Not the same. Can't have

any fun. It's like a prison camp . . ." he muttered blackly.

"I'll see you next time," I called, but he was busy examining my hand. "Aha!" he shouted as I left the hall.

The street was deserted when I got off the bus. The doors closed behind me with a hydraulic hiss, and the bus lurched noisily off, wheezing fumes. I started to walk, thinking about the oral history project. The truth was, I had become curious about that old murder. Maybe because of the connection with Three North.

I took a shortcut down the same lane Bear used. At the other end I was surprised to hear voices. It sounded like a group of older kids just past the place where the lane came out. I slowed down.

"He wasn't home," someone said.

"We'll come back in half an hour and try again."

I stiffened, recognizing Buddha's gravel voice.

"What's he done anyway?" asked a younger boy.

"Nothing. We're supposed to convince him to join the Gathering, is all."

Someone giggled and there was the sound of a slap.

"Idiot," Buddha snarled. "He said convince, not pulverize."

A horrible suspicion began to form in the pit of my belly.

"What does it matter if he joins or not?" someone asked.

"Mr. Karle thinks he might be a troublemaker. He wants him under control."

I swallowed a dry lump in my throat and began to back away.

"You keep an eye on him tomorrow, all of you. We have to find out who his friends are. Mr. Karle figures they might be the ones who broke into the museum. We don't want bad kids like them in Cheshunt."

They all laughed.

When I judged I was far enough away, I turned and hiked back down the lane and into the street. I thought of calling my mother, but knew she wouldn't believe me. I could hardly believe it myself.

Why was Mr. Karle trying to force me into joining the youth club? But, worse by far, he was trying to find out who I hung around with. Just as Nissa had feared.

I had to warn the others.

I started to run.

12

"What were the police doing at your place last night?" Nissa demanded accusingly.

"My mother called them because I was out so late." I explained about the altered shifts. "How did you know they came?"

"One of the school patrol kids was talking about it," Bear said.

"What did you tell them?" Nissa asked sharply. "You didn't mention any of us did you?"

"Name, rank, and serial number," I said, resenting the way she was interrogating me.

She scowled. "You think this is a joke? This puts all of us in danger."

I stood up angrily. "Maybe I better go then."

Bear touched Nissa's arm. "It's not his fault if his mother called the police."

"Maybe not, but if the Kraken suspects and starts watching him, we're all in trouble. Lallie said not to call any attention to ourselves."

"I didn't invite them! I told them I'd gone for a walk."

Nissa snorted. "I'm sure they believed you."

I suppressed a surge of anger because she was right about them not believing me. "I didn't tell them anything."

There was a loud clattering sound on the roof and I looked up.

"Rain," Bear murmured. "Lallie says it will go on all night." He looked across to the bed where the odd little blond girl lay staring up at the roof.

"What's the matter with her?"

"She's fine, no thanks to you," Nissa said.

I thought suddenly of Buddha staking out the house. Nissa had launched into me before I could tell them about it. The anger faded from her face as I told them what I had overheard.

Outside, the rain drumming on the roof increased in force.

"It still doesn't have to mean he knows Nathaniel is one of the ones called," Bear said slowly.

"It means he suspects. That's bad enough. For all we know, it might be all that he needs to figure out who we are," Nissa said.

"Buddha is one of the Kraken's fixers," Danny said darkly. "One of these days I'll fix him."

"Buddha said the Kraken wanted me in because I was a troublemaker."

"Troublemakers who join the Gathering get fixed," Danny pointed out.

I thought of something else. "I overheard the Kraken talking about me today. He knew about the police coming to my house too."

"The police told him," Danny said flatly. His pale eyes were like chunks of ice. "The Kraken set up the whole lot: the curfew, the Gathering, the community committee. They all report to him. And Seth's dad has been with him all the way. What with the community committee, Seth's dad's contacts, and every second kid in the Gathering, the Kraken knows just about all there is that goes on in Cheshunt."

"But why? What is he trying to do?"

"Lallie told you," Nissa said bleakly, coming back to the crate table. "He's looking for us."

A tingle of fear ran through my veins. "Why?"

Nissa's eyes went over to Lallie. "Because we chose to answer the Call. Because of the symbols. Because somehow our coming brought her."

"Look, maybe we ought to go to the police," I said. "Not the ones here in Cheshunt, but in Saltridge or Willington."

Danny's eyes blazed at me. "How do we know they're not with him too?"

Bear broke in. "Even if we did find some that weren't, what would we tell them?"

"That . . . that . . ." I stopped, seeing his point.

"Seth . . ." Lallie gasped suddenly.

We all turned to look at her. She was sitting bolt upright. Her breathing sounded wet and difficult.

"Be careful, Seth," she said clearly, then she fell back.

"Oh, no!" Nissa was instantly wild-eyed. She ran to the bed. "Lallie, is Seth in trouble?"

But Lallie didn't answer. She closed her eyes and seemed to sleep. On impulse I went over to the bed. Her face was dead white and there were black shadows under her eyes.

"She looks sick," I said softly.

"You don't believe she saw Seth, do you?" Nissa said in a hard voice. "You think she's some kind of basket case."

"I don't know what to believe," I admitted.

That seemed to defuse her fury, because she sat down on the side of the bed with a sigh. "You know, I was already living up here when she first came. I used to leave the school, then come back just about dark. Sometimes I'd go to the public library and study until it closed. One night I came back when I thought the coast was clear and she was there, just sitting on the library steps.

"I tried to get her to go home. I thought she was a bit simple." Nissa's storm-blue eyes were unfocused with remembering. "Then she tells me she knows I live in the library attic. I nearly died. She said she had come because I answered the Call. She told me I was the first and that four more would come." Nissa's eyes searched mine.

I had no idea what she wanted me to say. It wasn't even that I disbelieved her. My face must have shown my confusion.

"I know how this feels. You're a thinker and so am I, and thinkers aren't very good at believing," Nissa said.

"Why is Lallie scared of the Kraken? Did he do something to her? Does she know something about him?"

Nissa gave me a pitying look, then she gazed down at Lallie. "Lallie wants us to do something, and the Kraken is going to try to stop us. That's all I know. I keep wanting to ask her more, but when I'm talking to her it just doesn't seem important." She looked at me, miniature twin gas flames dancing in her eyes. "Lallie said tonight she would forge the symbols. Then she's going to tell us what we have to do."

"Forge?"

Lallie opened her eyes and turned her head to look at me. "The last to come must forge at last."

Nissa and I exchanged a startled look. Then Lallie sat up, her eyes wide. "Open the door."

Bear obeyed, dragging open the attic door and scrambling down the ladder. We heard him curse as the key would not turn quickly enough in the library door.

"Hurry," Lallie whispered.

There was a long silence and the rain pounded down. Then Bear climbed back into the attic. Behind him Seth Paul came through the opening *carrying The Tod!*

"Some kind of dogs are out there. If it wasn't for this little guy, I'd have been minced meat."

The Tod wriggled and Seth set him down. He ran across and jumped up, soaking wet, on my lap. Wordlessly Danny handed me a towel. My mind was reeling because it seemed like Lallie had been right about Seth being in danger.

"Guess that answers the question about where he came from," Seth said, his eyes summing me up. "You're Nathaniel, right? Nissa told me about you."

Seth Paul was even more perfect close up than at a distance.

He was built like an athlete, all toned muscle and fine lines. His eyelashes were long and as dark as the black hair plastered to his head. His eyes were a soft gray. Even his teeth were white and perfectly straight.

Seth wiped his hand and extended it. I put my own into it, feeling self-conscious. It was warm and firm. It would be. Seth Paul's hands would never sweat or feel like dead fish.

"I told you there were dogs," Danny said defiantly to Bear. He looked over at Seth and I was surprised to see a flicker of dislike in his eyes. "Black ones, right?"

"I couldn't tell. They were on the football field. I would have walked right into them if the dog hadn't warned me."

"Warned you?" Bear echoed.

"He started following me, then he stopped and growled. That's when I saw them over on the other side of the football field. About six of them slinking along the fence line. If I had kept going, I would have walked right into them." He looked at The Tod with genuine admiration.

I rubbed him down, wondering how he had gotten out. He'd been locked in the yard at home when I left that morning. It occurred to me that Buddha might have let him out. Getting my dog run over would be just his style. I felt a stab of fright at the thought of The Tod in Buddha's hands.

Seth turned to Nissa. "Sorry I didn't make it last night." There was a softer note in his voice now, but she just stared at him with subtle anger. After a minute he turned away and went over to Lallie, who reached up and touched his cheek, her eyes sad. "Show me what you have brought."

Seth fetched his sodden backpack, extracting a thin parcel nearly two feet long. Unwrapping a grubby oilcloth, he withdrew a slender, beautifully made silver telescope. "It's an antique. My father'd kill me if he found I'd stolen it."

"The eye that sees," Lallie whispered.

"What does it mean?" Seth asked.

She looked into his eyes. "It means seeing things that are not seen by others."

"He can do that all right," Danny muttered cryptically.

Lallie turned to face me. "Nathaniel?"

My heart started to beat faster as I dug the metal disc out. She looked at it on the palm of my hand, frowning. Her frown deepened as she closed her fingers around it.

She shut her eyes, but suddenly they flew open as if someone had slapped her hard. Her pupils were dilated so far, her eyes looked black, as if she were drugged or terrified.

"Hey," Nissa murmured uneasily. "What's the matter?"

"Nathaniel's symbol is the circle," Lallie whispered. "The sign of completion." She came closer, still looking into my eyes. "You took this from him."

In spite of my shock that she could know that, I was gratified by the look on Nissa's face.

"It is time for the Forging," Lallie announced.

She made us put everything in a circle on the table. It looked like a selection of junk from a garage sale.

"Join hands," she said, her breathing suddenly labored. "Around the table."

Nissa slid her hand into mine. It was narrow and calloused. Danny took my other hand and we grinned at one another sheepishly.

"Does this mean we're engaged," he asked me coyly. In spite of everything it was funny, or maybe I was getting hysterical.

"This isn't anything to laugh about!" Nissa snapped.

"It is," Lallie whispered. "Laughter is a powerful weapon, for it carries the light. To laugh is to defy the darkness."

I no longer felt like laughing. Lallie's words were too solemn. Too strange. I could not hear the rain now. Or maybe it had stopped. The lamp on the table in the middle of the symbols guttered faintly, throwing its light on our faces and onto the table.

Seth took Nissa's hand, then held his spare hand out to Lallie. But she shook her head.

Seth took Bear's hand instead. We should have felt ridiculous, but no one even looked embarrassed. It was like that moment of a seance when you are suddenly afraid something will happen this time.

"Here stand the five." Lallie's words were barely above a whisper, yet they seemed to reach into all corners of the shadowy attic.

An expectant silence followed, and I gasped aloud when the lamp flame suddenly shot up, extinguishing our shadows on the surrounding walls. From nowhere a violent gust of wind blew around us, sending the column of fire into a frenzied dance.

I realized my knees were shaking, and tried to tell myself not to get carried away by the atmosphere.

"Each symbol shows the strength and weakness of the Chosen," Lallie said, and her voice sounded eerily older. I was afraid to turn around in case more than her voice had aged.

"Heed the warnings:

"Danny, extinguish the dark flame of the past lest it consume you.

"Nissa, strength without compassion is soulless and cruel. Weakness too has its place, for it brings understanding.

"Seth, see the sorrowing earth. Seek your own vision. Trust it.

"Bear, only a wound brought into the light can be healed. That which is hidden will in darkness fester.

"Nathaniel, time is a circle, without beginning or end. Seek beyond the shadows of the past to know the truth of the future."

The bizarre warning sank into me like an echo going on and on forever as I understood that what was happening was real; was not a dream or hypnosis but some kind of magic. I felt a blast of pure joy because if this was real, what else might be real?

Then Lallie spoke again and her voice chilled my blood

because she sounded older still; a withered crone whose voice trembled with unspeakable grief.

"Long ago terrible wrongs were done in this place: sacrifice and torture and betrayal. These deeds bruised the earth and a cycle of darkness has grown here."

Nissa tightened her grip fiercely, arresting my instinctive movement, forcing me to remain in the circle.

"At the beginning of the cycle the darkness calls, drawing like to like, until one comes who is empty: a vessel who will gather the darkness to it and enable the infection to grow and extend like a cancer. The vessel has come, the darkness now gathers."

She gave a high-pitched moan of distress, but again Nissa's grip strengthened, forcing me to be still.

"But the light waits too. Long ago five gave their lives in this place, that a light would shine secretly, a sentinel in the heart of the shadow, calling like to like at need. Here stand five who have chosen to answer the Call.

"Each has brought an ancient symbol to the secret place. Now shall the symbols be forged into a Chain that will enable the five to drive the darkness from the sorrowing earth. Yet, once exorcised, the dark will seek a new home. Then must a second and greater Chain be forged, and as long as it is not sundered, it may bind the dark until the memory of the Chain is as dust in the wind."

Her voice changed again, and abruptly she sounded very young. "But if the Chain is broken, then shall the darkness infect the earth anew, its strength increased a thousandfold."

She took a deep, shuddering breath.

"Do each of you swear to keep faith with the others linked here, to heal the sorrowing earth, to cleave to the Chain that will bind the dark?"

The flame in the lantern guttered violently, though the air was quite still.

"I will," Danny whispered.

"Say it then. Speak the words."

"I . . . I swear to keep faith with the others." Danny said. "I swear to heal the sorrowing earth. I swear to cleave to the Chain that will bind the dark."

When my turn came to speak, I said the words too, and a wave of static electricity crackled through me, lifting my hair.

"Now and forever are you of the Chain," Lallie said. "Let the Chain be forged."

The lamp light went out.

There was an intense, soundless explosion of light, and in the split second before I was blinded, it seemed to me the objects on the table altered.

Then it was dark.

"May the Chain prevail long. . . ." Lallie gasped, then there was the sound of someone falling.

TWO

The Gathering

13

I ran home with The Tod close at my heels. It was still pitch-dark and raining, but that wasn't why I was running.

I ran because of what had happened in the attic and everything that had been happening since we arrived in Cheshunt. Coming out of the library into the last dark hours of the night, I had thought again, but with more fear than joy this time, that if what had happened was real, then what else might be real?

What nightmares might walk?

I wished I had suggested going home at least partway with Bear, but he and Danny had their bikes and they had ridden off together. Seth had gone the other way. Lallie was still in the attic. She had not wakened since the Forging. Hanging limp in Seth's arms when he lifted her onto Nissa's bed, she had looked more dead than alive.

By the time I reached the park, my imagination was working overtime. I kept hearing Lallie say Cheshunt had been bruised by evil, and that now an infection had grown that somehow we were supposed to heal using the symbols.

What did that mean?

And what did it have to do with Mr. Karle?

I kept thinking of the yellow eyes I had seen staring out from the park and worrying about what I would do if something jumped out at me. I walked on the other side of the street but that didn't help. I was still too close to the shadowy trees. I started thinking about the feral dogs, wondering if they had come to answer a Call too.

A dog barked in the park and I stifled a yell of fright.

My heart was galloping by the time I got to the door. I fumbled the key in the lock, then dropped it. When I bent over to pick it up, my neck crawled at the thought of Buddha creeping up behind me.

I was sweating hard before I got inside the front door.

I didn't want to be on my own so I brought The Tod in with me. I fed him and then made myself a hot drink. Doing those everyday things made me feel calmer, but even so the house seemed to crouch around me, filled with shadows and unexplained creaks.

I got into my pajamas, switched the late news on loud, and sat in the armchair, The Tod curled in my lap.

Nissa had warned us to forget about everything that had happened until she contacted us. She would do this as soon as Lallie was well enough to explain how we could use the symbols for the healing. Until then we were to wait patiently and stay out of trouble.

Which was easier said than done. Since coming to Cheshunt I had been in more trouble than I had been in my whole life before that. And after everything that had happened, we still had no idea why Mr. Karle was trying to figure out who we were. The one clue was the fact that Lallie had spoken of a gathering of the dark. Surely it was no coincidence that Mr. Karle's youth club was called the Gathering. That must be why Lallie was so frightened of him. I swallowed, wondering if Mr. Karle could be the one who would come to be filled up with darkness. And if he was, what did that mean exactly?

I fingered the metal disc in my pocket. It had been Danny's suggestion that if the objects could offer some sort of shielding power, we should keep them with us.

I forced my wandering attention back to the television where the announcer was talking about an escaped murderer in another state. Mr. Big, he called him. It sounded as if he was talking about a new kind of kid's toy. The Mr. Big doll.

The phone rang and I jumped. I had drifted off to sleep. The announcer had been replaced by a black-and-white cowboy movie, and a man in a purple stetson was aiming his gun at a green Indian. Rain was playing havoc with the reception.

"Mom?" I croaked into the phone.

No one responded.

"Mom?" I asked again, hearing the note of unease creep into my voice.

There was a faint crackle on the line. I listened a moment longer, then hung up. Suddenly the house seemed alien. I picked up The Tod, who immediately drooped back to sleep.

My grandmother had given him to me as a tiny puppy, saying I needed something of my own and overruling my mother's protests. I felt suddenly like howling my eyes out. With a stabbing ache of loneliness I thought of calling her up. At least the line would be busy. But what would I say? Hi, Grandma. I'm about to fight the champion of the dark. Just thought I'd call.

I wished my mother would come home, but there was little likelihood of that. Determinedly I dragged out the list of names I had taken from the library photograph. There was no way I could sleep yet, and doing homework was better than sitting thinking about Mr. Karle. The phone book listed all of the numbers for the three adjoining suburbs of Cheshunt, Willington, and Saltridge. The first name was Wilson. There were about a million Wilsons in the book. I decided to start by concentrating on the most unusual names on my list. There were five and I wrote them down on the message pad beside the phone: Jon Briody, Marta Tron, Zebediah Sikorsky, Afron Myall, and David Bellfrage. Then I pulled out the phone book and hunted them up one at a time, writing down all the numbers under those surnames. I ended up with four Briodys, three Trons, two Sikorskys, five Myalls, and two Bellfrages.

The phone rang again.

My heart thumped for a few beats as I waited a bit before picking up the receiver.

"Hello?" I said, faking a sleepy voice. I was determined not to let whoever was on the other end know I was rattled.

No answer.

"I'm sorry, if you can hear me, you're not getting through. Better call through the operator." I hung up and stared at the phone uneasily. Folding the list of names and phone numbers, I shoved them in my pocket.

The phone rang again and The Tod growled.

This time I backed away and stood there, listening to it ring and ring. The sound seemed to echo for a long time after it stopped, and I had to force myself to go over to the phone and take the receiver off the hook.

I felt cold and frightened, and wished we had stayed in the attic together until daylight. At least when we were together we could talk about things. And what did the phone calls mean anyway? The chances were it was just Buddha and he had gotten our number from the operator under new listings.

But what really scared me was the thought that maybe it wasn't Buddha.

I shuddered, turned off the television, went into the bedroom, switching on the radio to drown out the silence, then climbed into bed. I thought of Nissa in her drafty attic. It must be ten times creepier to be there. On the other hand, hadn't Lallie called the attic a secret place for the light? Maybe we should have stayed there.

I wondered sleepily what Nissa would have said if I offered to stay. I imagined myself being up there with her alone. Maybe she would be scared and I could put my arm around her. Then I pictured her face and wondered what it would be like to kiss her. She might laugh. I had never actually kissed a girl before. She might be able to tell. Or maybe she hadn't kissed anyone before either.

Sourly I thought of the way Seth's eyes softened when he looked at Nissa. He probably kissed perfectly too.

The rain on the roof seemed hypnotically soothing and I drifted into sleep.

Dreaming is a funny business. It's the one thing you don't have any control over. When you want to dream, you can't, and when it's a really good dream, you can't make it happen again. If it's a nightmare, you can't wake up fast enough, and if it's an exciting dream, you always wake up at the worst possible moment. Murphy's Law of dreaming.

So I dreamed. I was walking in a dense, leafy arbor. Pinhole shafts of light slanted in from odd angles, and the only sound was the crackling of dead leaves underfoot.

At the end of the arbor I could see a garden bathed in reddish light. I heard a snatch of a song and a burst of laughter.

It turned out the red light wasn't dawn or dusk, as I had expected. It was night and a bloody moon rode full and high in a starless sky, just like in the old monster nightmare.

Pushing through the tangled bushes and heading down a slope, I moved toward the singing.

"Dance with me . . ." sang a girl in the distance.

I came out of the tangles into a clearing where there were three people in old-fashioned clothes having a picnic. There was a dark-haired girl dancing around on her own and singing, and a girl with a long blond plait sitting on a tartan rug with a guy of eighteen or nineteen.

Somehow I knew they were no more seeing the bloody moon than they were seeing me. The blond girl had a frilly parasol as if to shade herself from the sun. For them it was daylight.

They were seeing one reality, and I another.

"Dance with me," sang the dark-haired girl to the guy. He had untidy blue-black hair and vivid blue eyes that reminded me of Nissa's. He shook his head and she danced off, eyes sparkling with anger.

"Dance with her," the blond girl said softly to him.

He shook his head. "I'd rather stay with you."

"Dance, dance, I dance with the wind . . ." sang the other girl, a bitterness under the words. The bloody light seemed to deepen.

Suddenly I heard a growling in the bushes behind me, and I knew the monster had followed me there. I swung around, but the hill was much steeper than I had realized, and I lost my balance and fell. Brambles clawed at me and I closed my eyes to protect them.

"Dance, dance . . ." sang the dark-haired girl.

I jerked awake with a gasp, and it was morning, pallid autumn sunlight streaming through my bedroom window.

Immediately I thought of what had happened in the attic. The Forging. It seemed even more unreal in the daylight than it had last night, and that reminded me of the dream where I had seen one thing while the picnicking trio had seen something else entirely.

The Tod whined at me expectantly so I got up to put him outside. It was too soon to get ready for school so I made myself some oatmeal, trying to forget about the events of the night. My mother's bedroom door was closed, which meant she had come in late and didn't want to be woken. I noticed the phone was back on the hook and wondered what she had thought, finding it off.

That reminded me of the phone numbers I had copied down the night before. It was early, but I decided to try a couple anyway.

I tried the numbers next to Briody to start with. The first was a grumpy shift worker who said he didn't know any Briody and that he rented through an agency so how the hell would he know who lived there before him. He hung up when I asked if he had the number of the agency.

The second Briody was a younger sounding woman who called me a lunatic halfway through my explanation. The third was a Saltridge number, and it was busy both times I tried.

Disheartened with Briody, I tried Sikorsky. No one answered.

I decided to try one of the Tron numbers. An elderly woman answered and I explained what I was after.

"What?" she asked when I'd finished.

I went through it again, raising the decibels.

"What?" she yelled.

I sighed and hung up. I'd have to scream before she would hear, and my mother would wake up.

I decided to try the rest of the numbers later. I fed The Tod and got my bike out of the shed. It had a flat, which was why I hadn't been riding it. I fixed the puncture, with The Tod hanging over my shoulder like a consulting expert.

I still had some time before my first class so I decided to ride to the public library and see if they kept back issues of newspapers. It had occurred to me that a murder case was sure to have gotten in the papers. If I could find it, I would be able to date what had happened.

I knew the librarian and he smiled through the window at me as I chained the bike.

"You're out early," he said. He was very plump, with a crew-cut and a lisp.

"Early bird catches the worm," I quipped back.

He grinned. "Got in a new book by David Gemmell. *Knights of Dark Renown*. It's about the knights who go on a quest against the dark."

I pushed away a chilly feeling of déjà vu and put a reserve on the book. While he was filling out the form, I asked him if the library kept old newspapers. I told him I wanted to go back about sixty years.

"We do have back copies, but not that far back. You'd want

to try the *Examiner* office in Willington." The *Examiner* was a free paper that circulated throughout the three suburbs.

"Would they have been around sixty or so years ago?"

"Not as the *Examiner*. It used to be called the *Tribune*. But it's the same paper. They might still have copies from those days for the journalists to refer to."

"Do you know if it's open to the public?"

He tapped his fingers, thinking. "If you tell them it's for a school project, you'll be fine. We were all students once."

I found it hard to imagine the librarian as a student, but I nodded. "Thanks."

It was too late to go over to Willington before school, so I put that on hold. It would be better to go on my way to Elderew for dinner one night. If I went straight after school, I could go to the *Examiner* and then bus across to Elderew afterward.

I cycled double-speed to the school and chained my bike alongside those already in the stand.

"What's a matter? Don't you trust us?"

I froze, recognizing Buddha's voice.

I turned slowly. He and two other big school patrol guys were slouching against the side of the bike shed nearest the door. The tall skinny kid with buckteeth looked like Brer Rabbit gone wrong. The other was a bullethead with a high-pitched voice.

"So, how's it goin'?" Buddha asked with exaggerated politeness.

"Fine," I said, wondering how far they would go in broad daylight.

"When are we gonna see you in the Gathering?" Buddha went on conversationally. He took one step nearer. His eyes were glassy and bloodshot, as if he had stayed up all night.

"I don't know if I'm going to join," I said, hoisting my

backpack out of the bike basket. "Those clubs take up a lot of time."

"You'd enjoy the meetings," Buddha said. He stepped forward again and carefully put his heel down on my foot. Hard.

My eyes started to water.

"You should reconsider, Nathaniel," he said. There was a sleepy smile on his face, as if hurting me really made him feel good.

Bullethead giggled.

"Cut it out," I gritted, trying to get my foot free.

Buddha leaned his full weight on his heel, grinding it into my foot. The pain was excruciating.

"What's going on?"

It was Nissa. She wore baggy tracksuit pants and a pilled brown sweater. Her red hair sticking up in all directions and lit from behind looked like a crown of flames.

"What's it to you?" Buddha sneered.

"Nothing, so long as you get your fat butt out of my way, lardo," she said savagely, staring right in his eyes.

I held my breath, but after a long tense minute Buddha backed down, stepping aside as Nissa pushed between us. She flashed me a disgusted, impatient look. "Go on. Get out of here."

Feeling gutless and ashamed, I limped away, wishing she hadn't seen me act so scared and cowardly. Why couldn't I have stood up to Buddha the way she had? First Bear had rescued me and now Nissa.

"You can't run forever . . ." Buddha shouted after me.

My foot was bruised badly, but I crossed the football field as quickly as I could. The air stank. It seemed incredible to me that a school had been built so close to a slaughterhouse. Worst of all, first period was gym, which meant being out in the stink and breathing it in.

It also meant facing Mr. Karle. The only good thing was that

Bear was in the class as well, and though we dared not talk to one another, it made me feel less alone.

We were supposed to play basketball, and Mr. Karle split us arbitrarily into two groups, ignoring muffled moans. He seemed preoccupied, which was fine by me. I kept seeing flashes of him walking through the night with the dogs, and then there was the way his room iced up when I was in there.

Three North had no indoor courts except the assembly hall, which doubled for drama classes and took precedence over gym for the space. So we had to play outside. It was sunny despite the cold and might not have been so bad except for the smell.

"Ugh," I grunted, getting a blast.

"What's up?" a boy asked me.

I stared at him incredulously. "The smell."

He looked at me as if I was mad. "I can't smell anything."

"Begin," Mr. Karle said.

I looked around and my heart started to race as I noticed his eyes on me. The circle in my pocket felt warm and I wondered if the heat might be some kind of warning. After all, it had felt hot when Mr. Karle turned up while I was in his office.

The ball came my way and I automatically jumped for it, gasping as someone elbowed me hard in the chest. I landed hard on my sore foot and went down.

"Foul!" someone else shouted.

"It's not a foul, you idiot. That's his own team." An argument broke out and was quashed.

"Are you all right, Mr. Delaney?" Mr. Karle asked. He always called everybody Mr. or Miss on the field.

I nodded, still gagging. Mr. Karle's eyes bored into mine. *Are you one of them?* his eyes seemed to ask.

He turned on his heel. "Play on."

The boy who had elbowed me gave me a flat, empty stare that made my blood run cold.

Bear gave me a warning look too, but there was nothing he

could do. I started to feel scared of what Mr. Karle might let happen.

Before the match was out, the same boy had trodden on my ankle, elbowed me in the eye, and punched me in the back.

"You're out of step, buddy," he said, helping me up.

And all the while, Mr. Karle watched unblinkingly, his bald head gleaming in the sunlight.

"You better do what they want," a girl whispered when we all took a breather.

I stared at her.

"Everyone knows they're out to get you. You're not the first kid who tried to say no. If you go once, they'll leave you alone. You don't have to do what they do."

I felt my mouth hanging open and closed it. "Mr. Karle can't make me join." A gust of icy wind swallowed up my words, and I turned, with a chilling sense of fear at the realization that I had said his name aloud.

He was looking at me, his eyes as cold as something that had been dead for years. And then he smiled and I felt light-headed with terror, because for a second his teeth looked as sharp and pointed as a vampire's.

Then he blinked and looked away.

The second half of the lesson was in the gym, and I was relieved to get inside, out of the stench. It seemed to be getting worse rather than better, and I wondered if I would ever get used to it, like everyone else seemed to have done. I was set up for medicine-ball situps with a burly blond guy.

Mr. Karle seemed to have lost interest in me, and the kid that had knocked me around on the court was on the horse.

"Ready?" the blond guy asked, poised. Like Buddha, his eyes were glassy and red-rimmed. The similarity bothered me.

"Hang on," I said.

He threw the ball as hard as he could at my head. When it connected, I actually saw stars. The last thing I heard as I passed out was someone giggling, and then I was down for the count.

I was somewhere, I was nowhere. I was conscious, but I couldn't feel anything or see anything. I was floating in blackness. It took me a minute to realize I was drifting, or being drifted toward a speck of whitish light. Somehow I went from floating to walking, and I was heading for what looked like a stone wishing well. I leaned forward to see if there were any coins. Not only was the well empty of money, it was empty of water. In fact, it didn't seem to have an inside. There was just a paleness, sort of like mist, but with more substance. It was like cloudy Jell-O. As I watched, the Jell-O grew darker and darker, and it began to smell like something rotten. The death smell.

Then a face looked out at me, dark and bestial with long yellowed teeth. *Are you one of them? Are you one of those baaad kids?* it whispered. Its eyes were black with huge pupils. It looked exactly like the thing I had imagined would come out of the closet and get me when I was a kid; the monster that chased me through the forest. And maybe that was real too. Maybe all the nightmares were real.

Then there was nothing and I was back in the blackness.

". . . get some water . . ." A voice drifted in like a station being tuned properly on the radio.

The darkness faded into light, into blobs of pink, into faces.

"Are you all right, Mr. Delaney?" Mr. Karle asked, his lips curved into a smile. His breath smelled terrible, like he had swallowed the whole slaughterhouse, or maybe the whole of Cheshunt. The death smell came out of his mouth on a hot tide at me.

I was too frightened to speak. I just stared up at him. Then he smiled his happy murderer smile and straightened up.

I sat up slowly, surprised to find I could move.

Mr. Karle assigned a kid to help me to first aid, where a brisk and bored home economics teacher gave me a couple of pills and told me to lie on the narrow cot. "Observation," she said. "Mild concussion."

"Great," I muttered.

14

At lunchtime the home economics teacher told me to go to lunch and come back after, if I still felt sick. My head ached and I wouldn't have minded some fresh air, but after what had happened in gym class, it seemed safer to go to the library.

I couldn't stop my eyes from going up to the roof in the lobby.

"Hi, how's the search going?" the librarian's assistant asked, then her eyes went to my forehead and the smile disappeared. "What happened?"

I reached up and felt the egg-sized bump on my head. "Gym accident."

I went over to sit in the private-study section, grabbed a book, and closed my eyes. They throw you out of the library if you sleep too obviously.

I jumped when someone sat down beside me, but it was only Danny.

"Bear told me some kid creamed you good."

I fingered the bump on my head ruefully.

"You think the Kraken set it up?" he asked.

I nodded, then wished I hadn't. "He knew what was going to happen. So did half the other kids there." I thought of something else. "Lallie said the symbols would hide us once they were forged into a Chain."

Danny leaned closer. "Unless he already guessed about you."

I shook my head gingerly. "He can't know for sure or he

wouldn't still be trying to get me into the Gathering. But he's suspicious, so he'll be watching, and he won't be the only one. Maybe you better not talk to me in the open like this. Remember what Nissa said about staying low."

He ignored that. "You know what I think? I think we're supposed to fight the Kraken."

I had a mad vision of Danny going up with his papier-mâché torch to duke it out with Mr. Karle. "Lallie didn't say anything about us fighting. She said we're supposed to fix whatever's wrong with Cheshunt. Heal it," I said doubtfully.

"She said laughter was a weapon. Why would you need weapons if there wasn't going to be a fight? I think the symbols are weapons too."

I frowned. "She said the symbols were meant to show our weaknesses and once they were forged, we're supposed to drive the dark out with them."

Danny nodded eagerly. "*He*'s the dark. The Kraken. And he'll try to stop us from this healing business for sure, so we'll have to fight him."

He had remembered Lallie's words far more clearly than I had, but still I felt he was taking the words too literally.

"Well, what about this second Forging? When is that going to happen?"

"After the Healing," Danny said triumphantly. "That's when the Kraken'll make his move."

I sighed. He had his mind made up that there was going to be a confrontation, but I didn't know what to think.

"One thing that bothers me is, why us? Why not five adults?"

Danny shrugged. "Maybe they didn't hear the Call. Or maybe they didn't answer it. We did."

"But *why* did we?"

He shrugged, his eyes disinterested. The Choosing was over, so he couldn't see the point in thinking about it. "You seen Nissa or precious Seth today?" He sneered.

"You don't like him, do you?"

"He's a pretty boy. All show. Underneath he's weak. I don't trust him. And then there's his father."

I was startled at the venom in his tone. "You can't blame him for his father."

Danny pretended to read a book as the assistant came over.

"I forgot to mention it," she said, "but I found an old scrapbook that a former teacher made about the school. Maybe you could use it for your assignment. It was in a box of books donated to us." She handed me a moldy-smelling folder.

"Bring it straight back to me before you leave." She hesitated a moment, as if she was already regretting giving it to me. It was the bump on my head that was making her nervous. She thought it meant I was violent and might start ripping out the pages and eating them. I nodded and smiled and tried to look as sane as I could to reassure her, and finally she went away and left me with it.

"What's this?" Danny asked, peering over my shoulder.

I told him about the oral history assignment.

"Let's have a look then."

I opened the folder. The edges of the paper were mouse-chewed and yellowing.

"Smells like something pissed on it," Danny murmured in disgust.

The front page read *Three North Cheshunt Secondary School*, in flowery handwriting. Underneath was written "Irma Heathcote."

Inside was a collection of dark brownish photographs that looked as if they had been processed by an amateur using old developing fluid. Some had captions written in the same fancy handwriting. "Ellis Bell wins the long jump" was written underneath the picture of a boy caught mid-jump above the pit, straining forward, his face screwed up with the effort. There were a lot of pictures of people dancing in couples. One showed two kids dressed in ball gown and suit, laughing as they whirled around. I studied their faces and after a minute it began to look as if they were screaming rather than laughing.

I shuddered, thinking I was beginning to see something distorted and horrible about everything.

On the next page were two newspaper clippings, yellowed and curling at the edges. One announced a fundraising fete, the other was little more than a picture and a brief caption.

"Hey, that's the library," Danny said.

He was right. It was the library building. The caption said: "The new Three North Cheshunt Secondary School building, constructed on the site of the old school, will be opened today by the Honorable Council Member, Mr. David Shropshire. Funds for the project were raised by the local community. It is hoped the refurbished school building and the return to school of local students will end the recent wave of youth-related crime sweeping the district." That surprised me, because I had imagined the library dated from before it had become a school. Especially the way Lallie talked about it being a secret, sacred place.

But maybe it was the site and not the building she meant.

The other clipping was dated almost exactly two years before the first. "A fete will be held to help finance the rebuilding of Three North Cheshunt Secondary School, destroyed in the tragic fire last month that took an elderly caretaker's life."

I sat back, feeling oddly uneasy. The fire and the caretaker again. And it had not happened just anywhere. It had happened in the library. I told Danny about the old murder.

"I guess the building must have caught on fire when he fell," he said, sounding subdued.

I flicked through the remainder of the folder. More clippings from the *Tribune*, and further in, pressed flowers from a nature walk and a snatch of a poem. Interestingly the poem was attributed to one of the people on my phone list, Zebediah Sikorsky. I wrote it down in my notepad. It was a soppy love poem comparing a girl to a flower with golden hair "that floats like buttery petals open to the sun."

I wrote the teacher's name down in my notes.

"Why'd you do that?"

"I'm going to see if I can hunt her down. She could be my interview."

"I thought you were going to talk to the old lady from the home." I had told him about Anna too.

"Apparently she's pretty cranky. Maybe she won't talk to me."

Danny shook his head. "I dunno how you can worry about this after last night."

"Takes my mind off it. Nissa said to forget about the Chain until Lallie can tell us more about what we're supposed to do." That was true, but even as I said it, I knew it was more than that. There was something compelling about that old mystery.

The bell rang and Danny left the library to go to class. I went back to first aid. Instead of the brisk home economics teacher, the school counselor was on first aid duty, beaming maternally. I groaned inwardly, wishing I had gone to class instead.

"So, Nathaniel. You've hurt your head." She had a slight accent.

"I didn't hurt it," I said indignantly. "Someone threw a medicine ball at it when I wasn't looking."

"You weren't paying attention then?" She dabbed the lump with disinfectant. "Was there something on your mind?"

Rain began to fall against the window, and in a moment the football field was blurred. Absently I thought how rain always seemed gray in autumn.

"Sorry," Mrs. Vellan said when I winced again. "You were saying you were distracted in the gym . . ."

"I was fixing my mat. The other kid thought I was ready, so he threw the ball."

"You're angry about that?" She was quick. I hadn't been able to keep resentment out of my voice.

"It hurt," I said.

"Do you think he did it on purpose?"

My heartbeat quickened. "He said it was an accident."

I closed my eyes. Maybe if she thought I was sleepy she'd leave me alone.

"It has been hard for you to move around so much, hasn't it, Nathaniel. Settling in is difficult enough, and there is the matter of your father . . ." she trailed off, expecting me to react to her knowledge, but I knew my mother had spoken to them about the car crash.

"Do you ever think about your father, Nathaniel? Do you ever wonder why you never saw him?"

I looked at her incredulously.

"People do not see clearly when they are young, Nathaniel. There is too much they do not know. Too much hidden from them. That is why children must learn to trust and respect their elders. The problem is that often young people think they know more than adults. Even that they can live without them," she droned on. "This can lead them into error and grief. Into disobeying rules."

She blinked, then smiled at me. I noticed the whites of her eyes were a dirty yellow. "Tell me, Nathaniel, that night when you broke the curfew, where did you go?"

"I walked," I said. My heart beat too fast and loud. It sounded like one of the poison pygmies out of the Deep Woods where the Phantom lives sending out a drum message. Be-ware, be-ware.

"We had a fight and I was mad, so I walked." I watched her warily as she put the disinfectant away and washed the bowl.

"You walked, but where did you go? Did you visit someone? A friend?" She shot a glance at me. "That is not the only night that you have broken the curfew, is it?"

My heart thumped because there was only one way she could

know that. Buddha must have told Mr. Karle I had not come home the previous night, and if Mrs. Vellan knew, he must have told her.

That meant she was working with Mr. Karle.

"A couple of times I stayed with my mother at the home where she works, and came home late with her," I said innocently.

Frustration flared in her eyes. "Did you ever see anyone out when you were coming home late at night?"

I started to say no, then I had a flash of inspiration. "I did see someone once."

She sat forward eagerly, unable to contain her excitement. "Who?"

"I saw that school patrol kid, Buddha."

There was a long silence.

"Well," Mrs. Vellan said at last. She rose and pushed the chair she had been sitting on back to the wall and left without another word.

I lay back, thinking Mr. Karle was using all of his resources to find out what I was up to. He was even prepared to let Buddha rough me up to make me join the Gathering.

Why?

Was it because if I joined the Gathering, I would be answering another darker Call? And if I refused, what would the penalty be? And if Danny was right, how could we fight him?

15

When I got home, the house was dark, but the kettle was warm. That meant my mother had just gone. There was a note from her telling me to go to Elderew for dinner again. My head was starting to ache, so I had another headache pill and fed The Tod. He jumped all over me and chewed on me. He still didn't accept school as a reasonable excuse for us being apart. I played catch with him for a while, but it started to rain so we came inside.

For a while I pored over the list of phone numbers I had written down the previous night, then dialed the second Sikorsky number. His name had gone up a notch in importance because it had appeared in Irma Heathcote's scrapbook, along with the newspaper clipping about the fire.

No one answered, so I tried the number that had been busy that morning. Either the person had the phone off the hook, or they were having a massive powwow because it was still busy. I tried a Myall number for a change.

A woman answered. I could hear a baby screaming its head off in the background.

"Hullo?" she asked in a frazzled voice.

"Hi, I'm trying to locate . . ."

A minute later I hung up with a sigh. The name meant nothing to the woman, who kept breaking off to yell at the kid. "Johnny don't, Johnny get off the stove, Johnny don't stick that in there." I grinned, thinking Johnny sounded like a holy terror. The next number I called was an older woman. I explained about the assignment and asked if she was any relation to Afron Myall.

"You'd be talking about my aunt," she said. "She moved to Europe years ago. I'm afraid she died over there."

I was reluctant to let her go. "Do you remember anything about her? Did she ever say anything about the school she went to?"

"No, well . . . I remember my mother saying they taught dancing at the school. You know, not the sort of thing kids do now. Proper dancing. Waltzes. But I don't suppose that's any use to you."

I thanked her and hung up, feeling it was hopeless. My best chance had to be Anna Galway. I decided to go over early to Elderew. Maybe I would be able to track her down.

I changed out of my school clothes and pulled on my favorite scruffy old jeans. My mother kept wanting to throw them out, but they were the most comfortable pair I had. She couldn't understand jeans were only ripe when they were falling apart. Every rip in them was a memory.

Thinking of memories reminded me of the things Mrs. Vellan had hinted about my father. Had there been some reason for us moving around, other than my mother's restlessness? And why had he never answered any of my letters or contacted me? Was it possible my mother had told Mrs. Vellan something she had kept from me?

I shrugged, because that was one mystery too many right now, and pushed the whole thing to the back of my mind. I locked The Tod up in my bedroom, thinking of Buddha on the loose.

I grabbed a notepad and pen, and arrived at the stop just as the bus came around the corner. Two blocks off, I sank down in my seat as we trundled past Buddha and a gang of kids heading toward my house.

Foiled, I thought. And The Tod was safe inside.

That put me in a good humor, though I realized the whole Buddha thing was just on hold, not dealt with.

The bus lumbered its way across town and I dozed, almost missing the Elderew stop. It was still daylight but chilly when I hurried up the path and rang the staff bell. An older woman in pink answered.

"So?" she said. "You are who?"

I was startled. "Uh . . . my mother works here."

"Mother?" she echoed, sounding mystified.

"My mother. Inside," I pointed.

"No can go," she said firmly. "Visiting hours over. You come back later."

Another head poked around the door. It was the girl from the dining room, Lilly something. "Hullo, Nathaniel. Here for dinner?"

The other woman stared at me, then at her. "Mother?" she echoed.

Instead of trying to explain, Lilly pulled me past her, giggling as we went down the hall. The lights were dim, but when we reached the dining room, she noticed the bump. I explained it had been an accident.

"Some accident. How's it feel?" Lilly asked.

"Not too bad." I refused her offer of company for dinner, explaining I was supposed to eat with my mother during her break.

"I'm going for a walk to kill time."

I slipped through the doors and into the recreation room. Mr. Pellman was sitting alongside a huge muscular man with black hair and a sallow monkey's face.

"Come over, Nat. There's someone you should meet."

"Hi, Mr. Pellman," I said.

"This is Patrick. He's an ex–hit man."

"What?" I gaped.

"It's true. Look at those hands."

Patrick beamed, holding out king-size paws for inspection.

"He . . . he tell you that?"

Mr. Pellman snorted. "Anyone can tell. Patrick's not shy. He says he only killed the bad guys." He leaned closer and winked. "He's Irish."

People on the other side were always the bad guys. I figured Patrick had probably been a taxi driver imagining himself as a secret I.R.A. operative. "Have you seen Anna Galway around today?"

"Now there's someone that deserves killing," Mr. Pellman retorted. Patrick looked at him with a bloodthirsty eagerness that made me think maybe he hadn't been a taxi driver after all.

"All right," Mr. Pellman said, mistaking my silence. "Yer not in a joking mood. I saw the old biddy in the garden. She threw a pinecone at me. I'm gonna get my lawyer after her for grievous bodily harm."

"Better she should be killed," Patrick said in a molasses thick Irish accent. Mr. Pellman stared at him, then burst out laughing.

I slipped away, deciding I'd better talk to Anna Galway before Mr. Pellman arranged for Patrick to take her out. I had heard someone say nursing homes were depressing because everyone went there to die, but Elderew was pretty lively.

Outside, autumn had started to turn the leaves of some of the trees brown and there was a rich fermenting smell in the damp air. It was no longer raining, but only a few people were outside because of the cold.

I stared around glumly, realizing I had no idea what Anna Galway looked like.

An old woman with her hair in curlers came past, but when I tried to speak with her she gave me a frightened look and a wide berth.

I sighed and looked around the wet, dark grounds. Then I saw a movement in a clump of trees. From the distance the woman looked too young to be Anna Galway, but she was alone.

I walked hesitantly toward her, thinking if it wasn't Anna, I would ask where she was. She spotted me, screeched, and launched a pinecone at me.

It was her all right. I held my hands up and walked toward her as if she were holding a gun on me. This confused her and she let me come right up to her.

"What are you doing?" she snarled. Up close she was in pretty good shape and her hair was still black, but her face was like a dark prune with deep-etched frown and scowl lines, her lips twisted into a perpetual sneer. Her eyes were hard and glittering in the leathery folds of her face.

"I . . . my name's Nathaniel," I began.

Her eyes swept down over my ragged clothes. "What do you want?"

"I . . . I just wanted to talk to you. I've got a school project and we have to talk to someone . . ." I stopped short of calling her old to her face.

"And you think I'm someone? Well, you're wrong. I'm no one. Once I thought I was, but it was all lies." An expression of bitter hate filled her face. She began to mumble to herself.

"You've lived around this area for a long time," I said loudly, thinking there was no point in trying to interview her.

She broke off mid-rant and stared at me with as much astonishment as if a cat had addressed her. "I've lived too long," she whispered.

My mind was working furiously. Anna had known the youth charged with burning the old caretaker. How could I get her onto that subject? "You used to live in Cheshunt," I said desperately. "I was wondering if you remember anything about it."

"It was a bad place." Her eyes slitted suspiciously. "Why do you want to know?"

"A . . . a school project . . ." I stammered, unnerved.

She reached out and grabbed my chin in her bony witch's grasp. "I think not."

"But it's true . . ." I gasped. "I . . . it's just an oral history project . . . for school."

"Which school?"

"Three North Cheshunt . . ."

She let me go abruptly and backed away from me. "What do you want?" she hissed, looking both terrified and insane. "Who sent you?"

I was astounded at the effect the name of the school had on her, but at the same time the security guard's voice floated into my mind: *"Some places are made for trouble. Years ago some bad things happened here."*

"Get away from me," Anna Galway whispered in a voice cracked with terror.

I was breathing fast, almost panting. I wanted to do what she asked, because suddenly I was scared of what she might tell me if I stayed. But something held me there.

"There was a court case over a fire at the school when you were there. A boy killed a caretaker and you were a witness. Do you remember?"

I expected her to start screaming, but she just sank onto the sodden grass as if her legs had no strength in them. "I was a witness, but in the end they didn't need me because he pleaded guilty."

That was the last thing I expected her to say.

Anna Galway looked up at me with desperate, agonized eyes. "He agreed that was what had to be done. So the rest of us could stay, one of us had to be sacrificed."

My heart was beating fiercely in my chest at that word. "Are . . . are you saying he didn't set the fire?"

Anna Galway began to weep soundlessly, tears running along the grooves and lines of her ancient face. "He loved the old man. He could not have hurt him." Now she was sobbing in earnest and I stared down at her, dumbfounded. She had just confessed to helping an innocent person go to jail for a murder he hadn't committed, an innocent man who had pleaded guilty.

"Then who . . . who did kill him?"

She did not bother to wipe the tears away. They ran unheeded down her face, soaking into the yellowing neck of her dressing gown.

"No one killed him. The old man poured kerosene over himself and lit a match. We all saw, but who would have believed us? We knew they would blame us, so he told them he did it. He took the blame, so the rest of us could stay."

16

"How did it happen?" my mother asked, looking horrified.

"I'm okay," I said. "I spent most of the day in first aid."

She leaned forward and shifted my hair so she could get a better look at the bump. "You might have a concussion. Maybe I better get one of our doctors to take a look at it."

"I'm fine," I insisted. I still felt dazed from what Anna Galway had told me.

"Well, we're both fine then. I'm on split shift again, so I won't be home till all hours of the morning." She sighed. "It's harder than I expected working shifts again. It was a lot easier just being a mother."

"It was good having dinner home sometimes," I joked, but maybe because of the business with Anna it came out more seriously than I had meant it to; she looked stricken.

"Oh, Nat, I'm sorry. But it won't be forever. There's a permanent day position coming up toward the end of the year, and then I'll be home every night. We can watch television together, go to the movies . . ."

"It's all right," I said, feeling guilty about making her feel guilty.

In the end she wanted to drive me home, but I talked her out of it.

Walking along the street later, I regretted being so noble. Dark clouds rushed along the face of the moon and blotted out all but a few stars. Cars passing by splashed muddy water onto the footpath, and I felt lonely and vulnerable.

By the time I reached the stop, my hands were blue and I was shivering, but it was another half hour before the bus came. By then my head was pounding and all I could think about was getting warm. The only other people on the bus were an elderly couple who stared at me as I went past them and down to the back.

A whole lot of kids were waiting to get on the bus at Saltridge Mall, and as they boarded, I recognized two of them as school patrol boys from Three North.

I slid down deeper into my seat, hoping none of them would see me. After getting bashed around at school the last thing I wanted was to be caught alone on the street at night.

I was startled to see Danny get on at the next stop. He didn't see me, but took a seat about halfway down the bus and across the aisle from the elderly couple. He had his backpack on, and something big was poking up out of it. His symbol.

The two school patrol guys moved up to sit in the seats directly behind him as soon as the bus started moving again.

"Hey, Whacko," a meaty redheaded kid called to Danny. "I didn't know they let loonies on public buses. Aren't there special buses for people like you? Ones with bars?"

Danny ignored this.

"Fruit Loop?" Redhead called. The other kids tittered. "Hey, you. I'm talking to you, Looney Tunes."

The old man turned to look pointedly across at Redhead.

"What are you gawking at, Gramps?" asked another kid nastily.

"Rudi," the old man's wife quavered. "It has nothing to do with us."

The man frowned at her, then turned back to Redhead. "Son,

there is no call to cause trouble. Why not just enjoy the bus ride?"

"Why don't you eat shit?" Redhead sneered.

The man flushed and looked angry. "You are from Cheshunt, but that does not frighten me. I know all about these gangs that come from Cheshunt to terrorize Saltridge."

"Sit down, Gramps, before you get hurt, and watch how you talk about Cheshunt," Redhead said threateningly. "Or else we'll pay you and your wife a little visit and teach you to respect the only decent neighborhood in this area."

"Decent," the man said angrily.

His wife tugged at his sleeve. "Rudi. Please." Rudi looked mad at her, but he gave in and straightened up in his seat.

Redhead chuckled loudly. "Smart move, Rudolph." He turned back to Danny when the old guy failed to bite. "What do you reckon, Whacko? Cheshunt is a good neighborhood, isn't it? Good school, good teachers, good headshrinkers . . . good cops."

Danny said nothing. I kept my fingers crossed that he would just ride it out. There were at least a dozen of them, and Nissa had warned us specifically to stay out of trouble, especially in public.

Danny seemed to remember that because he kept his mouth shut. Or maybe it was because the bus-line policy was to pull over and throw out all parties to any dispute, regardless of who was in the right. I saw the driver watching them all in the mirror, but he didn't say anything. He had become deaf too. Adults do that a lot when they think there is trouble they might not be able to handle.

Danny and the group of kids got out at my stop, which was almost the end of the bus route. The old couple had gotten out at the last stop in Saltridge.

I got off the bus last, with a feeling of impending disaster. The kids from the bus were already ranged around Danny.

"Did they give you any electric shocks in the nuthouse,

Whacko?" one of the kids asked. I thought I recognized him from Buddha's group.

"Weirdo," another said. It was like a whole flock of birds picking on one.

"Loony."

"Freak."

"Nutso."

One of the kids elbowed another and pointed to me. Danny turned and looked surprised.

"What are you gawking at?" Redhead demanded. "Buzz off."

I told myself to go. Nissa had said to stay away from one another and it was Danny's fight.

But I didn't move.

Redhead stepped toward me and a flash of triumph came into his eyes when he saw the shock in my face. Only it wasn't him coming up to me that made me look like that. I could feel something in my pocket heating up. The circle. A warning from the Twilight Zone.

"I said buzz off," Redhead said slowly, as if I were mentally retarded.

"Look, I was just going to say I saw a police car back there."

Redhead's eyes narrowed, but he looked around the street uneasily.

I pressed on, hoping I had put two and two together and come up with the right answer. "You better quit this. You know he doesn't like anything to happen in Cheshunt. And it's nearly curfew."

Redhead actually paled. "Yeah, I forgot for a second. You won't tell him, will you?"

"Definitely not," I said truthfully.

He looked relieved. Then he turned to Danny. "You just watch it, Freako. We don't need your sort in Cheshunt. It's open season on anyone who's not in the Gathering. Remember that."

I willed Danny to get moving while the going was good. The

125

other school patrol guy had started to look at me. Any minute someone would realize that I didn't belong to the Gathering either. You could only bluff so far and so long.

I stared at Danny pointedly, trying to make him go.

"Snotbag," Danny said to Redhead. Then he turned to a scared-looking kid and punched him square in the nose.

Redhead's face contorted with fury, but to my amazement he made no move toward Danny. Instead he looked around nervously before responding. "You'll keep, Whacko. Don't go into any dark alleys."

He turned and hustled the kid whose nose had been mashed.

We started to walk too. "What did you do that for?" I demanded angrily. "That little kid didn't say anything. He was just going along with the others."

"The ones who just go along are worse. They don't even have the guts to decide. I'm teaching him about gorillas," he mumbled. "It's my mission."

The anger in me faded. What was he talking about?

"That was pretty slick talking back there. You're okay, Nathaniel," he said, and in spite of everything I felt a burst of pride at his approval. It was as cold and dark as it had been before, but there was something comforting about not being alone. Especially in Cheshunt.

"How did you know that about the Kraken not wanting trouble in Cheshunt?" he asked curiously.

I shrugged. "It was a guess. What that old guy on the bus said made me think of it. And the fact that none of us have been beaten up outright. I think it must be some kind of rule he's set that no one is to cause trouble here."

"What happened at the home?" Danny said after a bit. "Did you get to talk to the old lady?"

I nodded and shivered, remembering the conversation with Anna Galway. "She was . . . a little mad. But she told me the guy who went to prison didn't kill the old caretaker."

"He was framed?" Danny said savagely. "The cops lied."

I frowned, wondering what his beef with the police was. "It was nothing to do with them. The kid gave himself up so the others wouldn't be blamed as well."

"If the guy didn't do it, who did?"

"Anna said he killed himself. Doused himself in kerosene and lit a match. She said no one would have believed the truth so this guy agreed to say he did it."

"There were a whole bunch of them then?" Danny said. "They should have stuck together. The police would have had to believe them."

We passed the park. It was silent and dark, and the wind made the swing creak eerily.

"A lot of weird things happen here," Danny said in a subdued voice. Suddenly he reached out and pushed me hard into a shadowy driveway.

"What the . . . ?"

"Shut up!" he hissed. "It's a police car."

I froze, thinking of Seth's father. Then I realized it was still a little early. "They can't do anything to us. It's not after curfew."

"I don't trust them," Danny whispered fiercely. "They make the rules, then they break them. Police can do anything they want. Who'd take the word of a couple of punk kids over a cop?"

We watched silently as the police car cruised slowly by.

Danny gave me a strange look as we came out. "You still see them as good guys, don't you?"

The moon went behind a cloud and the world grew darker, but he didn't seem to notice. He leaned closer and his pale eyes were almost luminous.

"One night, a couple of years ago, I was coming home from a party on a farm outside town. I didn't know the guy driving. He had borrowed the car from this other guy called Benno, who had lost his license. Benno had been in a lot of trouble as a kid, but he had a kid of his own and a wife, and he was trying to make a go of it and stay straight. Anyway, this guy was driving me along the beach road in Benno's car when a cop car spotted us."

Danny's voice dropped lower, but his eyes were distant. "We weren't doing anything wrong, so I figure they had checked on the registration and recognized Benno's name. They started after us. The guy driving the car freaked and took off. He said the cops had beat him up once before on a dark road." He smiled bleakly. "I figured he was probably lying because cops don't do things like that for no reason, but I just sat tight. When they were gaining, he swerved off the main road, bashed through a gate, and bogged the car in a field. Then he ran off."

It started to rain lightly, but Danny seemed oblivious to it. "The cops had a dog in the car and they let him go. That was when I ran, but the dog got me right away."

He stopped, as if picturing what he was telling me, fixing the details in his mind. Rain soaked steadily into us, but I was transfixed by the vividness of Danny's storytelling.

"The cops were hopping mad at having to run around in a muddy field and then getting no one but a kid," he went on. "I didn't know it then, but it's cop tradition here to beat up anyone who resists arrest or runs. I tried to tell them what happened, but all they wanted was the name of the guy who had driven the car. They thought it was Benno. I told them it wasn't him and that he was still at the party, but they didn't believe me. They told me if I didn't name Benno as the driver, they'd sic the dog on me."

He laughed. "I thought they were bluffing, and I guess they thought I'd cave in and say anything they wanted. I started to realize they didn't care who was driving the car about the same time they understood that I wasn't going to lie. So they sicced the dog on me. I punched it away, so they held me down, belted me with their sticks, and then they held me while the dog attacked me."

Danny brushed his hand unconsciously over his forehead and

the streetlight shone fleetingly on a wide twisted scar hidden by his blond fringe.

"Jesus!" I whispered, staring at his forehead in horror. I felt breathless and scared, and it seemed to me I could hear it all: the threats, the dog growling, and Danny screaming.

"I was a mess by the time they got the dog off me. I was all torn up on the head, and he had gotten my leg and shoulder pretty bad. But I still didn't say Benno drove the car." There was a faint tremor in his voice, and I wondered how close he had come to doing what they wanted. How near he had come to breaking.

"That was torture," I said incredulously.

Danny seemed not to hear me. "They dropped me outside the hospital, and later on another cop came to my mom's house to say I was being charged with breaking into that farmer's yard and destroying property."

He looked at my face, read the outrage and shock. "The lawyer my mom hired said it would be my word against theirs, and no one was going to believe a kid over a cop. He said if I didn't plead guilty to the police charges, I'd go to a detention center. He said to plead guilty and then I could charge the cops later for beating up on me."

He stopped.

"What did you do? Did you charge the police with bashing you?"

Danny smiled with unexpected gentleness. "Nathaniel, that's what I meant about you. Haven't you figured out by now that in the sleazy adult world there aren't any good guys? The lawyer told my mother to accept, so she did." His smile faded. "I pleaded guilty, and then we found out that the police themselves investigate complaints against each other."

"What?"

Danny nodded. "See?" He started to walk again, and I followed, but my legs felt unsteady. "For a while I was scared every time I saw a cop, because I figured if a cop could do that, then they could do anything, even kill me, and no one would do anything. I went a little mad for a while and I had to go to this place." He gave me a quick look. "A sanitorium. That's what those kids were talking about on the bus. The only reason they let me come home from the sanitorium was because I told them I made up the whole thing about the cops attacking me. They didn't believe me until I lied."

He gave a hard bark of laughter.

My mind groped toward something like a hand in the dark. A conclusion maybe; a light. But Danny's voice intruded, subtle as a shadow in the night. "I was pretty messed up. I felt like it wasn't over. It seemed like there was something missing. So I waited.

"Then, one day a cop came to Three North. It turned out to be one of the cops that bashed me. There he is smiling and telling everyone how the police are there to protect them. I thought maybe he didn't recognize me. But at the end of the talk he winked at me, like we knew a good joke nobody else did."

We had reached my house and I stopped, so Danny did too. I don't think he was seeing anything though.

"When he winked, it all came clear to me. I realized everything that happened was a joke. I had been thinking that what happened with the police was wrong, waiting for something to happen to make it right. But when he winked, I realized nothing was going to make it right. That's life. Nothing made any sense but to stay alive—survive. Justice. Right and wrong: It was all bullshit people made up."

He took a deep breath and stretched his arms out. "It's like that woman who went to live with gorillas in the jungle," Danny explained. "She had to turn herself into a gorilla to live with them. That's what you have to do if you want to survive. It's no good telling a gorilla who wants to tear your head off that he shouldn't do that because it's not fair. That's what the police are like. The power makes them into gorillas and you have to remember that's what they are. You don't talk to them or expect them to be fair. You run, or you climb up a tree, or you shoot them before they can get you."

Danny was telling me that what had happened in that dark field turned him into the wolf boy. He had become an animal so that he could survive.

As if he read my thoughts, Danny said, "I got a mission, see. That kid back there, I'm teaching kids like him what those cops taught me. I'm helping them survive because next time instead of trying to reason with the gorilla that wants to eat them, they'll run. I help them see how it really is—you live, and then one day the wild animals realize you're not one of them and they kill you and eat you. End of story. There's no such thing as bad gorillas or good gorillas."

You could tell he really believed that, but there was something wrong about what he was saying. Something that didn't jell. And I thought of Lallie's warning to Danny. She had told him not to let the dark flame of the past consume the future. "What about Lallie and the Chain? That's about right winning out over wrong."

Danny grinned at me, an engaging urchin's grin, and in spite of being horrified over what he had told me, I found myself smiling back. "Yeah. Well I'm an idealist."

"You *are* crazy." I laughed, shaking my head. I was surprised to find I no longer thought of him as a sort of trainee maniac. He seemed suddenly kind of heroic to me. I thought he was probably right about power making people savage, but not about it turning them into animals. Animals are better than people. Humans are the real savages. That's what people don't understand. Those police who bashed Danny weren't acting like animals. They were acting like humans.

We were leaning on the fence now, and without us noticing, the rain had stopped.

"I was crazy, until I met Lallie," Danny said quietly and seriously. "The first day I saw her I had just been in a brawl.

My mouth was all bloody, and everyone had scattered because a cop was coming across the football field. Lallie wiped the blood off my mouth. I can remember exactly the words she said too. She said, 'You have to believe in justice to make it happen. You have to believe in the light, or you live in darkness. Believing is the magic.'"

He shook his head. "It was as if she saw inside my mind and knew what was eating me up. Then—you're not going to believe this—Lallie said the cop couldn't see the truth because he didn't believe in it. That cop came right up to us and looked around. He couldn't see us! Spooky, eh?" He shrugged and seemed suddenly embarrassed.

"I still don't get why you belted that kid."

He shrugged. "It was because of what Lallie said about believing in justice. That little kid had stopped believing. He was just going along with those big guys because it was easy and safe. Only it's not safe. It's never safe to go along with what's wrong. You have to fight against it. I showed him that it wasn't safe to go along."

I stared at him, for the first time noticing that he was a lot shorter than me. His pale hair was darkened by rain and plastered to his head, his jeans and jacket dripping wet.

"I never told anyone that whole story before, not even Bear," he said suddenly. He looked up and his eyes were clear and bright. "I told you because you have to understand a guy isn't good just because he is a policeman. It's what people do that makes them good or bad." Danny sneezed and wiped his nose on the back of his hand. "Better go."

He frowned, staring over my shoulder. "There's a note on your door."

I turned to see an envelope stuck to the front door. My heart jumped and I hurried over, ripped it open, and read it with a feeling of trepidation.

Danny came up the path after me. "What is it?"

"It says we've all got to meet at Shelly Beach tomorrow at eleven. It's signed: The Chain."

Danny squinted at it. "Bear must have dropped it over. It says urgent."

"Maybe it's to do with Lallie. I guess there'll be one waiting for you too."

Danny nodded, frowning down at the note. Then he shrugged, pulled his jacket tight around him, and headed down the path. "See you tomorrow then."

I nodded. "Danny?"

He looked back, and the rain began at the same time, more heavily, streaming down his face in rivulets. "Yeah?"

I opened my mouth, not sure what I wanted to say. That I was glad he had told me what had happened to him. That it had made me sick and angry. That he had more guts than anyone I had ever known.

"You're all right too, Danny-O," I said at last.

He grinned again, sketched a wave in the air, and trotted away into the rainy night.

17

I let The Tod out of my room and into the backyard for a walk. He gave me a reproachful look for the weather, which he regarded as my area of responsibility.

Standing at the back step to wait for him, I watched the rain hammer down on the dark lawn. Behind me the house felt vast and empty, and I wished I had asked Danny to stay.

It was hard to remember how much I had disliked him less than a week ago. His oddball sense of humor, even his wild streak were neither good nor bad traits now. The longer I knew Danny, the more complex he seemed, the more sane his craziness became.

It occurred to me that this was why Danny had been called to the Chain. Maybe that was what Lallie had meant about being Chosen by our choices. In choosing to fight against evil, Danny chose to fight for what was right. But if that was so, why had I answered the Call? I had never fought against evil.

The Tod came back inside, shook himself vigorously, and went into the kitchen with an expectant look. Obediently I opened a can of dog food, then sneezed violently. I was still wearing the rain-soaked clothes. No wonder I couldn't think properly. I built a fire, changed in front of it, and made a hot drink.

But even then my mind would not settle. Random thoughts flew at me like leaves blown before a storm; Buddha standing on my foot, and Mr. Karle smiling while the blond boy threw the medicine ball. Mrs. Vellan questioning me, hinting things about my father and mother. The redhead kid on the bus telling the old man he would come and fix him. Lallie telling us Cheshunt had been bruised by an ancient evil.

And behind all of these I had a nightmarish image of Danny, who was scared of nothing, screaming while policemen held him in a dark field and a dog savaged him.

Lallie had said Cheshunt was bruised by evil—torture, sacrifice, and betrayal—and the more I thought of that, the more I could see the ancient theme repeating itself like echoes all around me.

Somewhere a dog barked, and The Tod lifted his head and gave a long, eerie howl in response. Then he looked at me with such a knowing, distant expression in his eyes that the hair on my arms prickled.

I pulled out the soggy note and smoothed it out on the carpet. It meant I would have to cut school. I had never done that in my whole life. My mother didn't even like me to be late.

The easiest thing would be to convince her I needed a day in bed after the bash on the skull. The bruise would be spectacular technicolor by morning, and it would not cross her mind that I might be faking. I was surprised to find the thought of cutting didn't bother me. I was probably a lot safer than at school, where anyone could brain me with a baseball bat and call it an accident.

I would stay in bed until my mother left, and then ride my bike out of Cheshunt along the beach road to Shelly Beach. I had never been there, but I knew it was just inside the boundary of Cheshunt.

I shivered despite the heat radiating from the fire, and a picture came into my mind of Anna Galway telling me about the caretaker killing himself. That had happened in Cheshunt. In fact, it had happened at Three North. Even back then, before Mr. Karle, the darkness had been here. Danny thought we had to fight the Kraken, but what was wrong with Cheshunt had gone on long before he came. That was what we were fighting. Mr. Karle was just its mouthpiece, its vessel. Maybe even one of many vessels.

The security guard had called the school a place where bad things happened. Whatever was going on with Cheshunt, the school was at the center of it, and I had the sudden conviction that whatever we were supposed to do would happen there too.

Later I found myself thinking of the guy that had taken the blame for the caretaker's death. How must he have felt all those years, knowing his life was slipping away while he rotted in prison for a crime he hadn't committed? I went to my jeans and pulled out the list of phone numbers with new resolve.

If I could find just one other person who had witnessed what happened, maybe I could write to the papers and get them curious enough to reopen that old case. It would be something to clear the guy's name after so long. In a funny sort of way I felt it would be a blow against the Kraken.

I could have kicked myself when I sat down at the phone and realized I hadn't asked Anna the name of the guy charged for the murder. I tried the Sikorsky number that had been busy all along, with a strong feeling that this was it. This time it barely rang once before a man picked it up.

"Yeah?"

I started to explain my search, but he cut me off, asking who I wanted. "I'm looking for Zebediah Sikorsky," I began.

"My name's Gertze and I never heard of any, what was it, Sokinski. He must have lived here before."

"Do you have a forwarding . . ."

"Nope." He hung up.

So much for hunches. I sighed, wondering how someone that terse had been on the phone for so long.

On impulse I looked up the name of the teacher whose scrapbook the librarian had let me read. If I could track her down, she might be able to tell me something about the fire and the other kids involved. There were five Heathcotes in the phone book. Three residential addresses and two businesses. I tried the first of the house numbers.

A kid answered. "Yeah?"

"Could I speak to your mother or father?"

"Yeah," he said, then he sang "Baa Baa Black Sheep" and hung up.

The second number was busy, and on the third try a girl answered.

"Heathcote residence." She was pretending she lived in a mansion with a maid. I grinned and explained what I was after. "You got the wrong number," she said importantly. "That lady lives in Saltridge. We've had calls for her before."

I nearly dropped the phone. Controlling my excitement, I asked if she knew Irma Heathcote's number.

It was the same as one of the business numbers I had written down: Heathcote Printery. When I dialed, it rang for a long time, before someone picked up the receiver.

"Irma Heathcote speaking," said an elderly woman.

My mouth felt dry. Swallowing, I apologized for calling so late and told her about the history project and the scrapbook.

She laughed. "Oh, my goodness. How on earth did it get back to the school? That was my very first school, you know. I was a student teacher doing my first rounds." She laughed again reminiscently.

"Do you think I could come and talk to you? I could bring the scrapbook." I crossed my fingers because I was unsure if the librarian would let me have it.

There was a pause. "I don't see why not, young man. Though I'm not sure how much I can help you. When would you like to come?"

I thought fast. "Would Sunday be possible?"

"This Sunday?" she sounded startled.

"If it's possible."

Another pause. "Well, I go to church, but if you came in the afternoon . . ."

"That'd be great." I took down the address, thanked her, and hung up feeling triumphant. My head started to hurt again, but I decided to call the second Sikorsky number. I was trying to imagine the sort of person who would write a soppy love poem when a man with a voice like gravel answered. "Yeah?"

Startled, I asked if Zebediah Sikorsky was there.

"Who wants to know?" He sounded middle-aged and rough. I told him my name and about the school project.

There was an odd pause. "Zebediah Sikorsky was my brother. He is dead," the man said gruffly, then he hung up.

I stared at the phone with an awful feeling, though common sense had told me some of the kids in that photograph must be dead. The phone rang and I jumped about a foot in the air. When I picked up the receiver, my hand was shaking.

"Hello?"

Silence and a faint echo of static. I thought I could hear the sound of someone breathing. I hung up.

The phone rang again. I just let it ring until it stopped, then I dialed the police.

"D 24. Police. Can I help you?"

I slammed the phone down and then took it off the hook before going to bed. I felt lousy, but I couldn't sleep. One minute I would think about Anna Galway and wish I had asked her the name of the boy. The next minute I would be worrying about what the phone calls meant and wondering how much Mr. Karle knew.

Calling the police had been instinctive, but then I had thought of Danny's story about them.

My mother was gone by ten the next day, having called the school to tell them I wouldn't be in. She had even made me a packed lunch so I wouldn't have to get up. Stifling guilt pangs, I gave her half an hour, then leaped out of bed and dressed. My head ached, but not badly.

I was supposed to be at the beach by eleven, according to the note. I stuffed the packed lunch and an orange in the backpack with a handful of dog biscuits and a bottle of water. Then I loaded The Tod in the bike basket and pedaled off, hoping Mom wouldn't turn back, having forgotten something. If she discovered me missing, it would be the end of glasnost. The Tod curled up right away and went to sleep.

It was a cold, gray day out, and looked like rain again. I had dressed warmly but taken a towel and bathing suit, just in case the afternoon cleared. Once I was out on the highway, I pedaled fast, reveling in the wind on my face.

All along the beach side of the road were factories. They were operating, but they looked old and derelict. Farther down, the factories gave way to fields of long, spiky salt grasses.

A factory horn blew to signal a coffee break. The noise woke The Tod and he hung over the edge of the basket and barked. I don't know what he thought the noise was. Maybe some big kind of bird that lives out there in the wetlands. He liked chasing birds.

By now I could see the ocean out in the distance. Suddenly the highway curved down toward the sea, and I was cycling right along the edge of the land. The road surface was about two feet above sea level. Gray-green bushes bordered the dark blue water, a choppy white froth riding the wave crests and blowing back on itself. I stared out at the sea and rode more slowly, savoring the salty tang of the air. The water seemed to go on forever, and the clouds were radiant at the edges where they were thinner and the sun shone through.

At last I came to the animal shelter, which my map told me marked the turnoff to Shelly Beach.

You could hear some of the dogs barking, calling out for their owners to come and get them away from there. The Tod listened, and then he started shivering and hunched right down in the basket.

I hated going to those places because I always wanted to take all the dogs home or let them all free, even though I knew most of them would go right out and be hit by a car or starve to death. I sometimes wished I could have a place where I could take those dogs and let them live. The Phantom had this sanctuary called Eden and all the animals there lived together, even tigers and baby deer, because they'd never learned it's kill or be killed. The meat eaters ate fish out of the lagoon and the island was protected by the Bandar poison pygmies and by the piranha fish in the lagoon. I would have liked there to be such a place for pets who had been dumped or abandoned. They could feed the owners to the piranhas.

I was so busy thinking of how I would organize my Eden that I didn't see someone running toward me. When the sound of footsteps grew closer, I cornered too fast, skidding in the gravel before I was back on the tar and riding as fast as I could.

"Nathaniel! Stop!"

I screeched to a halt, recognizing Bear's voice. He came running up panting hard, red spots of color in his cheeks. He was wearing cut-off denim shorts and a faded pink T-shirt, and his hair was hanging loose over his shoulders.

"Hey, Conan. You scared the hell out of me." I laughed.

He didn't laugh back. "The note was a fake."

I felt like someone punched me in the stomach. "What?"

He nodded, still sucking in air. "I went by Danny's place this morning and he asked me why I hadn't left him a note."

"But how could it be fake? Nissa might have left it."

He shook his head and looked up the road. "Then why wouldn't I have gotten one? And Danny? Besides, I asked her."

"But . . . it was signed: The Chain."

Bear gave me a bleak stare. "Danny told me. And that means there's only one person who could have left it."

"The Kraken?"

He motioned for me to get off the bike, then lifted The Tod out of the basket and dragged it over behind a clump of bushes and threw some leaves on it. "Nissa reckons it's to flush you out. If they get you, they'll make you tell about the rest of us."

I groaned and picked the dog up. "My mother called the school to say I was sick!"

"Don't worry about that now. If Nissa's right, someone should be coming along to catch you red-handed any time now. Lucky you were early. I only just made it. If you'd gone down to the point, there would have been no way back. They'd have had you."

We heard a car in the distance and dived into the bushes. I closed thumb and forefinger around The Tod's little muzzle, ignoring his disgusted look.

A minute later a police car pulled around the corner and sped off down the beach road.

"What a surprise," Bear whispered. I felt too sick to joke. If it hadn't been for Danny and Bear, I would have walked right into the trap.

"We'll wait until they go, then we'll cross the fields. The others are meeting us at Moonlight Head." He smiled at my puzzled look. "We figured since the Kraken was so good as to set up a meeting for us, we might as well take advantage of it."

"But, if we're all away from school today it'll be obvious who we are."

Bear's grin broadened. "Danny called the police anonymously and said there were three bombs hidden in the school. The whole place will be in an uproar for hours. There's no way they'll be able to say for sure who was or wasn't there."

It was almost an hour before the patrol car roared back past us and back around the corner, sending up an irritated spume of gravel.

When it had disappeared out of sight, Bear stood up and stretched luxuriantly. The Tod did the same and we both laughed. Moments later we were running across the overgrown field toward a dark plantation of pines, The Tod bounding along behind us like a mutated rabbit.

At the fence line Bear held the barbed wire up while I got through, and I did the same for him. The Tod scooted underneath, his ears pricked up with excitement.

We had to walk bent over to get under the pine branches, because the trees were so close together. There was a heavy silence in the deadness under them and it was unexpectedly dark, the smell of pine-needle sap almost overpowering.

We came out of the trees to a view that took my breath away. A steep rocky hill sloping down to a short, white curve of beach.

"Moonlight Head," Bear announced, smiling at my reaction.

A sharp wind blew the smell of the waves into our faces as we clambered down the rocks to the beach. The waves unrolled onto the shore with a silky whisper, and the clouds parted to bathe the beach in golden autumn sunlight.

"Unbelievable," I murmured.

Bear gave me a meaningful look. "It feels like we've come out of a dark cave, doesn't it. The road back there is the border of Cheshunt."

It might have been my imagination, but it did seem as though a great weight had lifted off my shoulders now that we had officially left Cheshunt. By the time we reached the sand, the waves crashing against the shore sounded deafeningly loud, as if they were a tidal wave building up steam.

"It's funny how people are about noises," Bear mused. "If that noise was a factory, people would complain it was too loud; but because it's the sea, we just think how great it is."

The Tod raced around in frenzied circles of delight, sticking his little snout in every hole or indentation. When he looked up at me, I burst out laughing because his nose and face were caked with sand. His black eyes stared at me out of the sand mask as if to ask what was taking me so long, then he raced off again.

"Hey!"

I jumped around and saw Danny waving madly from the far end of the beach. The Tod streaked off toward him, and we followed at a slower pace.

Danny punched me lightly in the arm. "You made it."

"Thanks to you and Bear," I said seriously.

He grinned. "Lucky I walked you home last night. So what happened?"

"Wait," Bear said.

Ten minutes later we came around a clump of seabrush and the rest of them were sitting on towels in a sheltered part of the beach.

"This is a good spot," Danny enthused. "The wind isn't too strong. Less sand in your sandwiches. And best of all, you can't be seen from above."

Seth was wearing faded jeans and a bulky hand-knitted cream sweater, one hand wrapped loosely around the neck of a bottle of coke. He looked like an advertisement for something—so perfect, he was not quite real. I wondered what was going on in his mind. There was a distant look in his eyes. His body was there, but his head was somewhere else.

Nissa was in her usual ragged jeans and huge sweater, and she looked at us expectantly. Bear told them economically about the police car.

"Police," Danny snarled. Seth said nothing.

"How's Lallie?" I asked Nissa.

She gave me an intense stare, squinting against the glare of the sun. "She came to see me last night. She was still pretty bad. She said now that the symbols were forged, the Kraken would use all of his power to find us." She gave me a shrewd look. "Maybe he already knows."

I felt defensive, but I kept my mouth shut because I was

beginning to realize that just because Nissa had an aggressive, direct way of saying things, didn't mean she was blaming me.

"Did she say what we do now?" Danny asked eagerly.

"She was . . . vague," Nissa said slowly. "Worse than before. She said Cheshunt is making her sick. But she did tell some things about the Healing. First we have to find the right spot to do the ritual. The place where it all started."

"How?"

"She said the eye that sees will know the earth that sorrows. That must mean Seth will figure that out somehow using his telescope." She frowned in her effort to remember the rest. "The sword has to open the wound. That's me, but I don't understand what it means."

"It must mean you have to fight. Cut someone," Danny broke in impatiently.

"No," Nissa said. "I'd better tell you the exact words: The farseeing eye has to find the earth that sorrows. The sword must open the wounded earth to release the poisons. The torch must sear the earth to close the wound. And . . . the bowl has to gather the cleansed earth and carry it to the sacred place for the Healing to be complete."

"What about Nathaniel?" Danny prompted. "What about the circle?"

"She said something about the circle suffering no obstacle to the Forging. It didn't really make sense because she was sort of drifting. I wanted to take her home, but she wouldn't let me. I don't think she wants us to know where she lives."

"Did she say anything about how we're supposed to deal with the Kraken?"

"She said he'll try to break the Chain so that we can't bind the darkness."

Danny gave me a meaningful look. "You see. We are meant to fight him."

"Fight him how?" I asked blankly.

"With the symbols, of course. That has to be it," Danny said eagerly. "Lallie will show us."

Nissa bit her lip and something in her expression made the saliva in my mouth dry out.

"I'm afraid not, Danny-O. The last thing Lallie told me was that she can't come into Cheshunt anymore. She said that it was up to us now. She can't help us anymore. She can't interfere."

18

"What do you mean, she can't interfere? She's the reason we're here!" Danny said angrily.

"No," Bear corrected gently. "We're the reason Lallie's here. Remember she said she came because we answered the Call."

Danny snorted derisively. "That's just words. She brought us together and said we have to fight him and now she's deserting us."

"Not deserting . . ." Nissa began.

Danny jumped to his feet, scattering sand. "If she's pulled out, what's the point in going on? All that stuff about healing—we don't even know what it means. What is the earth that sorrows?"

"Maybe this is some kind of test," I said.

He looked down at me searchingly, the wind ruffling his wheaten hair. I felt Nissa staring at me, but I held Danny's eyes. "It's like we have to figure out the clues."

"She said he's going to come after us. How are we supposed to defend ourselves? We've done nothing but run and hide from him and I'm sick of it."

"We have to be careful," Nissa said.

"He's the one who'd better be careful," Danny said savagely. Then he thumped the sand. "If only she'd told us how to use the symbols against him."

"Maybe they are just symbols," Seth said softly.

It was the first thing he had said, and because the wind was blowing toward me, I suddenly understood why he hadn't offered the Coke to anyone else. It was whisky or rum or some other strong alcohol, and perfect Seth Paul was high as a kite.

Nissa's hand snaked out and she knocked the bottle to the ground. Seth stared at her stupidly as whatever was in the bottle glugged out. Then he reached for it, but she kicked it out of the way.

"Weak shit," Danny said in disgust.

"You promised you wouldn't drink anymore," Nissa said icily.

"I couldn't help it." His bleary eyes turned to me and I felt a mixture of embarrassment and pity, and looked away.

Danny ignored him pointedly, turning to Nissa. "You've got the sword and that's a weapon."

Seth sat up clumsily. "The sword is to cut the . . . the earth for the healing."

"A sword is a weapon," Danny snapped.

"She can't fight the Kraken on her own. Lallie didn't say that," Seth slurred.

Danny laughed mockingly. "Are you offering to help her? You couldn't fight your way out of a paper bag."

"Just shut up, Seth," Nissa said disgustedly. "You're drunk."

He flushed. "I just meant maybe we're not supposed to use the symbols that way," he mumbled.

I felt a stab of pity for him and wondered how I had ever thought he was perfect. But, drunk or not, he was one of us and there had to be a reason for it. I thought of Lallie's warning to him. She had told him to seek his own vision.

My own warning had been a cryptic command to understand the past. The only thing I could think it meant was that I should try to figure out what the ancient evil was that had bruised Cheshunt.

I tuned back into the conversation to find Danny telling them about the business on the bus. The way he told it, I came out like some kind of hero.

"You think the Kraken told the kids in the Gathering to

behave themselves in Cheshunt?" Nissa asked me.

"I think it's more than that. I think he sent them out to cause trouble in the other neighborhoods."

"Why?"

"To make Cheshunt look good, so the other suburbs will listen to him, so he can spread the darkness."

"Maybe it's time we took a look at what goes on in those meetings they have," Bear said. "There's one on this weekend."

A chill ran down my spine.

Nissa bit her lip. "I don't know, Bear. Lallie said the darkness would gather to give him strength. It would be too dangerous for any of us to join."

"Who said anything about joining?" Bear asked, with Danny's recklessness in his eyes.

Nissa looked worried. "I don't know. If he catches you spying, I don't know what he'd do."

Danny grinned. "I'll come with you." He looked at Seth and his expression grew cold. "What are you going to do?"

"Nothing," Nissa said coolly. "He's going to invite me over to his house so I can snoop around and see if I can find out where his father fits into all this."

"What if his father realizes what you're up to?" Danny asked.

"You just worry about your part of it," Nissa snapped. She glanced at me. "You're the thinker, so you can try to figure out what all that stuff about the healing means. Okay?"

I nodded, wondering if she thought I would be too frightened to do anything because I was quiet.

The sun had come out of the cloud about fifteen minutes earlier and it was getting hot.

"What about a swim?" Bear suggested.

We all went in, even Seth. He, Nissa, and Danny dived right in, and Bear and I walked in slowly. I watched Nissa swim strongly, parallel to the shore.

"She's pretty good, isn't she?" Bear asked. "I'm hopeless."

"I'm not much better," I admitted. But I was thinking about how Nissa had looked without the sweater and jeans. She wore a bathing suit bottom and a T-shirt, and she was not the least bit skinny or shapeless.

We had gotten as far as the armpits, and I was trying to get up the nerve for the rest. Bear took a deep breath and ducked down, and I eased myself under, gritting my teeth.

"It's harder that way," Bear said. Then without warning he lurched sideways, a look of horror on his face.

Danny surfaced beside him, grinning like a maniac. "Da-da da-da da-da . . ." He sang the theme from *Jaws*.

Bear howled in fury and splashed him. Danny ducked and the water got Nissa square in the face. In a second we were all at it, splashing and screeching like a bunch of ten-year-olds. When we got out, we were shivering and grinning with blue-tinged lips.

But near-hypothermia didn't stop me from noticing you could see right through Nissa's T-shirt when it was wet. Then I was hot as well as cold. I wondered suddenly what it would be like if we were alone at the beach, if there was no T-shirt.

I looked up and she was watching me, a strange expression on her face.

I started drying myself furiously, waiting for her to say something nasty about me staring at her breasts like that. When I was brave enough to look again, she had her sweater back on and was pouring hot tea out of one of the thermoses.

I slid my hand into my jeans to get a tissue and something burned me. I yelped and whipped my hand away.

"What is it?" Bear asked.

I didn't have to put my hand in again to know what had burned me. Somehow the sun had made the circle in my pocket boiling hot. Then I remembered how hot the circle had felt in Mr. Karle's office that day.

Maybe it hadn't been the sun after all.

I jumped to my feet and looked around. The others looked up at me, as if I had gone mad. I ran my eyes frantically along the beach and up the rocky cliff.

Then, swinging around, I noticed something a long way out in the water. I frowned and squinted.

The others stood and followed my gaze, then Nissa gave a cry.

"It's Seth!"

He must have been swimming out ever since we got into the water. Nissa didn't hesitate. She threw off the sweater, dived in, and started to swim out after him. Danny was close behind her, his arms churning. Bear and I swam too, but we were nowhere as strong or fast.

After we had gone a little way, Nissa yelled something back to Danny, and he turned and yelled to us.

"Spread out," Bear panted.

"You stop here," I puffed, seeing he was probably the worst swimmer among us.

His eyes were dark with fear, but he nodded and started to tread water. I swam out until I started to feel tired, then I floated, conserving my strength for when it was needed. Danny and Nissa were still swimming strongly. Beyond them, seemingly miles out, was Seth's dark head.

Moments later Danny had stopped, and I could see his stomach. He was floating too. Now it was up to Nissa, and she showed no sign of slowing down, though it was hard to tell at such a distance. A piece of seaweed brushed against my leg, and I gasped in momentary fright at the thought of sharks circling in for the kill.

There was a distant shout, and I looked to see Nissa had reached Seth. They seemed to be struggling. My heart began to pound. What if he ended up drowning them both? There was no doubt in my mind that Seth was trying to kill himself.

But then they were beginning to come back. I watched with

bated breath as they inched toward the shore. Nissa was slowing then, obviously tiring. Danny swam out the last few yards and they began to come in again, dragging Seth between them.

When they finally got close, I could see Nissa and Danny were at the end of their strength. Seth lay on his back between them, his face dead white. My heart thudded as I swam forward to meet them and I fought a surge of panic when both Nissa and Danny grabbed me and I went under.

I sucked in a mouthful of salty water in shock, kicked my way to the surface, and yelled to Bear to help us.

In seconds he was beside me and we were swimming together, Bear and I swimming awkwardly between the rest of them, all of us gasping. By the time we reached the shore, none of us had the strength to walk, and we dragged ourselves out onto the sand, panting and coughing.

Then someone was crying.

I struggled to sit and realized it was Seth. He was lying on his back, racked by great gasping sobs. Gradually the others sat up, and we were all staring at him helplessly. Then, to my astonishment Nissa gathered the sobbing Seth into her arms and hugged him.

"It's all right, Seth," she croaked. "It's all going to be all right."

Her eyes met mine, and I noticed the pupils were so wide her eyes looked black. Without thinking I leaned forward and wrapped my arms around them both, my eyes burning. Then I felt arms around me as the others hugged us too.

All I could think about was how close Seth had come to swimming out and dying without any of us even noticing. I felt so sad for him that my chest and throat ached, because no matter how bad things had gotten, I had never been so without hope that I wanted to die.

Nissa was the first to speak, and I realized she was the only one of us whose eyes were dry. "Seth, why?"

He shook his head minutely, as if even that movement was almost beyond him. She opened her mouth to say something else, but Bear shook his head at her.

"I think we all need a hot drink," he rasped.

She nodded and went meekly over to the blankets. The rest of us rose, half supporting Seth. Bear wrapped a blanket around him, and Nissa poured from the second thermos. The first one had drained away during our dash to save Seth.

She drank from it first, then offered the steaming cup solemnly to Bear.

He drank, then gave it back to her. She gave it to each of us like that, silently, with the air of a priestess at some ancient ritual. And last, she offered it to Seth.

He looked in her eyes, his face haggard with despair, then his head slumped.

"Drink," she urged him softly.

An hour later we were all on our way home, Bear carrying Seth on his bike and Nissa with me, her salt-stiff hair brushing against my face as we headed back into Cheshunt. As we rode, I felt the heavy wrongness that lay over Cheshunt in my bones and blood.

I felt a surge of fear, but at the same time the nearness of the others made it easier to bear going back. Something had happened that afternoon, a queer sort of meshing, and when we stopped at a stand, to let Seth catch a taxi home, there was a closeness between us that had not been there before.

After the taxi had taken Seth away, the rest of us stopped a minute before going in our separate directions.

"You think he'll be okay?" Nissa murmured.

"I don't know," Bear admitted.

"It was my fault," she said grimly. "It was the way I talked to him. The way I treated him. I put too much pressure on him."

"So what happens now?" Danny asked.

"We go on with it," Nissa said in a hard voice. "You and Bear find out what you can about the Gathering, Nat figures out the Healing."

She walked away without looking back, her shoulders slumped, and as she did so, I felt afraid for her and for all of us and what we planned to do. I shivered and zipped up my jacket, but the cold had gotten inside my skin.

Bear and Danny stirred and climbed back on their bikes, pushing off.

"Be careful," I called.

"Daniel into the lions' den," Danny yelled blithely.

I watched them go, feeling bone tired and wrung out. Before today everything, even me getting pushed around, had seemed like some kind of black game. But the afternoon and Seth's almost successful attempt to kill himself brought it home to me that it was no game. Seth had come close to dying that afternoon, and while I didn't think the Kraken knew Seth was one of us, maybe the bit of weakness in Seth that Lallie had warned us about was already working against him.

We had to find out what was eating away at Seth before it destroyed him.

A couple of girls carrying clipboards came out of the corner house and gazed at me. I climbed on my own bike, wondering if everything that had happened that day had left its mark on me. I pushed away from the curb and pedaled away fast. I was nearly home before I remembered I was supposed to be in bed sick. I would be in serious trouble if my mother realized I had been out all day.

As I reached the park, a patrol car coasted by, going in the opposite direction. I felt the policemen inside look out at me, their eyes filled with dark magic.

19

I slept badly that night, despite The Tod's comforting presence curled into the back of my knees, my dreams full of dogs barking in the darkness and policemen with faces hidden in shadow.

I woke in the morning to the sound of my mother talking on the phone and I listened to the tone, trying to gauge her mood.

". . . I know, but I just feel it's better to let sleeping dogs lie," she was saying as I came out.

When she saw me, she mouthed that it was her mother. There was a deep furrow between her brows as she listened. For some reason talking to my grandmother always made her tense and upset.

"Yes, well, I'll do it in my own way and time," she said tightly. "Look, Mother, Nathaniel's here now. Do you want to say hello to him?"

There was another long burst of talk and her frown deepened. "I know what you think, but it's my decision. Here's Nathaniel. I'll talk to you soon." She handed the phone over and I wondered what they had been arguing about.

"Hi," I said into the receiver.

"Hullo, darling. How are you liking your new school?" my grandmother asked.

The sound of her voice brought me astonishingly close to the edge of tears, and I might even have told her the whole thing, if I hadn't sensed my mother listening. "It's okay," I said guardedly.

A sigh came through the phone. "Nathaniel, I know you're a long way away, but remember I'm always here. Call me whenever you want someone to talk to." She paused. "Try to talk with your mother. She needs you."

"I will," I said.

We talked for a little about The Tod, then she hung up.

Over breakfast my mother said a day in bed didn't seem to have done me much good because I looked washed out. It turned out she *had* called during the day, but had assumed I was sleeping too soundly to hear the phone. She stared at me for a long moment, and I resisted the urge to squirm with guilt, but it turned out she wasn't wondering what I had been up to because out of the blue she said I shouldn't go to detention while I was still recovering, and then she called the school to say so.

Even more surprising, she said I needed a day out in the fresh air and suggested we go to the zoo in the next county. I was only too happy to go, but I couldn't help wondering what was going on. My mother rarely did anything for no reason, and generally I got the feeling she preferred work to spending time with me. The only thing I could think of was that her mother had been at her to spend more time with me.

The zoo was about an hour's drive, and we didn't talk much on the way there, but for once it was a peaceful silence. It was a cool day, though the sun was shining and a slight breeze stirred the sodden banks of autumn leaves under the great shady trees that flanked either side of the entrance to the parking lot as we pulled up.

Looking up at the sky through the canopy of rusty foliage, I had that peculiar feeling you sometimes get of coming somewhere for the first time and feeling you've been there before.

Standing behind my mother at the ticket booth covered in a peeling jungle-book mural, I found the sense of familiarity increasing.

We had not been to the zoo since I started high school, but we automatically headed for the monkey enclosure, the way we had always done. My mother liked the panthers and tigers, while I preferred the bears. The monkeys were a compromise because we both liked watching them. It was their similarity to humans that made monkeys so fascinating. As usual, they were clustered in family groups, baby monkeys chattering and swinging from dead branches while the older monkeys busily groomed one another. Nearest the enclosure wire was a huge dark gorilla. Two smaller monkeys were industriously picking fleas off the backs of his hands.

"It's the monkey manicure," a young woman told her boyfriend. He laughed and so did the other people standing around him.

"They're his slaves," said a little girl of about three, standing with her mother and father.

"They're his friends," her mother corrected. "That's Magilla Gorilla."

"Magilla's Manicure," the boyfriend said.

I glanced around at the enclosure, and again it seemed to me that I had seen it before, right down to the gnarled tree growing at the center. I looked up at my mother, but she was laughing at the antics of two small monkeys playing hide-and-seek. It struck me that she almost never laughed aloud.

"Mom, did we ever come here before?" I asked.

She gave me a startled look and hesitated before answering. "We did, but I'm surprised you remember. It was a long time ago." She paused again, as if weighing her words. "We lived over in Pendleton for a while."

Pendleton was the district beyond Saltridge. Less than fifteen miles away from Cheshunt.

"You never told me we lived near here before."

"I didn't think it was important," my mother said, walking ahead. "We only stayed a little while." She closed her mouth with a snap, as if to keep something inside.

I had a fleeting image of fear, and then of running, but it

156

was too vague to put into words. "Is that why you took the job at Elderew?"

"No. Well, perhaps partly, to lay some old ghosts to rest." Just then her eyes grew wide with horror, and I followed them to the enclosure.

The big black gorilla suddenly grabbed one of the monkeys and threw it to the ground, baring long yellow fangs in a savage grimace.

"Mafia Magilla," the boyfriend quipped, laughing.

"The hairy godfather," said his girlfriend.

The black gorilla got up and started pounding its great fists into the other monkey who just cringed and whimpered, making no attempt to escape. A few people cried out in shocked surprise.

The toddler shrank against her parents' legs. "The bad monkey is hurting the baby monkey. Why doesn't it run away?"

"It's too frightened," my mother murmured.

I gave her a startled look, but she didn't see me. Like everyone else, her eyes were riveted on the gorilla. It had now begun to kick the other monkey, which rolled onto its back and was no longer even shielding its head.

"It'll kill it," someone murmured worriedly. "It's an evil monkey," the little girl said, and started to cry.

"They're probably just playing," her father said, and led her firmly away. But the girl didn't look convinced and kept craning her neck to look back.

At last the gorilla spat on the smaller monkey, to cries of disgust from the watchers. Then he went back to his rock. The second monkey that had just stood and watched the whole thing came scurrying over to go on with searching for fleas. The small monkey just lay blinking and panting, not daring to move. Every now and then the gorilla would give it a look of pure malice, and I thought the girl had been right about it being evil.

"Do you believe in good and evil, Mom?" I asked, when we were looking at the seals.

She had seemed preoccupied after we left the monkey enclosure. "That's a pretty heavy subject for a Saturday morning."

I was silent and she smiled wryly. "Well, let me see. I don't think a monkey can be evil. I just think they do things for territorial reasons. Out of instinct."

"I don't mean the monkey."

Her smile disappeared so suddenly, I thought she was mad at me, but instead a serious look came into her eyes. "You mean people? I believe people can do evil things and I guess that would make them evil."

"But I mean evil as a sort of force that you could fight."

She frowned. "Evil and good are potentials in all of us. You have a choice whether or not to be evil, because you can choose not to do evil things," she went on, almost as if she were talking to herself. "Sometimes it might be tempting to do a bad thing and if you resist, then that's fighting evil. But a force outside human beings?" She shook her head.

"Anyway, even the terms good and evil are too black and white because they don't take into account the grays in life."

"Grays?"

She nodded. "Sometimes you just can't label this as evil or that as good. It's not that simple, so then it becomes a matter of the lesser of two evils."

It was just the sort of explanation an adult would have. My mother could only see evil in a mundane way, like stealing or lying or cheating on your income tax.

One of the zoo assistants came to feed the seals, and a lot of people gathered to watch, saying how cute the baby seals were and worrying about them getting the same amount of dinner.

But my mind was not on the feeding. I was thinking that kids could see things that adults couldn't, because they weren't hampered by ideas of the way things ought to be.

The more I thought about it, the more it seemed to me that this lay at the core of what was happening in Cheshunt. Lallie had said to Danny that believing was a kind of magic, and believing was something kids could do better than adults. Maybe that was why five kids had responded to the Call instead of adults. An adult who heard the Call would explain it away somehow, and dismiss it.

You couldn't respond to something you didn't believe in. You couldn't see what you couldn't believe in.

Then a more astonishing thought came to me: *You couldn't fight evil if you didn't believe in it!*

"You're very quiet," my mother said. "What were you thinking about?"

"Salmon," I said at last.

She looked puzzled and said she doubted the zoo had salmon.

We went to look at the elephant. It had a baby, and a zoo assistant, stripped down to shorts and sneakers, was giving them both a bath.

"He's having his bath," a man told a group of wide-eyed children in scout uniforms. They were young, but I was sure that if Mr. Karle passed by, they would see him for what he really was. They wouldn't say it was impossible, because to kids that young everything is possible.

As if she had been thinking along similar lines, my mother suddenly said. "Nathaniel, people who . . . who are bad didn't start out that way. Sometimes it gets to be a vicious cycle. A child who is bashed can grow up and become a murderer. But it doesn't have to be that way. Sometimes being a victim of evil makes you stronger."

Lallie had said whatever was wrong with Cheshunt had started with an ancient evil that had bruised it. Maybe the same went for people. A person bruised by evil always had a dark patch that could get infected.

"Nathaniel?" my mother asked. "I wish you'd tell me if something is bothering you."

I looked into her hazel eyes and had the overpowering desire to tell everything to her. But common sense kept my mouth shut, because if what had been going through my mind was right, she would not want to hear. She would think I was having one of those teenage breakdowns you read about in the paper.

"I'm just hungry, I guess."

Her face cleared and she looked relieved. "Let's go eat then."

There was a restaurant in a pavilion, and we chose a sunny corner sheltered from the wind.

"I think it's going to rain again," my mother said. Then she shook her head, as if she were mad at herself. "Listen to me, talking about the weather to my son." She gave me an apologetic look. "Nathaniel, I want us to be able to talk more. To say things to one another, but it's hard for me. Most of my life I've spent learning how to hold things in."

"Because of your father?"

My grandfather had been a tyrant who had ruled his house with an iron hand, and hearing the occasional story about him from my grandmother over the years had made me glad he died just before I was born. My mother had never said it exactly, but I had gotten the feeling that part of the reason she had married my father so young was to escape from her father's house.

But to my surprise she shook her head. "That's part of it, but that's not the whole story." She stopped and began to spread mustard on her sandwich. "Sometimes situations shape a person and even when the situation changes, it's hard for a person to get out of old habits." I gathered she meant herself and wondered what she was trying to tell me.

She fell silent again, and we watched a skinny albino peacock stalk by.

"Poor thing," my mother said sadly.

Two policemen walked by laughing and talking, and I turned to watch them, wondering how Seth Paul's father would fit into my theory.

"Do you think a policeman could be evil?"

She turned to stare after the policemen as well. "I think anyone who has power over other people can be evil. 'Power corrupts and absolute power corrupts absolutely,' " she quoted. "I think it's easier to be evil when you have power, when you're strong." She reached over and ruffled my hair, as if I were six. She was smiling, but I saw unease deep down in her eyes. "But I suppose they don't set out to be evil. It's just that the power they have to control, ends up making them want to control everything. I think wanting to control things is where evil begins." She tilted her head. "Nathaniel, what is all this about good and evil?"

"It's something we were discussing in class," I said glibly, but she was not so easily diverted.

"There's nothing wrong at school is there?" she asked.

That brought me to my senses. I didn't want her to go up to the school and start nosing around. In fact, I wanted her as far away from Mr. Karle's influence and his creepy hypnotic eyes as I could get her.

"No," I said lightly. Changing the subject to distract her, I told her about the history project and tracking down Irma Heathcote.

"You're quite the detective," she said, as we came to the alligator pool. The sign said he was called Charlie Chomp, and he gave us an impassive stare out of ancient yellow eyes.

I told her about my attempts to find one of the students who still lived locally by using the phone book.

"I'm glad there were no long-distance calls." She laughed.

I grinned. "Oh, I forgot, there were two calls to Alaska, but you'll have to take it out of my pocket money."

We smiled at one another, and I felt a sudden rush of love for her and a desire to protect her.

"Speaking of calls, I had a couple of funny ones late last night." She turned her back on Charlie and moved to the turtle pool alongside. There was no sign of Tim the Turtle, and the sun suddenly disappeared into a bank of dark clouds that had been building on the horizon.

"I noticed you left the phone off the hook the night before. Did you get any crank calls?"

"I must have knocked it off. Did you call the police about the calls?"

She looked around at me quickly. "No, I . . . I didn't."

I nodded and we were awkwardly silent for a moment.

The first few spots of rain fell, and we headed back to the car. The Tod had been asleep, but he barked frantically when we opened the door. I let him out on the grass for a walk. By the time we were driving back down the highway, it was coming down in sheets, thundering on the roof.

"Just made it to the car in time," my mother said. She suggested we see a movie together and have a pizza after we had changed at home, but when we got home, there was a message on the answering service from Elderew asking if she could work the night shift. She sighed and looked tired as she returned the call to say she would come.

"We need the money," she said apologetically.

Thirty minutes later she drove off toward Saltridge. Waving at her, I noticed two girls coming out of a house farther up the road.

As they passed, I recognized one as the girl who had warned me against holding out during the basketball game. Marigold, her name was. I lifted my hand to wave, but she looked away.

Feeling stupid, I went inside, wondering why she had snubbed me. Belatedly I realized she might not have responded because she didn't want anyone to think we were friends. As if she knew being a friend of mine were dangerous.

20

"Hey," Bear called.

I swung around in surprise to find him sprawled under a tree in the park.

"Where's The Tod?"

"Locked in the laundry room. I have to go to Willington and I can't take him with me, but I'm too scared to leave him in the backyard with Buddha lurking around."

"Willington?" Bear echoed.

I told him my idea for the assignment, and about Irma Heathcote. "What are you doing here anyway?"

He grinned. "Waiting for you. Nissa wanted me to tell you we're meeting tomorrow night."

His voice seemed to echo oddly and I looked around at the park. Unlike the zoo garden, there was a desolate, unkempt air about it. "I hate this place," I said, surprised to discover I meant it.

Bear looked around. "It's kind of creepy, but it's probably just all the rumors about it. You never see anyone playing here."

I thought of telling him about the eyes and the way it sometimes seemed bigger at night, but Bear got to his feet and pulled on his backpack. "So you didn't go to detention yesterday?"

I shrugged. "My mom called the school. It was all her idea. We went to the zoo."

"The zoo!"

I grinned at his expression. "Yeah, I thought that too when

she suggested it, but it was fun. We used to go a lot when I was little." I frowned. "I think she wanted to tell me something, but she couldn't get up the nerve. What about you and Danny? Did you find out anything about the Gathering?"

"Postponed," Bear said disgustedly. "So, have you had any ideas about the Healing?"

"Not really. Did Nissa say how things went at Seth's place?"

He frowned. "She didn't end up going. Seth went away with his father for the weekend."

I frowned, thinking about Seth and his father. "Why do you suppose he's the way he is?"

"Who knows. His mother left, you know, and his father got custody."

"I wonder how he feels being on the other side of his father?"

"I wonder that too," Bear said pensively. "You know, the very first night he came up to the attic, he was drunk out of his mind. Lallie brought him. You know Danny. He wanted to know what we were supposed to do with him. Nissa was most worried about his father, because even then everyone knew he was the sort of policeman people were scared of. But Lallie just said the Chain needed Seth."

"Poor Seth," I said softly, thinking of the way he had looked at Nissa at the beach. Another thought occurred to me. "Have you ever wondered what will happen if we lose?"

"Like Lallie said, the darkness will spread."

I shook my head. "I mean what will happen to us."

He gave me a somber look as we turned into Ende Crescent and stopped at the bus shelter. He sniffed and grimaced. "What a stink."

I looked at him in surprise. "You can smell it?"

"Are you kidding?"

"I thought I was the only one. My mother said I'd get used to it."

"*Hey!*"

We swung around to see Buddha and a group of school patrol guys coming across the field at a run.

"Shit," Bear breathed.

"Where do you two think you're going?" Buddha demanded as they crowded around us. His eyes were as red as Seth's had been the previous day, but there was no alcohol on his breath.

"None of your business," Bear said.

Buddha just laughed and punched Bear as hard as he could in the stomach. Bear grunted and doubled over, but to my surprise, he didn't try to hit Buddha back.

Buddha frowned and shoved him in the chest. "Come on, you big weak shit. Fight."

He didn't even flinch when Buddha slapped him hard across the face, and I wondered what was the matter with him. He was easily as big as Buddha, and even I could see that if he beat him, none of the others would take him on. For a second I had a vision of the monkey lying down while the gorilla pounded it.

"Cut it out," I yelled, hoping someone in one of the nearby houses would hear and come out. There was something frightening in Buddha's face, an emptiness that turned his eyes into black holes. Maybe Mr. Karle had not just told Buddha to rough us up. Maybe he had said anything goes. Or maybe Buddha was just too damn crazy to care.

Buddha spun on his heel without warning and punched me in the stomach as hard as he could.

"Where were you two going?" His voice was perfectly calm and seemed to have nothing to do with his eyes.

Winded, I gasped and heaved, struggling to get some air into my lungs. It felt like my chest was on fire. "To Willington," I managed finally as he was shaping up for another punch.

Buddha frowned and relaxed. "Why?"

"To have dinner with my mother." There was no point in refusing to answer.

"You're supposed to be sick. You didn't go to detention yesterday because you were sick," Buddha said, and I wondered how he knew that.

He smiled, showing his teeth as he looked down at Bear. "I guess we're just going to have to teach you both a lesson."

Right then the bus came around the corner and stopped to let out a whole group of people in football jerseys. As they poured around us, I grabbed the front of Bear's shirt, hauled him after me up the bus steps, and paid for us both. We sat right up front near the bus driver, but we needn't have worried.

As the bus pulled away, I could hear them all arguing because none of them had enough money to go after us.

I looked back to find them glaring balefully after us. All except Buddha. He was smiling.

"You know, I wasn't scared of fighting him," Bear said.

"You don't have to explain."

He seemed not to hear me. "When I was seven, my mother left me to look after my little sister Jenny. She was five. I was watching her play on some swings when these older kids came up and started calling me names."

Bear's face was bleak and stony reflected in the bus window. "I could have just ignored them, but I didn't. I got mad and I started fighting. I was a lot bigger than they were, so it was no contest. I won."

He stopped abruptly, a pulse above his collarbone hammering madly. Beyond him the streets flicked by, and people got on and off at stops, but it felt as if all of that was happening in another dimension.

"I was so busy fighting, I didn't see my little sister had climbed on top of the monkey bars. The next thing I heard was someone screaming."

Bear was silent for a long time.

"Did she fall?" I prompted at last.

"She slipped and hit her head." Bear looked up, straight at me, and I was shocked to see tears in his eyes.

"Did she . . . die?"

He shook his head. "She was in a coma for a week, and when she woke up, she wasn't the same. She used to smile and laugh all the time, but now she doesn't smile or look at you. She just stares. It's as if I did kill her, but the body was left behind."

The bus lurched to a stop, and just in time I realized it was my stop. We both got off and watched the bus pull away.

Above us the sky sagged heavily, as gray and laden with moisture as a wet tent. I was right on time, but I was uneasy about going off and leaving Bear feeling so low, especially after what had happened at the beach with Seth.

"You might as well come with me," I said casually, keeping my fingers crossed that it wouldn't put Irma Heathcote off from seeing me.

Bear nodded, but his mind was not on the present. "You know, I never told my mother the truth about that day. I . . . couldn't. If I'd been watching her, it wouldn't have happened. I might just as well have killed her. Sometimes I think it would have been better for her if I had. And every time I do anything, I think to myself that it's something Jenny will never do now. Because of me."

"Is that why you wouldn't fight Buddha? Because you were fighting when . . . when that happened?"

"No," Bear said in an exhausted voice. "I don't fight back because I deserve to be hurt. Because of Jenny. That's my punishment."

I stared at him incredulously. "But you were just a little kid. You didn't mean to do it."

He laughed bitterly. "Murderers say that. Soldiers who kill civilians, policemen who shoot innocent bystanders. 'I didn't mean it.' Only that's no excuse, is it? Anyway, I don't expect you to understand. It's not why I told you, I just wanted you to know I'm not a coward."

"I never thought you were," I said.

I knocked at number 45 Pitman Street, reminding myself of why I was there.

Almost at once the door opened and a fragile-looking elderly woman with white hair twirled in a bun on the top of her head looked out of a dark hallway.

"Mrs. Heathcote? I'm Nathaniel and this is a friend of mine from class."

She gave Bear a long look. "I'm pleased to meet you. What is your name?"

"Frank," Bear said, before I could answer. He shook her hand politely, managing not to stare at the purple-tinted fingers.

Once in the brightly lit kitchen I could see her properly. Irma Heathcote was wearing rubber boots about fourteen sizes too big for her and purple-stained overalls.

She left us to sit at a neatly scrubbed wooden kitchen table while she changed. The air was filled with gleaming pots and bottled herbs, and had the unmistakable scent of freshly baked bread.

I looked at Bear. "What did you tell her your name was Frank for?"

"Because it is."

Irma Heathcote came back wearing pink slippers and a flowered dress, her hands were only faintly blue now, and she carried a bucket full of blackberries.

"I know they're a noxious weed, of course, but I didn't plant them. I'm just reaping what someone else sowed. No doubt I'll be arrested one of these days and put in jail."

It was a grim joke, considering why I had come, but she didn't know that, so I smiled wanly. She hummed to herself as she emptied the blackberries into a double boiler. "You have to get the moisture out before you put the sugar in." She peered under the lid, then looked up at me. "I daresay you're thinking what a gossipy old woman I am."

I felt the blood rise into my face and she burst out laughing.

"It's true. I am. I talk the ear off the few visitors I have." She sighed and there was a flash of sadness in her faded green eyes as she looked from me to Bear.

"My husband died three years back, and since we didn't have children, there are no grandchildren to fill the space he left. I never thought of that when I decided against having my own children."

"You . . . you probably had enough of kids, what with teaching . . ." I said, trying to steer her toward her former career. She gave me a bright, curious, intelligent look that told me she knew exactly what I was talking about.

"I loved teaching," she said simply. "I felt that if I had my own children I wouldn't give as much of myself to it. You see, for me it wasn't just a job. It seemed to me the most important thing a person could do was to help shape the minds that would someday direct the future."

I nodded, trying to imagine what it would be like to be taught by someone who thought kids were important. Then, with a chill I realized Mr. Karle understood the importance of kids. Whatever he was planning started with kids.

"My mom had eight kids, and she says she wonders if she didn't miss out on another life because of that," Bear said surprisingly.

"Eight!" Mrs. Heathcote said admiringly, scooping a pile of sugar into the blackberry soup, a delicious rich, sweet smell curling into the air. She sniffed appreciatively as she turned down the flame under the boiler, then plugged in the kettle.

"Time for a cup of tea. Would you boys like a snack?"

Bear nodded for us both and looked pleased when she began to slice some bread and cover it with blackberry jam. She set the steaming mugs and the platter of bread and jam on the table and beamed at the expression on our faces.

The bread was still warm and the jam, from a previous batch, she murmured, was sweet and tangy and a long way from the jam you buy at the supermarket. Mr. Karle and the Chain seemed to belong to another world.

"Did you bring the book?" she asked suddenly.

The bread stuck in my throat. "I'm sorry. I haven't been to school since I talked to you."

"But you called me on Thursday. Didn't you go to school Friday?"

"I . . . I was . . ." I stopped before her knowing look.

"You skipped school, didn't you?" Her voice was stern and I couldn't help myself. I nodded and I felt Bear tense up beside me.

She relaxed. "Thought so, I always could tell when children were lying. And something tells me lies don't come easily to you, Nathaniel." She looked at Bear. "You too?"

I expected him to shake his head, but he nodded.

She looked from one of us to the other. "I assume that the reason you took a day away from school was a very important one."

"It was," I said, trying to understand how we had come to tell so much to a stranger. "I don't usually cut. My mother'd kill me if she found out."

"I doubt it," Mrs. Heathcote said dryly. She sipped her tea and stared at me over the rim. "So, why did you call me?"

"I'm trying to find out the name of a student who went to Three North when you were a teacher there," I told her.

She frowned. "A student's name? From my first year out? It was a long time ago. Why this particular student?"

"Do you remember any of the kids on this list?" I asked, handing it to her. "They were under that photo I told you about, the one in the library."

She smoothed the note carefully, staring at me as she did so.

"Mmm, the names do bring back faces . . ." she murmured. "Why this one student?"

I hesitated and she rapped the table imperiously. "Come, Nathaniel. How can I name anyone unless you tell me something more?"

"It's just . . . well you might not approve of what I'm trying to find out." She waited patiently. "I'm looking for the boy who was supposed to have murdered the caretaker."

"Ahhh."

"You remember him?"

"I remember. Of course I remember. You said 'supposed to have murdered.' He was convicted, you know. He actually pleaded guilty."

"I know, but he didn't do it."

Her eyes glittered. "How do you know that? He did plead guilty to the charge."

I ignored that. "Which one was he?" She looked down at the list, pointing to one of the names, and a sick dizziness came over me.

"My goodness, Nathaniel. Are you all right?" She stood and came around to stop beside the chair. Bear had stood up too and was staring at me worriedly.

"What's the matter?"

"I'm all right," I said, but my voice felt far away. I looked up at them both, feeling a terrible rush of sorrow. "Zebediah Sikorsky is dead."

"Dead . . ." she murmured. She sat again.

"Anna told me he didn't do it and I wanted to . . . help him," I said. I had not meant to tell her that. It was the shock.

"Anna?"

There was no point in holding back when she knew so much. I told her everything Anna had told me about the caretaker's death. "She said a group of kids witnessed what happened and that he, Zebediah, agreed to take the blame."

"A group?" Mrs. Heathcote echoed, but it was her own

memory she questioned. Finally she nodded. "Yes. They were all seen near the school that day, the group of them. Gang you'd say now. They were friends, though they were an odd lot. Anna was one of them. She was a pretty, dark-haired girl with a quick temper. . . ." A distant bell rang in my mind, but I was too rattled to pursue it. "I remember how strange I thought it was that Anna spoke out against Zeb." She smiled. "That's what everyone called him. Not Zebediah. Zeb."

"Why strange?" Bear asked curiously.

Irma Heathcote gave him a long look. "Because she was in love with Zeb. She was from a wealthy family. The only reason she came to Three North was because her father thought pampering children made them weak. Anna was pampered all right, but she was anything but weak. She had a streak of iron in her, underneath all the frills and fluttering eyelashes. The first time she set eyes on Zeb, she decided he belonged to her. He was a handsome boy. He liked her, but I don't think he was in love with her. He was the son of a Polish immigrant who couldn't speak a word of English, and as far as I know, he had two shirts to his name. But he was a clever boy and he knew his mind."

She examined the list again, then shook her head. "So they decided between them that Zeb would take the blame. How dreadful that they did not feel they could simply tell the truth."

"Do you . . . can you think of any reason why the caretaker would have killed himself like that?"

There was a long silence, and Irma Heathcote's eyes were shadows in the dimness of the kitchen, for it was close to dusk.

She sighed deeply. "You know, I was only at that school for a short time, but it has remained one of my clearest memories, and not just because one of my ex-students was arraigned for murder. I was not a superstitious girl, nor was I then, I fear, a very religious one. That came after, perhaps because of Three North. Yet I felt, the first day I came there, that it was a place that harbored evil. Things could happen there that would happen nowhere else."

She sipped at the dregs of her cold tea. "There was a dance instructor who had come to the school shortly before I did. He was charming and very handsome, but after he came, there was a lot of trouble and his name would always be at the center of it. Hysterical girls throwing themselves at him, claiming he had encouraged them, boys fighting and half killing each other over something he had let slip." She frowned. "I saw him talking to Sam—the caretaker—a few times. He was a good talker, and you often found yourself confiding things you did not mean to say to him. Sam had been in the war, and I recall someone once telling me he did not like to speak of it; that he felt a great deal of guilt because he had once been ordered to burn down a building that turned out to have women and children in it. They all died. I could imagine someone working on his guilt, inflaming it until . . ."

"But . . . why would this dance instructor want to make the old man kill himself?" Bear asked.

She sighed heavily. "It sounds insane even as I say it, but I think he liked to cause trouble. He enjoyed strife. He even had some of the town board members at one another's throats."

"What . . . what happened to him?" Bear asked.

Irma Heathcote blinked. "He became headmaster eventually, but I had left by then." She shook her head. "Poor Anna and Zeb. I wish . . . I wish I had known. Perhaps if I had stayed . . ."

"Mrs. Heathcote . . ." I began, but she rose.

"I don't think there is anything more I can tell you, Nathaniel," she said with sad finality. "I can't help either Anna or Zeb now, and neither can you. I don't live in Cheshunt and I want to forget I ever lived there, because it was like living in a shadow." She switched on the light, and only then did I realize how long we had been there. It was verging on dark. Bear stirred too, saying he had a bus to catch.

I stood up and pulled on the jacket I had discarded. "I'd better go too. My mother's expecting me for dinner."

Mrs. Heathcote nodded. "It is getting late."

At the front door I thanked her, as if the whole strange afternoon had been no more than tea and blackberry jam. As I reached the gate, she called out my name. I turned slowly to look at her, but she was little more than a pastel shadow in the deepening twilight.

"Nathaniel, be careful," she said softly.

THREE

The Forging

The Foreme

21

On the bus ride to Elderew and during my meal with my mother, I felt as if someone had switched the vacuum cleaner on "blow" and put it inside my head. Everything was flying around. My head was full of voices. I kept hearing Irma Heathcote saying that Cheshunt was a place that harbored evil. And then Lallie telling us we were supposed to heal the sorrowing earth.

And then I'd think about what Bear had told me, and Danny. They had experienced such terrible things. Nissa too, and Seth. The worst that had happened to me was that my mother and father had separated, and then my father died in a car crash. I had always felt sorry for myself over that, but the things that had happened to the others made my life seem like paradise.

Just before Bear's bus came, we had talked about Irma's story of the dance master and how many strange, unrelated things had happened in Cheshunt over the years.

"Except I don't think they're unrelated," Bear said. "I think that dance master was drawn here, same as a lot of other bad people. I think everything that has happened in Cheshunt is related to everything else because it comes from a sort of core."

"The earth that sorrows," I murmured now. The place where the evil had bruised the earth.

It was such a strange concept to think of the earth being bruised, as if it were alive and could be hurt. Well, you could poison water with chemicals, and a nuclear bomb could poison the ground for thousands of years. Why shouldn't it be possible for the earth to be poisoned with evil?

But where was the place we had to heal, the sorrowing earth? Over at Elderew my mother was too busy to stop for more than a quick bite to eat, though she did ask how I was feeling. For a minute I had no idea what she meant. Getting knocked unconscious at school seemed to have happened weeks ago. In fact, it was hard to believe we had been in Cheshunt less than a month.

My mother seemed distracted too, as if the trip to the zoo the day before had used up her weekly ration of words. She ate and went back to work, leaving me to finish alone.

When Lilly came to drive me to the bus stop, she had some news that drove everything that had happened that day out of my mind.

"Anna Galway is dead," she told me. "I'm sorry, Nathaniel."

I felt winded, somehow empty. "H-how?" Wildly I wondered if Patrick the ex–hit man had murdered her. "Was it . . . I mean how did she die?"

Lilly tilted her head. "She was old."

I thought of Irma Heathcote in her rubber boots picking blackberries. "Not as old as all that."

She gave me a funny look. "No, I suppose not in years, but in her heart she was old. Your asking made me remember some things. I couldn't have said them before, but now that she's dead, I don't suppose it matters. She tried to commit suicide three times since she came here. She never married, and in all the time she'd been with us, no one visited her. She was a very unhappy person."

"Did she . . . die in her sleep?" I said, but I was thinking: *Did she finally succeed and kill herself?*

"She was sitting in a chair in the sun when they found her.

The only thing she liked was the garden. Once—" Lilly smiled at the memory. "Once I saw her dancing around and around by herself. She was singing. . . . I suppose she was remembering something that made her happy."

I tried to imagine Anna as a young girl who loved dancing, but instead I thought of the photograph I had seen in Irma Heathcote's scrapbook, and her story about the dance master. Then a dizziness came over me. A blurring of focus, as if I were seeing two things at once.

A picture came into my mind of a dark-haired girl dancing around in a tangled hillside garden. The dream in which I had ended up falling off the side of a mountain.

The hair on my neck stirred.

Was it possible I had actually been dreaming of Anna as a girl? Maybe being in the Chain made it happen. Lallie had told me to seek the past. Maybe that somehow gave me the power to see back in time?

If that had been Anna in my dream, it struck me forcibly that the dark-haired youth must have been Zeb Sikorsky.

I shook my head, suddenly convinced I was letting my imagination run away with me.

But then Bear's words at the bus stop came back to me: "*I think everything that has happened in Cheshunt is related to everything else.*"

If the dreams were coming for a reason, then what might that reason be? Were the dreams meant to show me how destructive the darkness infesting Cheshunt was? Or how long it had been here? Or was it something more than that? Lallie had told me to look beyond the shadows of the past. Was I meant to see something in this old tragedy between Anna and Zeb and their friends? Was it a warning?

I shook my head, suddenly exhausted. It had been such a long day and I felt so drained. I was beyond thinking.

"Are you all right?" Lilly asked, pulling up at the bus stop.

I nodded, and as I opened the car door, an icy gust of wind blew into the car and fluttered a pile of papers on the floor. "I'd better go."

I was the only one on the bus. I stared out the windows at the empty streets, thinking I would write up everything that I had discovered for my assignment, including what I could recall of my conversation with Anna. I would just leave it without answers. It would be like the Bermuda Triangle. Mr. Dodds had said himself that there were no easy final answers in history, just questions and more questions.

My mind was a weary blank as we came into the outskirts of Cheshunt, and the heavy darkness of the place fell over me like a shroud. I pressed my face against the window. There were huge trees growing densely on all sides. I must have gotten on the wrong bus somehow.

I blinked wearily and it was just Cheshunt again, neat and tidy and silent. I was so tired, I was starting to see things. Or maybe it was Cheshunt causing the visions. Irma Heathcote called it a place that harbored evil. Only it was worse than that because it didn't only harbor evil. Cheshunt called it.

That night the phone didn't ring once, and that seemed more ominous than the crank calls. I went to bed, thinking it would be hard to go to sleep. I had let The Tod out for a walk, but now he was curled up on the bed beside me. He had known something was wrong, the way dogs do. He had stood up on my knees and looked in my eyes as if he were searching for something there. I stroked his silky ears, thinking of all the things I had learned, and before I realized it, I had fallen into a dream.

Just like that I was back in the overgrown mountainside garden in the red moonlight. I could hear the singing. Anna Galway's voice, I thought dreamily.

Once again I moved toward the voice, but this time I came

out of trees to find myself beside a broad, swift stream. There was a river raft floating by, carrying the two girls I had seen in the field picnicking. The dark-haired girl was singing, her voice melodious and strong.

"You have a lovely voice," the blond girl said.

I could hear her clearly, though they were some distance off. The dark girl stopped singing, with a haughty toss of her curls.

"*He* doesn't think so. He only sees you, and what am I to that?"

"There is no competition," the blond girl said.

"Tell *him* that," Anna said, her eyes slitted with jealous anger. I shivered at the flash of savagery in her expression. "If you don't care for him, tell him." She paused. "Or *do* you care for him?"

"I care for all of you," the blond girl answered, but I could see, as Anna could, that she was avoiding the question. Anna Galway, I whispered the name to myself. Anna who loved Zeb Sikorsky. But he had not cared for her.

I thought of the handsome young man preferring to sit with the blond girl rather than dance with Anna. That was Zeb, I was sure of it. I stepped forward onto the bank in my eagerness to hear more and the blond girl turned to stare at me.

"What is it?" Anna asked, turning too.

"That boy."

"What boy?" Anna demanded, staring straight at me, but even as she moved toward me, her face changed and thickened, and she was the monster, its eyes full of insane rage.

"Children should be seen and not heard," it snarled in a guttural voice, and its great fetid paws closed around my neck with lethal killing strength, yet I didn't struggle or try to pull the paws away so that I could breathe.

I just stood there, letting it kill me. A black cloud blotted out the garden then, and somewhere miles away I heard a woman scream. Then a little girl asked, "Why doesn't he run away?"

181

"Because he's too frightened," my mother murmured.

I woke up gasping and choking, thrusting the nightmare out of my mind.

Riding to school, my eyes felt heavy and my throat sore. I was still terribly tired, but I had come up with a simpler explanation for the dreams. Maybe they had been sparked off by a combination of my research and what had been happening in the attic. The simplest way to find out if I had been dreaming of the actual past was to see if Anna and Zeb's faces in my dreams matched up with the faces in the library photograph.

I decided the first chance I got, I would go and examine the photograph.

I was late, so I had to go straight to class. The morning passed in a blur. English was with Mrs. Bunburry, who was one of the few teachers who really loved what she taught. Normally I liked her classes, but there was too much on my mind for me to concentrate.

"To sleep, perchance to dream . . ." Bunny read, in a voice that belonged to someone taller, younger, and more beautiful.

My mind went off on a tangent at the mention of dreaming. I dragged myself back at the sound of my own name and stood to read out my paraphrasing of Shakespearean speech. It got a lot of laughs. Even Bunny smiled at my dithering version of Hamlet's "to be or not to be" speech. Asked what had inspired me, I told them I thought Hamlet was a guy who just thought too much, the way I did.

"You think and think, and you're too busy thinking of everything to do anything or to see the things right in front of you," Bunny said.

At the end of the class she announced that it was not too late for anyone who wanted to see a performance of *Macbeth* that night with the twelfth graders.

Science was just before lunch, and it might as well have been Sanskrit for all I heard.

At lunchtime I went straight to the library to look at the photograph.

I had half convinced myself I was not dreaming of the real past, so when Anna and Zeb looked out of the photograph at me, my heart jerked violently against my chest bones.

I felt dizzy with shock. It was one thing to suspect you were dreaming of the past, and another to know it for sure. I spent lunchtime in the library, pretending to read to stay out of Buddha's way.

Lallie had told us the library, or at least the spot the library was built on, was sacred, so I figured it was by far the safest place in the school.

At the end of lunchtime, just before the bell, my name was called over the school PA system. "Nathaniel Delaney, report to the office please. . . ." I packed up my books with a feeling of doom.

It turned out to be the weekend-duty teacher, who hauled me over the coals for skipping detention, penalizing me with an additional detention on top of the one I still had to work off. I explained about getting knocked out in gym on Thursday and staying home sick Friday. I gave her a truckload of words. It was like feeding bones to a savage dog, until it's too bloated to be bothered biting you. She warned me to make sure I didn't get sick next weekend. To be there. It didn't make any difference to her that my mother had called in.

After lunch I had history, which meant I could legitimately think about Anna Galway and Zeb Sikorsky. Mr. Dodds told us to work on our assignments and gave anyone who wanted it a pass to study in the library.

"And what about you, Nathaniel? Have you decided on a topic?" He was working his way around the room, asking everyone the same question. I told him about the photograph in the library and the phone calls I'd made, trying to locate the old students. I told him I had found out one of the students died in jail on a murder charge, while another had died in an old age home in Saltridge.

He was impressed. "Even so, you'll still have to find someone who's alive to interview, in order to complete the demands of the assignment."

I told him about visiting Mrs. Heathcote and the old book in the library. "That's better," he said, looking really interested. "So what is your next move?"

I had a flash of inspiration. "I thought I'd go to the *Examiner* offices after school to see if the paper has any stories about the fire."

"Very good work, Nathaniel. Very thorough. But you know, I don't think the *Examiner* is open after four."

We looked at one another for a minute.

"If I gave you a study pass, you'd go straight there, right? And not fool around?"

That told me he genuinely liked the work I had done, and in spite of everything, it made me feel good. I nodded eagerly. "That would be great, sir, but I'd have to get the next bus and that leaves in fifteen minutes."

He hesitated fractionally. "All right. No time for a study pass. Off you go then. If anyone questions you, refer them to me. Don't let me down."

The bus was filled with mothers with shopping baskets who stared at me as suspiciously as if I had walked into the wrong restroom. I got out of the bus right in the shopping area of Willington and went down the pink-painted stairwell into the reception office of the *Examiner*. This was pink too, and a receptionist in a pink uniform looked at me expectantly.

"Yeeeess?" she said.

I told her what I was after, half expecting she would say it was impossible.

"We do have a morgue. But it's not really open to the public."

I stared at her incredulously and she burst out laughing. "I'm sorry. I forgot. The morgue is just what the journalists call it."

I grinned sheepishly and loosened up, hoping the papers might offer some information that would explain why I was dreaming of Anna and Zeb. "Is there someone I could ask?" I gave her my best earnest-schoolboy look.

"Well, as a matter of fact . . ." Her eyes went over my shoulder, and I turned to see a big man with a potbelly and a mop of hair that made him look like a cartoon composer, slouched in the doorway.

"You after a job, kid? We have one internship coming up next year and that's it. We get twenty applications for every opening, but you've got as good a chance as the next. Better, if you can use that talent for getting information and belly laughs out of hardened newspaper office receptionists."

"Mr. Sharone." The receptionist giggled. "You should eavesdrop properly. He's not after a job. He's after information."

"Then he *should* be after a job," Mr. Sharone declared. He looked me up and down with a measuring glance, then beckoned for me to follow. I went, feeling as if I were being swept along by a tidal wave.

His office turned out to be a dingy, smoke-stained room piled with back copies of newspapers and stacks of spiral notepads. Old clippings were stuck up on the wall along with a picture of a baseball player bending over to catch a ball, his pants split right along the seam to show he wore no underwear.

Mr. Sharone roared laughing when he saw me staring at the black-and-white blowup. "That's to remind me that sometimes getting the story is a matter of being in the right place at the right time." He chuckled hugely to himself. "Now, what did you want?"

"Uh . . . I wanted to know if I could have a look through your old papers. The morgue," I added.

He grinned. "Learning the jargon already, eh? You're quick. Ever thought of being a journalist?"

"Journalist . . ." I echoed uncertainly.

"Yeah. Like Clark Kent, only you don't get to wear blue tights, but sometimes you fly all right." He grinned to himself.

I was startled at where things were heading. I had just used the *Examiner* research as a way of getting away from school early. I seemed to have wound up in a weird sort of job interview.

"What are you after anyhow?" he asked.

I plunged in, explaining as concisely as I could about the photographs, about the assignment. I told him about the fire, but not the murder. "So, what I want to do is see if I can find any of the stories about the fire. It wasn't the *Examiner*," I added, remembering. "It was the paper this used to be. The *Tribune.*"

"Hmm. Three North High School, you say?" He gave me a quick, searching look. "We do have back files from the old rag." He hauled his bulk out of the chair, and I was left to follow him down another corridor and down some stairs into a room piled with huge stacks of red-bound volumes.

"They're the back copies of the *Examiner*. Look for green covers."

We found them in a closet and lifted a pile out onto a low table. Mr. Sharone pulled up a chair and waved me to another, already flipping pages. A thick, musty paper smell floated out from the volume.

"Date?"

I told him about Irma Heathcote's book and the two clippings pressed inside, along with their dates. He looked at the spines of the volumes, sorted four out, and returned the rest to the closet. "You look through those and I'll take these," he said, dividing the pile in two.

It took us about an hour. He found the first story, which turned out to be a straight announcement about a fire that had gutted the school building. He read the article out loud, then looked up at me with a frown that reminded me of Mrs. Heathcote. "This says someone died in the fire, and that it was lit deliberately. You know about that?"

I tried to look innocent, but his cynical, questioning eyes made me give up the struggle. I told him how Zeb had pleaded guilty to the murder of the caretaker and Anna's story of what had really happened.

The journalist's nose practically twitched with excitement. "What a story it would make if we could print the truth and get him out. Would this Anna talk to us?"

"She's dead and so is he," I said flatly. I told him how Anna died before I could talk to her again.

"Tough luck," he said. I wasn't sure if he meant for the paper, for Anna and Zeb, or me. Maybe for all of us.

To my relief, the receptionist stuck her head around the stairwell. "Mr. Sharone, someone to see you."

He grunted and got up. "Back to the fray. Listen, good luck. Lemme know how it comes out. You got me curious."

I nodded noncommittally.

"Kid?" I looked up again. "Maybe you should think about that internship."

He left before I could frame a reply. I went back to the papers.

The story he had located was brief. It said a body had been found and that there were suspicious circumstances. An article the next day expanded the story with an eyewitness who claimed to have seen kids messing around on the school grounds earlier on the day of the fire. Then there was a short sensational article saying police had identified the body as Samuel McLainie, the school caretaker. The story said he had been a soldier decorated in the first world war. The picture that went with the article was taken off an older photograph and showed Samuel in uniform, smiling.

At the very end the article said the old man had left everything in his will to a teacher at the school, a man called Koster Laine.

Only two days later there was a story about Zeb being taken into custody by police. The article pointed out he had been one of the students spotted at the school the day of the fire. It reported that Zeb had refused to speak, except to say it was his fault.

There was no mention of Anna, but another article said a schoolgirl had been helping police with their inquiries. In summing up after the brief hearing the judge presiding called it a hideous crime in the light of the previous friendship between the pair, sentencing Zeb to life imprisonment.

There were a couple of rehashed versions of the story after that, and the final articles about the school being rebuilt and reopened that I had already seen in Irma Heathcote's book.

Skimming the papers following the whole affair, I was struck by the amount of violent crimes that had happened in and around Cheshunt after the fire and court case. Especially after the court case. It was as if that death had triggered off a wave of violence that swept through the following years.

Until about a year back when things had changed—or so everyone said—Mr. Karle had come to town, and suddenly there was no delinquency, no crime, no hooliganism.

There was just the Gathering.

22

It was a dark, foul-smelling dusk and the streets were empty, the gray sky swollen looking and purple tinged when I got back to Cheshunt.

I turned the corner into the park street and suddenly my heart started to pound because in the dark opening of a garage, I heard breathing and saw the flare of yellow eyes. A big cat or a dog.

Whatever it was growled and it didn't sound like a cat or a dog. Maybe it was one of those feral dogs that had chased Seth. Obviously they had been drawn to Cheshunt too, answering some dark Call.

I heard running footsteps and whirled, half expecting to see the monster of my dreams come to strangle me. But my mouth fell open.

It was Nissa, and her face was white with horror. She ran straight into me, and I realized she hadn't even seen me. I held onto her or she would have run on.

"Nissa?"

She struggled violently, panting and trembling from head to toe, and her bare arms felt clammy.

"*Nissa!*"

At last her eyes focused. "Nathaniel." She shuddered, her fingers digging into my arms.

"What is it? What's happened?"

We were right alongside the park, so I took her to sit down on the bench. She leaned heavily on me and I thought she would have just fallen down if I weren't there.

"Are you okay?"

She laughed and there was a definite edge of hysteria in her voice. "I'm fine, I'm great."

My arm was resting along the back of her seat, against her shoulders, and I felt self-conscious. I wanted to leave it there and I wanted to take it away. I didn't know what had scared her. What I did know was that I was on my own with Nissa and her defenses were down. She wasn't giving me that sarcastic half smile or that cool, smart look of hers. Then I was ashamed of having those thoughts while she was so scared.

"What happened?" I asked again.

She gave me a ghostly, hollow-eyed look. "It was a man. At least, I think it was a man."

I took my hand away. "What? Some kind of pervert or something?"

"I was just sitting at the bus stop, killing time. Waiting to go to the library. This man came up to me and I . . . I knew him."

I was confused. "What do you mean? A teacher?"

"A man I knew from before my mother left." Her lips were pale and trembling. She bit down on her bottom lip and then took a deep breath.

"It was my first year of high school. My mother was still around then, and that meant there were always men calling in. There was this one guy she liked a lot. A singer, or at least that's what he told us. He was probably a traveling vacuum-cleaner salesman," she added with a flash of cynicism. "He didn't seem as affected by her moods as the others. That made him more appealing to her, and she took a lot of trouble fixing herself up when he was coming around.

"One night he came, and my mother had gone out. He said

he knew she was with another man, but he wasn't angry. He just thought it was funny. He asked where Mrs. Kennett was, and I told him she was at her flower club."

Nissa pulled her knees up and folded her arms around them, resting her chin on one bare kneecap.

"He told me he hadn't been coming to see my mother. That he loved me." She ran one hand through her ragged hair. "My mother was always the center of the universe to everybody. People treated me the way they did because of her. I was just this smart, ugly kid they had to put up with. His saying it was me he came to see . . . well, I . . . it felt good. He started putting his arms around me." She stopped abruptly and looked right into my eyes with a kind of nakedness. "I would have done anything for him just then," she said in a hard voice. "Mrs. Kennett came home and put an end to what might have happened. She called me a dirty little slut and . . . well, the usual sort of stuff. I . . . I told her we were in love." She laughed harshly.

"He couldn't get out fast enough. He told her he had just been having a little fun, that I had been more than willing. He said, 'Like mother like daughter . . .' "

She looked angry at herself and hurt too. I wanted to protect her from her own contempt. I wanted to tell her I loved her, and that I didn't care about her mother or Mrs. Kennett.

And then my heart beat like bongo drums because I realized where my thoughts had brought me.

But Nissa was oblivious to my reactions.

Awkwardly I put my arm around her. It was uncomfortable because she was taller, but I could feel myself shaking because I was so close to her.

She stiffened and I thought she was going to shove me back. I was prepared for that, but then she just relaxed and leaned into me.

My blood felt like it was rushing backward in my veins. I

patted her back and stared over her shoulders at the street, not knowing what to say.

"Ah hell," Nissa said at last. She sat up. "Life's shit sometimes."

I don't know how I looked, but she burst out laughing. Then I was laughing too, I don't even know why. I laughed so hard, it hurt my stomach. In a weird way I was also laughing because of putting my arms around Nissa.

"You know, it changed me. Not the thing with him," she said when we stopped laughing. "It was realizing I wanted so badly for someone to see me for myself that I would do anything. I made a vow to myself then that I'd never love anyone again. Not like that. From then on I relied on nobody and took care of myself." She shook her head and took another deep breath.

"Anyway, it was that man."

I blinked, then remembered her running toward me. "He chased you?"

She shook her head and the fear came back into her eyes. "He came up to me. I thought he was going to ask directions, then I recognized him. He said hello and asked how I'd been. I pretended I didn't know who he was. I was halfway through saying he must have made a mistake when he said there was no mistake. He said he had been thinking of me a lot. Dreaming of me. In the end he decided to come back to Cheshunt and see if he could find me. He said I had called him." She shuddered with loathing. "I just got scared then and ran. Like he was the boogey man." There was disgust in her voice, but I thought of the monster in my nightmares and shivered.

"You don't believe me," Nissa said flatly.

"I do," I said. "I just don't know what it means."

"It was him saying I called him that really scared me. . . ."

"I don't think you called him. I think Cheshunt did."

"But why?"

"To have exactly the effect it did. To scare you. Maybe worse."

192

Abruptly Nissa stiffened and held her finger to her lips.

"What is it?" I whispered. I looked around, suddenly conscious of how dark and shadowy the park was. You couldn't even see the bathrooms or swings, and the trees seemed too close and thick. I remembered the eyes that had flared yellow at me and stood up, my heart pounding.

Nissa must have felt the same, because she stood too and said I might as well come to the library with her. We didn't speak again until the park was behind us, then she asked if I had remembered my symbol. I pulled down the neck of my sweater and showed her how I had knotted it onto a thong of leather around my neck. "I keep it under my clothes so no one can see it."

"I don't think it would matter," Nissa said pensively, hoisting her backpack higher. She shook her head impatiently at my offer to carry it. "The sword fell out of my bag at lunchtime right in the middle of the yard. I had a story ready in case something like that happened, but no one mentioned it. Their eyes just seemed to slide off of it. I bet it's the same with Bear's bowl and that torch of Danny's. We're the only ones who can see them."

We got to the library and up into the attic without mishap. Nissa made us a snack while we waited for the others, and I found myself telling her about the death of the caretaker and Zeb's admission of guilt in spite of his innocence. Before I could stop myself, I was also telling her about the dreams.

She just listened. When I stopped, she looked at me sideways, her face serious and calm. "It's this school, isn't it, Nat? That's what you're saying? That unnatural things happen here?" Her eyes widened. "Of course! The earth that sorrows. It has to be right here. I've been racking my brain, but it must be here."

I thought of the caretaker dying and the dance master, and I thought she was right. "This is the core of the evil. This is what has to be healed!"

"There's something else," she said, the triumph in her eyes

193

fading. "You told me there was a red moon in that garden you dreamed about?"

I nodded.

Her face looked very pale in the lantern light. "I've seen a moon like that here. Some nights I look out of the window and it's red like that. Blood red."

I opened my mouth to tell her the red moon had been a feature of my nightmares long before we had come to Cheshunt, but the others had started to arrive and she went to let them in.

Seth arrived last and was out of breath but sober, to my secret relief. No one mentioned what had happened at the beach.

As soon as we were all together, Nissa told the rest of them about my dreams. "We think they are meant to show us the sorrowing earth is here," she said. "Do the rest of you have any better suggestion?"

Bear shook his head. "Makes sense. Everything bad revolves around the school, doesn't it?"

"Then I say let's do the Healing tonight," Nissa said.

But Danny disagreed. He wanted to talk about how we were going to fight Mr. Karle.

"The Healing comes first," Nissa said.

"I know that, but Lallie told you he would try and stop us from forging the Chain that would bind the dark. I think we need to figure out what she meant by that before we do any Healing. And in case he attacks as soon as we start the Healing, we have to be prepared."

"Maybe the Healing is what gives the symbols power as weapons," Bear ventured. "The only way to know is by trying it."

Outside, the night was still and chilly, and clouds blotted out the stars and veiled the moon, but we agreed it was safer to do the Healing on a dark night when we were less likely to be seen. I thought of The Tod and wished he was there too. After all, he had answered the Call just as we had. If the truth be known, he had brought me there.

I hung the circle outside my sweater and the others held their symbols, then we stood self-consciously in a ring.

"What do we do first?" I whispered.

Danny giggled and Nissa gave him a sharp look, opening her mouth to tell him off. Then she closed it and frowned without saying anything, and I guessed she was remembering what Lallie had said about laughter being a weapon against the dark.

"It's cold," Seth said.

"All right," Nissa announced. "Now let's just think how it went before we start."

"I have to burn the earth," Danny said.

"Earth doesn't burn," Bear objected.

"It must mean to light a fire," Seth offered.

"Don't be stupid!" Nissa snapped. "On a night like this the flames would be visible for miles. How are we going to explain to the fire department that we're just healing the earth. They'll think we're trying to burn the damn school down."

"Maybe it's just symbolic," Bear said. "The torch for fire."

"We'll try it both ways," she decided. "First without fire and then if that doesn't work, we'll do it the other way."

"How will we know?" Seth asked.

We all looked at him.

"How are we going to know if it's worked?"

"There'll be a sign," Danny told him with such certainty I hadn't the heart to voice my doubts. Besides, maybe it was time I stopped being like Hamlet and started doing instead of always thinking.

"We'll just try and see how it goes," Nissa said, looking around worriedly. "But let's not forget where we are. Stay alert in case the police come."

"Or worse," Danny echoed. "In case *he* comes."

23

Nissa lifted the rusty sword high, then looked around. "What should I say?"

"Something about healing," Bear said.

She shook her head. "You're the one doing the healing. I'm making a wound so the poisons get out."

"Say that then."

Nissa took a deep breath. "I, the bearer of the sword of strength, smite this earth . . ."

"Sorrowing earth," Danny prompted.

Nissa gave him an angry look. "Don't interrupt!"

"Start again."

"I, the bearer of . . . this sword, smite the sorrowing earth to . . . to let out the darkness," she finished with a flourish, then she let the sword fall and slice into the frozen ground, opening a trench. Immediately it began to weep with muddy water.

"It looks like a wound," Seth murmured.

"Shh!" Nissa said sternly. "Now it's Danny's turn."

He held up the torch. "I, the torchbearer, smite this sorrowing earth with fire," he intoned solemnly. Then he touched the edge of the torch to the gash in the ground. There was a hiss and a thin ribbon of smoke as fire met water.

Bear knelt and scrabbled a bit of the muddy dirt into the stone bowl. "Ugh. It stinks."

"Concentrate," Nissa said.

"Say something," Danny urged.

"Uh. I, the bowl bearer. No, I who bear the bowl do . . . do take this sorrowing—no—this healed earth to the sacred place and . . . and it will be healed."

"You said it was healed already."

Bear scowled at Danny. "All right Mr. Know-it-all. I take this sorrowing earth to . . . to the sacred attic to be healed."

Back in the attic Bear set the bowl on the crate table.

"What now?" Seth asked timidly.

"Nat's turn," Nissa elected. "Remember? The last to come *must* forge at last."

I swallowed, because I had forgotten that. "I guess we should stand around the bowl like Lallie had us do, and hold hands."

"What about the other things?" Danny broke in. "We should put them in too."

This done, we held hands again, and I racked my brains to remember what Lallie had said. "We, the five who brought the symbols that are the Chain do . . . bring this bowl of sorrowing earth to . . . to be healed." One phrase seemed to echo suddenly in my thoughts.

"May the Chain prevail long!"

Nothing happened.

"It didn't work," Danny said in a disgusted voice.

"How do you know it didn't?"

He pointed at the things on the crate table. "They didn't change."

"We don't know that they will," Nissa said, but she sounded disappointed too. "Maybe it was too close to the library?"

We went through the whole ritual, this time right down near the cafeteria.

When nothing happened again, Bear suggested we may not

have been meant to take the dirt back to the attic. "Maybe we're supposed to do the whole Healing on the spot, then take the dirt to the attic."

We tried that.

Nothing happened again, except that it got colder. We went back to the attic and had a hot drink to warm up, trying to figure out what we were doing wrong. Seth had started sneezing and I felt as if my bones were icicles.

"Maybe it is meant to be the football field," Nissa said pensively.

"Maybe it's not the school at all. It could be anywhere in Cheshunt."

"Maybe we're just not saying the right words."

"It could be the wrong time," Seth suggested.

Nissa gave him a weary look. "We just have to keep trying, that's all."

"Maybe it's because Seth isn't doing anything!" I said.

"Yeah! That must be it. Now what did she say about him?" Danny said grimacing with the effort to remember. "Something about seeing things right?"

"No, throwing off the shadows of other men's visions. Was that it?" Bear suggested.

"No," Nissa said. "I know! Lallie said he has to see the sorrowing earth."

We all looked at Seth.

"I don't understand. You already know where it is. What am I supposed to do? I don't know what to do."

Danny shoved him in the arm. "Maybe it's not the right spot."

"Maybe he's meant to look through the telescope?" Bear said.

That sounded right so we all trooped outside and waited with bated breath while Seth looked through the telescope at the ground.

"It's too dark to see anything," he said.

We tried another couple of spots, and even crept out on the football field to try it there. It didn't work, and we dared not use real fire until we were certain it was the right place. Danny was convinced this was the missing ingredient.

"We'll have to risk fire if that's what we're supposed to do," he insisted. But none of us had matches and it was getting late.

It was creepy too, even with all of us together. Every second we were on the field was dangerous. Being out in the open and vulnerable reminded us of the danger, and suddenly trying to figure out Lallie's clues was no longer a game but something deadly serious.

Freezing and exhausted, we decided to call it a night and go home. Before we parted, Nissa told us she would try to find Lallie the next day to see if she could get her to be more explicit about how the Healing was supposed to be done, and exactly where.

We agreed to meet again Wednesday night in the attic and left five minutes apart. I went last because I lived nearest.

"See you then," Nissa said. "And thanks for before."

She ran lightly across the field toward the school and I wondered why she hadn't told the others about the man. Maybe she was embarrassed. I watched until she reached the light and disappeared around the edge of the building, then turned and jogged home.

When I reached the park street, I looked over automatically, thinking of sitting on the bench with my arm around Nissa. A feeling of pure terror shot through me at the sight of a multitude of gleaming yellow eyes watching me from the shadowy wilderness of the park.

Feral dogs. They started to growl.

I bolted.

I pounded along the path and heard them coming after me,

the great thuds of their paws on the footpath, the rasping of their breathing.

I tore around the corner into my street, knowing I had no hope of making it to my house. I turned to face them, pulling the circle out from under my sweater and thrusting it at them, hoping it would do something.

The darkness was like a mist, and I could see nothing more than their eyes and the ivory gleam of sharp teeth. Somehow that made them more terrible than if they had been completely visible. They slowed fractionally when I swung to face them, then began to slink forward again.

The circle slid out of my fingers, but my legs wouldn't move. I felt dazed with fear.

"Begone!" cried a voice behind me.

The dogs snarled and stopped, startled.

It was Lallie and she held The Tod in her arms. Horrified, I watched her bend down and set him free. I tried to grab hold of him as he bolted past me, barking wildly, but Lallie stopped me.

Incredibly, the dogs in their dark fume backed away. Perhaps they wondered what he was. The moment they gave way, he charged again, and they turned and fled.

Then they were gone.

"Jesus, Lallie," I gasped and scooped The Tod up. He licked my face and blinked at me proudly. "Jesus," I said again, hugging him. Loving him. "What if they hadn't run!"

"They smelled your fear. That's why they came after you. Чe was not afraid," she said, patting and nuzzling him and laughing softly. Her breathing was heavy and labored.

"Are you okay?"

She did not answer, but followed when I walked the few houses back to mine. I sat on the fence because my legs were like jelly. For a second there I had been sure The Tod was going to be killed.

"How did you get here?" I asked, suddenly struck by her timely appearance. "And how did you get The Tod?"

"The beasts were hungry," Lallie said, gasping a little. Her eyes seemed unfocused and her lips faintly blue.

Alarmed, I asked again if she was all right.

She appeared not to hear my question. "They come to feed because they know the darkness gathers. If you fail, there will be fear and blood, and they are hungry." Her breath was wheezing in and out.

"Did . . . did the Kraken send them?"

A ghost of a smile crossed her features. "He has no power to call. His power is in illusion and fear. Don't you understand? He was called, just as the dogs were." The smile faded. "But they were attracted by your fear. The darkness is very strong now. They might have killed you. The Healing must be done soon, or it will be too late."

That reminded me of the abortive events of the night. "Lallie, where are we supposed to do this Healing? Tonight we tried and . . ."

"Where the earth is saturated with fear and death. The signs of it are all around you," Lallie murmured. Her eyes drifted.

"Can't you just tell us! If there's so little time . . ."

Her face was a pale blur in the darkness as she turned to face me. "There is no time."

"But how are we supposed to fight him!" I burst out. "Are the symbols weapons?"

She blinked, as if I'd startled her back from wherever her mind was wandering. "You are the symbols. The symbols are you. The circle is the symbol that links the Chain to bind the dark. It has great power, for it will accept no obstacle to the linking."

"I don't understand. Are you saying it's not a weapon? That there won't be a fight?" A cowardly little bit of me hoped she would agree.

But instead she sighed. "If the Chain breaks, the dark will win. See the true battle, Nathaniel."

"True battle? I don't understand. Can't you explain properly?"

She shook her head. "I am not to interfere. There will be payment even for this night." She knelt down, took The Tod's muzzle in her hand, and looked into his eyes, poisoned by whatever was wrong with Cheshunt.

He was very still for a minute. Then he whined, as if he was in pain, and shrank away from her.

"I am sorry," she whispered. He wagged his tail but his ears were down.

Then she turned and began to walk away down the street. Her breathing sounded as if her lungs were filled with water, and I remembered what Nissa said about Cheshunt making her sick.

"Lallie! I'd better come with you."

But she was gone.

24

I got into bed a bare hour before my mother came home from night duty. I lay awake listening to her come in, shower, and go to bed. I felt exhausted, but I was too unsettled to sleep. Even after she was quiet, I lay listening to the creaks and groans of the timber house settling, my mind running over and over everything that had happened in the long night: getting the news of Anna's death, trying to do the Healing at the school, the feral dogs chasing me, and Lallie's miraculous appearance.

But in the end it was Nissa I thought about. I had actually had my arms around her. My wrist seemed to tingle where her bare neck had brushed against it, as if her skin had printed itself on me like the Phantom's good ring. For keeps. I thought of the way her breasts showed through the T-shirt at the beach, and drowsed, feeling restless and feverish. The bed sheets kept tangling around my feet or sliding off to one side.

I tossed and turned finally into a dream.

I was walking along the footpath. I didn't recognize the street. It looked blurred, as if I were seeing it through rain, but I thought it was somewhere in Cheshunt.

I felt bone-achingly tired and disoriented. Weak. I barely had the strength to move my feet.

I walked to the edge of the curb to cross the street, and at the same time I heard a car engine.

I looked up and the car was coming straight at me, its headlights shining yellow like some great animal. The death smell filled the air.

I tried to run but my legs were weak, uncontrolled.

As the car bore down on me, I saw the man behind the wheel change into my father, his face contorted with fury.

"Children should be seen and not heard!" he growled.

I screamed as the car plowed into me.

I sat up in the dark, my heart pounding, running to beat the pain barrier. It had been so real. I felt as if I had yelled out loud, but there was no noise from my mother's room. The queer reverberating scream that had ended the dream had been part of it.

It took me a long time to fall asleep after that. I kept seeing the look on my father's face before he ran me down. And he had said that same thing about children being seen and not heard as in the other dream. Maybe he had once said that to me, and for some reason my mind had dredged it up. Somewhere far off I heard a dog barking, but the barking sounded like laughter too.

The next day my mother seemed sluggish and distracted, so she didn't notice how quiet I was.

"I think I'm getting a bug," she said in a nasal voice as we climbed into the car. Her cheeks were flushed and her eyes seemed kind of unfocused.

"Maybe you should stay home."

She shook her head. "I'll get one of the doctors there to take a look at me."

Outside, the stench was incredible, but she was oblivious to it, and to the heavy metallic gleam of the sky. The cloud cover completely blotted out the sun, casting a bleary light over Cheshunt.

As we drove past the park, I thought of the dogs that had come from there, attracted, Lallie said, by my fear. Last night the park had seemed wilder and darker, but today it looked almost normal. It was weird the way things seemed to change, but maybe that was part of the distorting effect of the darkness.

My mother pulled into the curb opposite the school and let me out.

"Come to Elderew for dinner," she said. "I'll call the school if I decide to come home. Okay?"

As she drove away, two girls came out of a house with a clipboard. One of them was from my English class. She slid a sheet of pink paper into her pile, and suddenly I thought of the pile of pink papers I had seen on Mr. Karle's desk the day I had been called to his office.

Without thinking about it, I went over and asked the two girls what the survey was about. The one from class, Marigold, looked frightened and tried to walk around me. The other girl scuttled off, as if I were a leper.

"You might as well talk to me," I said determinedly. "If you don't, I'll hang around you so much, people will think you're one of my friends."

I was stabbing in the dark, but the color drained out of her cheeks and she gave me a look filled with dread.

"What do you want?" she whispered.

I pointed to her clipboard. "What are you doing with those? What is he trying to find out?"

"It's a survey," she whispered, looking around to see who was watching her talk to me. "Please. It's dangerous."

"What is? Talking to me?"

She nodded, and my blood ran cold. "Then tell me. It's the fastest way to get rid of me."

"He gave us a list of all the kids' addresses at the school. We have to go to all of the houses and get these sheets signed by kids' parents. They're surveys about setting up a youth militia in Cheshunt."

"Marigold!"

It was one of the school patrol girls. "What is going on here?"

Marigold looked too frightened to speak.

The older girl glared at me, but her eyes were red and vacant-looking, as if she were high on something. "Well?"

"I asked her out," I said. "She told me to go away."

Marigold's eyes flashed with dumb gratitude.

"Then get moving," the big girl snarled. Marigold bolted, and I sauntered across the road to the school, feeling the school patrol girl's eyes boring into my neck.

A youth militia. Like Hitler's *Jugend*. Something told me this was how Mr. Karle planned to spread the darkness once he had disposed of us. The school patrol and the Gathering set up to control kids were only part of it. The other side were the gangs he sent to cause trouble outside Cheshunt. It didn't make sense that he was creating trouble and fixing it.

But I was less concerned about that than the fact that the survey was taking in every student. What would happen when they called at Nissa's address and found she was not living there?

I would warn her and maybe she could use my address, or say she lived in Saltridge and use Elderew. Surely the survey wouldn't go that far.

But I couldn't find her or any of the others before the bell rang. It was a weird day. The kids seemed like my mother, sluggish and kind of dopey. And even the teachers acted odd. Every now and then, in the middle of a sentence they would just stop talking and tilt their heads as if they were listening to something. The whole class would just sit there with blank looks on their faces, until the teachers picked up where they left off.

At lunchtime I saw Buddha and some of his gang way down at the end of the football field playing some sort of game. From a distance they looked like a pack of animals scrapping.

I spent recess and lunch in the study cubicles right in back of the library because there, at least, no one could accidentally on purpose try to brain me. Besides, it was probably the one safe place in the school, maybe in all of Cheshunt. It was home free, sacrosanct in a place that harbored evil.

Then I thought of the caretaker being burned there, and shuddered because in this game it was possible there was nowhere safe. No home free.

I had started to think none of the others were at school when, at lunchtime on my way to the library, I noticed Seth and a bunch of seniors starting their mural on one of the brick walls of the science building.

Seth was joking with one of the others. He sounded carefree and happy, and it was hard to believe this was the same Seth that had been drunk and crying on the beach.

I couldn't see his symbol anywhere, but maybe he had put it in his locker.

When I came back after the lunch bell, he and the other kids had gone, and I got a good look at the mural design.

My blood turned to ice because, even barely begun, it showed a garden on a hillside just like the one in my dream. Looking at it made me feel sick and confused.

The last class was with Mr. Dodds, but he just told us to get on with our projects. He didn't even ask me how the visit to the *Examiner* had gone. His eyes were bloodshot and he looked at me as if he had trouble seeing me.

After school I felt a rush of relief at seeing Bear crossing the football field and ran to catch him. I expected him to tell me off for coming up to him like that where anyone could see us, but he only stared at me, his face grim.

"What's the matter?"

"I came to get you. It's Lallie," he said.

I was relieved. "I saw her last night."

Bear just stared at me, his eyes as cold as chips of ice. "What did you say?"

"I saw her. She turned up just in time to stop some of those feral dogs from getting me . . ." I faltered, seeing the look of incredulity on his face.

"What is it?"

"This morning Lallie was found in the yard by the security guard. . . ."

"Oh, no!" I whispered, knowing it was my fault she had come back into Cheshunt.

25

The others were waiting in the public library for Bear to bring me back. We huddled together in the windy courtyard because the cold meant no one would come out to disturb us.

The plump librarian had smiled at me as I came in, but I cut him off halfway through news of a book I had asked him to order. He looked hurt, but I was too numb to care.

All I could think about was Lallie saying there would be a price for her intervening to stop the dogs from getting me. Was this the price? Her life for mine? Guilt tasted sour. Especially since it must have happened right after she left me.

If only I had taken her home.

Seth was ashen and stunned, the laughing golden boy nowhere in sight. On the way Bear had told me he found Seth at the end of lunchtime, but hadn't seen me in back of the library study area.

"How could this have happened?" Seth was saying in hoarse disbelief. "Why would she come back here when she said she couldn't?"

I knew, but the words were locked up in my horror. Even when the feral dogs had chased me, I had never really imagined anyone would be seriously hurt or killed. Not even when Lallie said the dogs might have killed me.

"It was *him*," Danny said. "Somehow the Kraken did this to her so we'd be on our own. We should kill him."

I thought confusedly of Lallie telling me the Kraken's power lay in the darkness inhabiting him, and was an illusion. She had underestimated the forces holding Cheshunt in thrall, and now she was dead. Maybe that was not the only thing she had been wrong about.

"She might wake . . ." Seth said.

I stared at him incredulously. "Wake? You mean, she's not dead?"

They all turned to face me.

"I thought I said," Bear murmured, shocked. "She's in the hospital in a coma. She was hit by a car. An ambulance came and took her away. They don't expect her to come out of it."

I thought confusedly of his sister and knew, as if I could read his thoughts, that he was thinking there were worse things than dying.

"She's not dead," Nissa added sharply.

"He saw her last night," Bear said, sitting down beside Nissa.

The wind whistled a desolate refrain, stirring the potted plants in the courtyard, reminding them of freedom. Somewhere I heard a girl laughing. In another universe maybe, where laughter was possible.

"It was after I left you at the school last night," I said. "I was on my way home and these . . . feral dogs came out of the park and chased me. They were gaining and I had no hope of getting home, so I turned and tried using the circle to defend myself." I shook my head. "It sounds stupid now, but last night it seemed like the only hope I had. It didn't work of course, but before they could get me, Lallie turned up with The Tod."

I told them the whole thing. Then I told them what Lallie had said about there being a price for helping me.

"What did Lallie mean about his power being an illusion?" Nissa asked.

"An illusion to distract us from concentrating on fighting him," Danny said.

"Why would he bother?" Seth asked. "We don't have any

idea how to fight him. We can't do anything without her. We'll have to wait until she recovers."

"You'd like that, wouldn't you, hero," Danny raged. "You probably wish she would die so you can just go dive in a bottle and drown your sorrows."

"Shut up," Nissa flared.

"You shut up," Danny snarled.

I sensed then that the whole thing was in danger of coming unglued. Without Lallie we were on the verge of flying apart like atoms.

"Maybe we can heal her," Bear said softly. "With the bowl."

The arguments stopped instantly, and Danny's eyes glowed with fierce hope. "Let's go now."

But Nissa reminded us that hospital visiting hours were strict in intensive-care wards; only immediate family could visit. "Better to go in the morning before school. There'll be more people around then and we'll have a better chance of sneaking in."

I felt uncertain about the healing bowl working on Lallie. The circle hadn't stopped the dogs, and Lallie had said the symbols were just that. Symbols. But I said nothing, because the rest of them needed to believe there was hope for her.

Even so, Lallie had said the darkness was getting stronger and we should act soon. "What about the Healing? Lallie said we had to do it soon or it would be too late."

"Tomorrow night, like we planned," Nissa snapped irritably and went on telling us what hospital it was. It seemed she had learned about the accident that morning.

Only Seth looked as if he had any doubts, but he would not meet my eye. Perhaps he felt as guilty as I did that I could not truly believe Bear's bowl would bring Lallie out of her coma.

The others were arranging excitedly to meet at the Willington bus stop the following morning to go to the hospital. We would all be late for school, but the thought of school seemed irrelevant.

After we parted, it was so late I caught the bus straight to Elderew for dinner.

I picked at my food, rearranging it to look like I had eaten something, but my mother was too sharp. "Are you sick, Nat?" she asked. "You've seemed out of it since that bump on the head. Maybe I should get you a checkup."

"It's fine," I said.

She frowned. "Nathaniel, if something were bothering you, you'd mention it wouldn't you?"

I nodded, crossing my fingers under the table.

Again I had the feeling she wanted to say something, but I was too worried about Lallie and the Chain to pursue it. I promised myself I would explain to her, somehow, when it was all over.

As I left to catch the bus home, I heard a voice calling my name. I turned to find Lilly Astaroth running down the path after me, her cape flapping in the wind. She was carrying a pile of notebooks. When she stopped, she was panting and out of breath.

"I was hoping to catch you before you left. You remember I told you Anna Galway had no one? That no one ever visited her? Well . . . she didn't have much, but I thought you might like to have these. They're her diaries. They'd just be thrown out and it seems so sad that no one cares. Anyway, here they are, if you want them."

She thrust the pile of scruffy notebooks into my hands and hurried back up the path toward Elderew.

I looked down at them, feeling dog-tired. If I lay down now, I felt as if all the skin would slide in a heap off my bones and I'd never get back up. The week before I would have been overjoyed to get my hands on something that might tell me more about the mystery of the caretaker, but with Anna and Zeb dead, and Lallie lying in a coma in hospital, the whole thing seemed unimportant.

I stuffed the books into my backpack and ran to catch the bus.

At home I sat on the floor in front of a fire with The Tod on my lap, stroking him. He seemed jumpy and every now and then he would look out the window and tremble.

Maybe it was just me, communicating my black mood, but in the end his eyes looking up at me seemed full of fear and sorrow.

I stared into the flames, wishing I could turn the clock back and walk Lallie home.

The Tod whined and I looked down at him.

He had gotten off my lap and was sniffing at my pack. I patted my lap but he ignored the invitation. He sniffed again, then whined and pawed at the bag.

He paused and looked up at me, then he whimpered again and pawed frantically at the bag, and suddenly I knew what he was doing.

He was trying to get at Anna's notebooks.

The hair on my neck stood up on end, and I felt as if someone had poured ice water down my back.

I reached over and dragged the bag toward me, undid the flaps, and got the musty smelling notebooks out. The Tod sniffed the edges excitedly, and I calmed down because it was possible he had just smelled mice on the notebooks. As if to give credence to this, once he had sniffed the books thoroughly, he settled down to sleep.

Without thinking I opened one of the notebooks.

It took only a page to know it was as rambling and confused and bitter as Anna herself had been. Worse, it switched back and forth fluidly between the present and the distant past, as if all the veils that separated one time from another had disintegrated in her mind. One minute she would be writing as a young girl, and the next she was a bitter old woman full of hate and spite.

As a girl she seemed less spiteful but just plain willful and spoiled. As an old woman she was eaten up with grudges over petty, probably imagined slights.

I skimmed until I came across a small passage, where she mentioned the first time she had seen Zeb Sikorsky: *The moment I saw him, it was as if some missing piece had slid into me, and he was a quietness, a stillness in my heart.*

After that the pages were filled with complicated schemes to get him alone. And then suddenly she would be writing as an old woman, cursing him for not loving her.

It was petty, ugly reading and made me feel depressed.

Rubbing my eyes, I thought of the serene blond girl in my dreams who had tried to make Zeb dance with Anna and wondered who she had been, and if she too had agreed Zeb should take the blame for what had happened.

I read until my mother's car pulled into the driveway, then jumped up, doused the fire, and got into bed, jamming the notepads under my mattress. I couldn't bear the thought of sitting there, acting as if everything was fine.

I pretended to be asleep when she came into my room, and she stood for a long time, looking down on me. At last she sighed and went away.

That night I dreamed I was in the library, only it was night and the lights were out. I was hiding down between two shelves and I could hear people shouting.

I peeped around the corner and saw Zeb and Anna and a couple of other kids. There was an old man who looked vaguely familiar to me, and they were facing him, pleading with him.

"Sam, don't do this. It wasn't your fault," Zeb cried.

The old man shook his head. "You don't understand, lad. I deserve to die. For the children. I threw gasoline on the wall and I burned the hut. I didn't mean to, but I killed them, and now I have to die too. A life for a life. I die just like they did."

"How could you know they were in there?" Anna protested, but the old man struck a match and even in the minute glow I could see his face and body were glistening darkly. His eyes were red-rimmed and rheumy.

My heart started to beat so hard, I felt faint.

"It's justice . . ." he whispered. "Just like he said."

"Sam, for God's sake! Don't!" Zeb cried, but it was too late, and there was a terrible scream from the old man as he went up in flames.

I woke, shivering and sweating with horror.

26

It was a bleary morning, where a gray sky intermittently drizzled a gray, misty rain and dark clots of cloud hinted at a pending thunderstorm.

My mother was asleep. I had poked my head in the door to say good-bye, but she didn't wake. She looked small and young, curled on her side with her hair all over the pillow. Once my father had slept curled with her, but now she lay alone and maybe she would be alone forever until she got as old as Anna Galway.

The Tod howled as I closed the gate. I hesitated, thinking I ought to put him inside, but I looked at my watch and realized I would miss the city bus if I didn't go right away.

The others were standing at the bus stop in an assortment of raincoats and parkas, all except Seth. Just as I arrived at the stop, the bus trundled around the corner, its tires hissing on the wet road.

"He's not going to come," Danny said disgustedly.

Nissa scowled at him as she climbed on the bus, and then we were heading toward Saltridge, Willington, and St. Mary's Hospital. It was too late for school kids, the bell having rung fifteen minutes earlier. The bus driver watched us in his mirror.

It took us no time to find the hospital. It was on the corner of a big intersection right on the Cheshunt border, a big gothic-looking place with fake turrets and cupolas. At the desk Nissa asked the receptionist where Lallie was.

"She's our sister," Danny said with such guileless innocence, he appeared almost half-witted. The nurse frowned around at us, then told us to wait while she went to get a doctor.

"I don't think we're going to be allowed to see her," Nissa said. "We better see if we can find her ourselves."

Danny found her and fetched the rest of us.

She was in a small room with three other people on flat hard-looking beds. They were all hooked up to monitoring equipment; Lallie, a pale splinter under stiff white sheets. In spite of the small beeping noise from her monitor registering a heartbeat, she already looked dead, her face cold and waxy. Her breathing was so erratic and difficult that listening to it made me feel breathless. Strangled.

"She sounds awful," Danny whispered.

"Get on with it," Nissa hissed, pushing Bear toward the bed.

He stumbled like a sleepwalker, took a deep, steadying breath, and set the bowl down. It must have had mud on it from the night before, because it left a dark smudge on the snowy sheet.

He took Lallie's thin, limp hand and tried to hang it in the bowl, but it fell away with such lifelessness that I felt sick.

"Hurry," Nissa said urgently, looking over her shoulder at the observation window.

Bear clenched his teeth and picked up the bowl, running it gently over her whole body. I heard him whisper fiercely, "Heal Lallie, please."

At that moment the receptionist bustled in with a security guard. She yelped at the sight of Bear and his bowl, and flushed with exasperation as Bear blurted out that we were going to heal her.

"Religious maniacs," she muttered, and commanded the security guard to get us out of the hospital and make sure we stayed out.

"It didn't work," Bear said in a desolate voice, oblivious to the rain.

Someone tapped me on the shoulder.

I turned to find the *Examiner* editor, Mr. Sharone, looking down at me. "It's Nathaniel, isn't it?"

I nodded and the others melted away, signaling they'd meet me at the bus stop. Mr. Sharone's sharp eyes ran over them, then came back to me. "Skipping school, eh?"

I opened and shut my mouth without saying anything.

He smiled quickly. "I'm not going to report you. Fact is, I've been thinking a lot about you since you came into the office."

It was raining harder, and he squinted up and grimaced, then drew me under a narrow awning over a flower shop.

"I'm glad I ran into you because I've been wanting to talk to you."

"Why?"

Mr. Sharone stared into my eyes for a long moment, as if he were trying to read something there. "You know, there's always a lot of stuff collected for stories that never makes it into print in a newspaper. Sometimes because it's too weird, or it can't be proven, or because it's too sick." He hesitated, as if trying to decide what to tell me.

"During the last few months I've been researching a story on youth crime and violence in Willington and Saltridge. No one is willing to be quoted, but the word is that the gangs come out of Cheshunt. Some say right out of that school of yours— Three North. You can imagine, then, that I was interested when you walked in my door."

He looked around, and that made me feel uneasy.

"Your looking up that old murder case made me curious because, apart from the fact that it happened at the school, you didn't act like a kid doing an assignment." He shrugged. "Still, that might not have gotten me because, though I'm a journalist, I don't believe in minding other people's business for them. What really got me was reading through the old file of non-printed stuff about the time of that fire of yours."

He squinted out at the rain, which was really hammering down now. "You see, what is happening now happened back then. Exactly the same, but on a smaller scale. Gangs of kids from one side of Cheshunt came over to the other and ran amok, burning, stealing, attacking people.

"I read the articles too, Nathaniel. Koster was the guy the caretaker left all of his money to. The interesting thing, though, is that the old man's death seemed to be the start of all the really bad violence. Before, it had been petty stuff, but after his death it escalated. Terrible things happened, sick things that never got in the papers for fear of copycat crimes: devil worship using people's pets; dead animals found with their heads cut off, dressed in women's clothes; rape and torture. Even people going berserk and killing their whole family, claiming they were possessed; triple suicides. Cheshunt came to be a very dark place indeed.

"That went on until about a year back. About the time I came to take over the paper. Then it all just stops, and almost overnight Cheshunt becomes a squeaky-clean model neighborhood. And then, about a month back it all starts up again. Kid gangs, bashings, robbery, intimidation, all coming out of Cheshunt and that school of yours. And so I think to myself: *What if it was some sort of cult then, and for some reason it's started up again?*"

He stopped, as if he expected me to say something. After a minute he shrugged. "Now, I might be off base, but just theoretically, what if some sharper-than-average school kid looking into the past comes across this stuff and sees the connection? This kid has the inside edge because he goes to the school where the gangs come from. And what if he gets the idea in his head of building a case to expose the whole mess?" His eyes widened speculatively and went beyond me to the bus stop where the others were waiting. "And maybe he enlists the help of a couple of other like-minded kids."

"I don't know what you mean," I said. "Cheshunt is a quiet town."

"Maybe it is," he said quietly. "Then again, maybe it's the eye of the storm."

His choice of words made me jump and he noticed. "What do you think, Nathaniel? You think there might be some storm clouds swelling over Cheshunt?"

I shrugged, too scared to trust my voice. There were storm clouds all right. They were gathering over my head, and it felt like all hell was waiting to break loose. My heart was hammering away so loudly, he should have heard it. Mr. Sharone was watching me closely. I don't know what he saw, but he nodded.

"I'm not crowding you, Nathaniel. I'm just letting you know that if it gets too big for you kids to handle, give me a call. But remember, you don't want to let it get as far as it did all those years back."

"I . . . don't know what you mean."

"I think you do," Mr. Sharone said with gentle certainty. "I think you know a lot of things you're not saying. The paper has a file about Three North now too. We started it when I did a story about the curfew. There are some letters in the file that suggest the curfew was set up so that demons can roam in the streets. Then there are letters claiming that the gangs that operate in Willington and Saltridge come from Cheshunt. Same as before. There are even letters that say the school is evil. Or that something in the school is evil. They're crackpot letters all right, but no smoke without fire. Excuse the pun. And I read these and I think to myself: *What if whatever is happening now is connected to what happened then?*"

Mr. Sharone took my silence as an answer. "All I'm saying is, if you need help, call me." He took a card out and reached across to slide it in my pocket.

I opened my mouth, but he held up his hand to silence me. "My home number is on that card too." He turned and walked away without looking back, turning up his collar against the downpour.

I watched him disappear into the veil of gray rain, my mind in turmoil. I couldn't help wondering if the man that had frightened Nissa the other night, and the one driving the car that had hit Lallie, and Mr. Sharone had all been drawn to Cheshunt just the way we were; called by what was best in them, to the light, or called by what was worst in them, to the dark. The lines of battle being drawn up.

And who knew how many others, dimly sensing the Call of light or dark had been drawn to Cheshunt over the years?

In the end I didn't tell the others.

They were still shattered about Lallie, and I felt guilty at having completely forgotten about her for a minute. Besides that, I had no chance to tell them anything. Rain was thundering down on the tin roof of the bus stop with a deafening racket, and Nissa barely had time to remind us to meet her that night, to try the healing again, before we had to get on the bus. It was packed so I just stood there, rain from my wet hair dripping down my neck. When we got off the bus, the school siren for the next period was sounding, so we had to run for it.

I don't know how I got through what remained of the morning classes. It was all a blur. At lunchtime I went to the library to get away from the other kids staring at me, wondering and fearful, knowing me to be marked. It made me think of that book written by the guy my grandfather and then I were named for: Nathaniel Hawthorne. In the book there is this woman who has to wear a big red A sewn on her dress so that everyone will know who she is and despise her. The librarian's assistant gave me an uneasy smile because somehow she saw the big red A on me.

I found myself drawn back to the wall where the photograph hung. I looked at Anna. She looked proud and strong-willed. Determined. Zeb was beside her and on his other side I was startled to recognize the blond girl from my dreams.

And suddenly the hair all over my body stirred because *I recognized her!*

The blond girl with the bright serene face and the sad eyes was Lallie as she would be in a few more years. It was seeing her look older in the hospital that made me able to recognize it.

But what on earth did it mean? Was she related to the girl in the photograph? Had she somehow been reincarnated?

I sat down before I fell down.

The older Lallie seemed to be looking straight at me, her eyes burning. Urging me to understand . . . what?

I thought of Anna's diaries and the way The Tod had tried to make me read them, and suddenly I was convinced there was some secret hidden in them.

The remainder of the day passed in a frenzy of impatience. Leaving the school after the bell I noticed the senior mural had been worked on. A lot of trees had been blocked in and some wild-looking mountains. But the thing that chilled me was the red moon painted above the scene, shedding its garish, bloody light.

I was almost running by the time I reached my street. I broke into a jog as soon as I could see the house, relieved to see the driveway was empty. It wasn't until I was inside that I remembered The Tod was out.

In spite of everything, I felt guilty at the thought of him getting rained on earlier in the day because I hadn't put him in. I called but he didn't come, which meant he was mad at me, sulking in his outside kennel. I went down the side path whistling, trying to ignore the wretched foulness of the air. It was incredibly strong, a putrid, decaying stench. The death smell.

"Grab him!" someone hissed, and I found myself locked between two big boys from the school patrol. My heart shuddered in panic.

"What are you doing?"

"Bring him around the back where he can see," Buddha called.

There were three more boys and an older girl, all from the school patrol. The girl was holding The Tod, patting him, but he was cringing away from her hand.

Fear and anger warred in me. "Put him down!"

The girl just smiled, a baring of crooked teeth, and something in her expression made me feel sick with fear.

I looked at Buddha. "What are you trying to do?"

Buddha smiled too. "We're not *trying* to do anything. We're doing it. We're teaching you a lesson. Holly?"

The girl came forward and held The Tod out. He started to whimper as Buddha poured something over him.

The smell cut through the putrid slaughterhouse stench.

Gasoline!

A dread more terrible than any I had ever experienced clawed into my chest. I was shaking violently, unable to tear my eyes away from the dark liquid glugging out over The Tod, darkening his honey-colored fur.

"B–Buddha . . . please," I breathed. "Please don't. I'll do anything you want, but don't do this."

Buddha smiled and his eyes were dark and cruel. "You say you'd do anything, but you don't really mean it. You see, Mr. Karle knows you're one of those bad kids. He knows, but instead of turning you in he's trying to save you. . . ."

He screwed the lid onto the container and put it on the ground.

"He said you need to be taught a lesson you won't forget." Buddha reached into his pocket and held something up.

I stared at it with a feeling of indescribable horror.

A box of matches.

I started to struggle violently, screaming. "No! Help! Don't. Don't. Tod!"

The Tod started to struggle in the girl's arms. She held him tighter.

"Take him back there and put him down," Buddha said, and Holly went down to the back of the yard.

"Please. Please. I'll do anything." I moaned, tears pouring down my cheeks.

"I could almost believe you, because that dog means a lot to you doesn't it, Nathaniel? Mr. Karle told us that. He said people need to lose something precious before they become properly . . . what was the word he used?" He smiled. "Receptive. That was it." Still smiling, he turned to Holly. "Put him down."

Even before The Tod's feet touched the ground, he was struggling to be free; to get to me.

"No! No! Run, Tod. Run away!" I screamed.

But it was no good, he pelted toward me, drawn by the fear in my voice.

Buddha lit a match.

I struggled savagely, kicking and screaming. I managed to get one boy away from my arm and I punched at the other, raked my fingernails down his face. Tried to gouge his eyes out, but the other boy grabbed me again, punching me in the ribs.

I pulled forward, tried to drag them with me, a wild notion in my mind of shielding The Tod with my body.

But the match flew through the air just as The Tod drew even with Buddha.

"Nooo!"

I screamed in utter horror, helpless. The match landed in his tail and flames swept forward up over him. Devoured him.

He arched and coiled, yelping in pain and fright, and then he screamed, a long inhuman howl of agony and terror. For one terrible second his eyes looked at me from out of the flames, bulging and pleading.

And then there was nothing but the cracking sound of burning meat.

"Next time it won't be a dog," I heard Buddha say, and dimly I registered running footsteps.

The boys holding me let go and I flung myself at The Tod, beating my hands on him with some insane idea that I could still save him. The flames burned my hands, seared them, but the pain was nothing compared to the terrible sorrow threatening to choke me.

At last the flames were extinguished, and incredibly I thought I could feel him shudder under my hands.

"Tod! Tod?" As I turned him over, I found myself praying to God. Pleading the way I had with Buddha. "Please. Please. Please let him be alive. I'll do anything."

But if there was a God, He was as incapable of undoing what had been done as I had been of stopping it.

The Tod was dead, the fur seared off him leaving charred, blistered flesh. His tongue, pink and obscene, lolled out from blackened jaws.

And all I could think of was the dismal way he had howled at me when I left him that morning, as if he knew what was coming to get him.

I screamed.

27

It rained then, and somehow that was the worst thing. Five minutes sooner and it might have saved The Tod.

I cuddled his limp, gruesome body to my chest, rocking backward and forward. My hands stung and I wanted to cut them off, thinking how much more agony The Tod must have felt. I cried until my stomach and my throat and my eyes hurt, all the time getting wetter and wetter. I couldn't bear to think of the way I had looked at my watch and left him out because I had been late for the bus. If he had been locked inside, they could not have gotten him.

The rain stopped and a fly came and buzzed around his body in the curdled air. I brushed it away with a feeling of hopeless rage, knowing it would not matter to The Tod that it flew over him, knowing nothing would matter to him ever again. He would never smell a story in the wind or growl at the stars or go to a stranger who called him in her windy voice. He was dead, and there was nothing more final than that.

Then a picture came to me with a jagged, tearing force: Lallie staring into The Tod's eyes and saying she was sorry. And The Tod cringing away from her.

Guilt was like acid, burning me as I remembered Lallie saying there would be a price for her helping me. Now she was in the hospital and The Tod was dead.

I cried again in fury and misery, because it was too late.

Hating Lallie for failing to warn me. Hating my mother for bringing us to Cheshunt. Hurting. Hating.

A cold hate filled me and at last I got up, shivering, and wrapped The Tod in my coat. I couldn't bury him. Not yet. So I carried him into my bedroom and laid him on the bed.

Looking down at him, Lallie's similarity to the girl in the photograph and Mr. Sharone's words came together and showed me what I had been too stupid to see before.

Zeb and Anna weren't just connected to what was happening now. They *were* what was happening now. They had been a Chain, as we were. But their Chain had failed. The simplicity of it took my breath away. I didn't understand how it could be, but I knew I was right.

And I didn't care.

I wanted to kill Buddha. I wanted to set him on fire, and Mr. Karle. I wanted them to feel pain and scream. My hands throbbed in dull pain.

I went out in the street, heading for the school. It was dark, and I realized hours must have passed while I had sat on the ground with The Tod. I walked the way a man shot will go on, not realizing half his guts are on the street behind him. Dimly it seemed I would find the Kraken at the school.

Bear, Danny, and Seth were outside the library when I arrived, reddish shapes in the neon light. As I drew nearer, I noticed Seth was swaying and his breath reeked of alcohol.

Before I could tell them what had happened, Danny clutched at my arm. "Nathaniel, Nissa's disappeared."

"Seth said she came to his place to remind him to come tonight, and then she left. That's the last anyone has seen of her," Bear explained.

I struggled to understand what they were telling me.

"She could've gone to the hospital again," Danny suggested.

The fact of Nissa's absence and The Tod's death came together, and suddenly I was more than scared, remembering what Buddha had said.

"Next time it won't be a dog."

I saw the caretaker in my dreams in flames, and superimposed over him, Nissa. For a minute I thought I was going to vomit. Fear for her almost suffocated me, and panicky thoughts skittered through me like leaves before a hurricane. I told them everything then. It all just spilled out in a tangle; Lallie in the school photograph; what Mr. Sharone had told me; and finally, in stark, dreadful words I told them what had happened to The Tod.

All three looked aghast.

"He'll be sorry," Danny swore.

Bear came over and put his arm awkwardly around my shoulders. But I shoved him away. "Don't you understand? He said next time it wouldn't be a dog. What if he meant next time it would be Nissa!"

Bear paled with shock.

I swung to face Seth. "You were the last to see her. There must be something she said about where she was going."

"I . . . I was drunk," Seth whispered, his face chalk pale.

I grabbed him and shook him. "You know! You must know!"

"Nathaniel!" Bear pulled me away from him.

I slapped his hand away, feeling as if the old, thinking Nathaniel had gone up in flames with The Tod. A strange thought came to me. "What did you see last night when you looked through the telescope?" I asked Seth.

He backed away. "Nothing. It was too . . ."

"In your mind, Seth. What did you see in your mind? What did you tell Nissa?"

Now he was shaking visibly. "I couldn't see anything

but . . . I remembered my father saying he was going there once. She said I must have seen something and I just . . . I told her but . . ."

"Where?" Danny snarled, grabbing him by the front of his shirt. "What did you tell Nissa?"

"The slaughterhouse," Seth whispered. "I saw the slaughterhouse."

28

"I can't come with you," Seth whispered. "I've had too much to drink. I'd hold you back."

Danny grabbed him by the front of his shirt again and shook him. If it had not been such a grim matter, the difference in their sizes would have made the gesture ridiculous.

"You're always drunk, you weak bastard. And you probably will hold us back, but you're coming with us. It's all for one and one for all, and we might need all."

"My father . . ." Seth began, but Danny shook him; the wolf boy had hold of a grizzly, but the grizzly was tranquilized.

"You're part of this too, and it's your fault Nissa went there alone instead of all of us together."

Seth nodded and Danny let him go.

We ran to start with, hugging the shadows and staying out of streetlights, Seth stumbling at our heels. But the slaughterhouse was on the other side of town, and Bear reminded us a group of kids running would attract too much attention, so we slowed to a walk. I felt a blind fury at myself for not having realized sooner where the earth that sorrows was. Lallie had even told me the evidence of it was all around me, and so it had been. Cheshunt was saturated with the death smell.

I was glad when Bear started filling us in on the slaughterhouse, because when we were silent, my mind started replaying

The Tod's death, and I felt I might truly go crazy if I thought of that too much.

I listened to Danny and Bear, moving like a sleepwalker.

Bear said he knew a lot about its history because his class had done an assignment on the slaughterhouse.

"It's old and it was built years ago from the ruins of an older rammed-earth building. Somebody said it used to be a church, but the book I read said it had been some kind of meeting place. There's an unused railway line that runs along behind it, that used to be for transporting carcasses to town in freezer cars. The whole place is practically derelict, but it's still used as a local slaughterhouse. It's got one solid, bolted door, as well as the chute doors for the cows and high windows with bits of glass cemented along the tops of the sills to stop anyone from climbing in."

"Why would they bother making it so hard to get into unless there was something there to hide?" Danny wondered.

"The books said it was because of cattle thieves in the Depression."

Danny turned to Seth who was as silent as I was. "Why did your father go there?"

"Dogs," he said. "Someone called the police and said that's where the feral dog pack had been hanging around. They were attracted . . ." He paled further. "They were attracted by the smell of the blood."

Bear and Danny exchanged a look, and I read my fear for Nissa in their eyes.

The moon and stars were veiled in cloud or smog, reducing the night world to a dim place of blurred shadow against deeper shadow. There were more and more overgrown vacant lots in this part of Cheshunt, gradually giving way to fields and the hills.

The slaughterhouse was on its own, sitting like a stone fortress on a low hill, others rising up behind it. As I stared at it, the black tentacles of despair gave way to a superstitious shudder of fear. The field we crossed to reach it was choked with blackberry and onionweed, but Bear said we would be fools to approach it along the well-lit road in case someone was keeping watch.

We stopped under a clump of diseased-looking bushes a few yards from the slaughterhouse.

"We have to figure out what Nissa would have done," Bear said.

Danny nodded. "Going on what Seth said she probably came here to see if he was right. To look for proof or a clue. She must have gone inside."

"Maybe she didn't come here," Seth whispered.

"Shut up," Danny snarled at him. He pointed to the holding yards that led into the slaughterhouse. There were a series of hinged timber doors.

"Locked from the inside," Bear said. He looked at me. "What do you think?"

I blinked at him stupidly, but my mind was blank.

Bear frowned. "Nathaniel, you have to forget about The Tod."

I felt a blind, violent urge to strike out at him. Seeing it, Bear backed away.

Danny stepped between us and looked into my eyes. "Bear's right. You have to forget about The Tod. For Nissa's sake."

I took a deep breath, and bit down hard on the inside of my mouth. Pain brought tears to my eyes and a moment of clarity.

"I know," I said. Even to my own ears my voice sounded strange. Flattened out and empty.

"Nat, the best way to get revenge for The Tod is to beat the Kraken," Danny said.

A hard ball of hate and anger settled over my chest. "You're right. Let's get on with it."

He looked at me a moment longer, then nodded. "All right, now let's go through it again. Maybe we've got the wrong idea. She might not have sneaked in. Maybe she just marched up and asked to look around for some school assignment."

I nodded. It was just the sort of blunt, fearless thing she would do.

But Bear shook his head. "She could ask until she was blue in the face, but no one would answer. The slaughterhouse only operates every couple of days during the daylight."

"There's no one there then?" Seth sounded relieved.

Bear shook his head. "I said the slaughterhouse was closed, I didn't say no one was there. I meant no one official would be there."

"Well, let's get closer and see if we can find some sign that she's been here at all," Danny said with sudden authority.

We crept around the whole building until we came to one of the windows where the rammed-earth wall was badly eroded. Here there were fresh scuff marks.

"Bingo," Danny said grimly. "I'll take a look."

He scaled the wall, using cracks as toeholds. Then he reached up and hoisted himself onto the sill.

He cried out in pain and fell backward, slithering to the ground as he fell, slithering down to us, his palms covered in blood.

"I forgot about the glass." He grimaced. Then his face changed. "But I saw her. At least I think it was her. She's lying on the floor under the window."

Seth gave a strangled groan and launched himself at the wall. He scaled it faster than I would have believed possible, until I remembered he was a champion athlete, vaulting over the windowsill and disappearing inside.

Bear was wrapping tissues around Danny's fingers, so I went up after Seth, ignoring the pain in my own hands. I used my jacket to pad the top and climbed over the sill onto a wooden shelf set in the wall at window level. Kneeling on it, I leaned forward.

At first I couldn't see anything, it was so dark, but gradually my eyes became accustomed to the dark. In the reflected glow of streetlights out front I saw Nissa lying directly below the sill. Seth was leaning over her, shaking her gently and trying to wake her. When she didn't move, he stared down at her. Perhaps he spoke, but it was too soft for me to hear. I felt a vicious stab of anger as he leaned forward and kissed her on the mouth. She stirred and groaned, wakened like a princess by a kiss.

Bear had climbed up beside me. "Don't move her yet," he called down sharply. "Something might be broken."

He climbed down into the shadowy darkness, squatted beside Nissa and ran his hands down over her body, checking for broken bones. "I don't think anything's broken. Let's get her out of this place."

Danny climbed onto the ledge so fast, he almost head-butted me off.

"We've got company," he said in a low voice, glancing back.

I looked outside to see an enormous dog slinking through the long grass toward the slaughterhouse.

We climbed down onto the floor just as Nissa sat up and shook her head with a groan.

"Are you . . . what happened?" Bear asked her.

"I . . . I came to see if this was the . . . the place where the earth sorrows." She glanced at Seth. "I guess you told them. I just got up on the sill when I heard a growling noise. A dog, I think. It startled me, and I lost my balance and fell."

Danny and I looked at one another but before we could speak, Nissa jumped to her feet and started hunting around anxiously. "The sword! I had it with me."

It had fallen under a low bench. Nissa took it into her hands and examined it.

I let my eyes wander around, taking in the shadowy partitions and benches and a faint gleam from suspended hooks. The whole place had a dry, dusty, bone smell rather than the terrible reek I had come to associate with it.

"You realize this is it, don't you?" Nissa said eagerly. "I don't know why we didn't think of it right away. It's so obvious. The earth that sorrows. We can do the Healing right now."

"I haven't got the bowl," Bear protested.

As it turned out, only Nissa and I had our symbols with us.

"All right, we'll go back and get them," she decided.

"We saw a dog slinking around out there," Danny said uneasily.

Nissa snorted derisively. "I'm not afraid of any mongrel dog. It surprised me, that's all." She held the sword up, removing the guard plug at the end of the blade. "I don't think we'll have too much trouble fending it off."

Outside, it had grown darker, but there was no sign of the animal. The overgrown fields and shadowy holding yards were empty.

"It must've gotten sick of waiting," Danny said, relief in his tone.

"Look at the moon," Bear murmured.

It was one of those rare, low, bloated orange moons, and because we were all looking up, none of us saw the dark, shaggy shape break away from the shadows near the wall.

A dog the size of a small bear exploded out of the night, growling savagely.

Nissa sprang forward to meet it, brandishing her sword. The creature snarled and focused its attention on her. She was so quick and fearless, I realized she must have practiced using the sword.

The dog stopped and gave an eerie ululating cry, and there were answering howls in the distance.

"It's calling them!" Danny hissed. There was another howl, fractionally closer. Nissa might be able to hold one off, but not a herd of feral dogs. If she could just get in a stab, the dog might be incapacitated long enough for us to get away. If we didn't get away, we were in deep trouble. I gritted my teeth, thinking there was no way I would give the Kraken the satisfaction of finding us penned like a lot of frightened sheep.

The dog lurched forward at Nissa, but the sword hissed as she swung it, forcing the dog to retreat, snapping and snarling in frustration. She couldn't get in a decent stab because it seemed uncannily able to anticipate her moves almost before she knew them herself. What she needed was a distraction.

I tensed in readiness, and when the dog began to move in, I lurched forward, shouting wildly. The dog twisted to face me with the same lethal swiftness but immediately seemed to realize what I was about and swung back to Nissa. It raked its talons down her arm, opening up deep gashes even as her point slashed along its side.

It yelped and fell back, but Nissa staggered after it, driving her blade deep into its mottled haunches.

It let out a bellow of agony and fell with a wet-sounding thump. Nissa reeled and stumbled to her knees.

"Catch her!" Danny cried.

I moved instinctively, wincing as she fell against my hands.

"She's probably got a concussion," Bear said.

"We better get away from here."

But it was already too late. We could see a pack of dogs of varying sizes pelting up the road leading to the slaughterhouse. It would be a matter of bare minutes before they discovered us.

"We'll have to climb back inside," Danny cried, panic lighting his eyes.

"No," Bear said firmly. "I'll run and they'll follow me. Then the rest of you get Nissa home."

The fear drained away from Danny's eyes slowly, leaving a queer, rigid calmness in its wake. "We'll lead them off. Nat and Seth can get Nissa home. Okay?" He was looking at me.

Even numb with grief, I felt a rush of admiration for their courage. "Be careful!"

Danny nodded. "You be careful. And tell Nissa what happened."

Then, incredibly, he laughed, and he and Bear ran, cutting across the field toward the old railway lines. Almost at once the dog pack spotted them and gave chase. They passed us snarling and panting, their eyes gleaming red in the moonlight. Crouched in the shadows, I held my breath, certain they would catch the dead dog's scent and circle back.

They flew past without so much as glancing at the slaughterhouse.

We waited until their barking had faded into the distance, then made our way back across the fields and through the streets to the school. Nissa was conscious but unsteady on her feet.

As soon as we were in the attic, I made her lie down and bandaged her arm, glad of something to occupy my mind. She was asleep almost at once.

It was an hour before Bear and Danny turned up, and I let them in with a surge of relief. They climbed into the attic, their faces flushed with exertion and triumph.

"We lost them," Danny said, his eyes glowing.

"We could have come a while back, but we thought we should lie low just in case," Bear put in. "No sense in leading them here."

The racket woke Nissa, and she insisted on getting up. She was still pale, but her eyes were clear. She made us explain all over again exactly how we had found her and what had happened. Incredibly, she had only a hazy recollection of fighting the dog.

"It's too late to go back tonight," she said at last. "But we'll go and do the Healing tomorrow night. We'll get in before the Kraken knows what's happening."

Danny and Bear looked at me, the excitement dying from their faces as they remembered the earlier part of the night. A leaden ache settled into my stomach at the thought of home and The Tod. As if the pain were linked to the event, I became aware of the burns on my hands.

Nissa followed my eyes and exclaimed as she took up one of my hands and examined the blistered palm. I winced involuntarily and took my hands firmly away.

"What happened to them?"

There was a long silence and the wind muttered at the eaves. Seth met my eyes with a skittish look, like a horse about to bolt. His eyes skated away as he stood up. "I have to go home."

There was an awkward silence as he left.

"What I'd like to know is why he didn't tell us sooner about the slaughterhouse," Danny said tightly, as soon as he had gone.

"He didn't believe in what he saw," Nissa said sharply. "He thought he had imagined it. He can't help the way he is."

She got out some ointment and began to stroke it with gentle efficiency onto my palms.

"I'm going too," Bear said.

Danny rose as well, looking over at me. "Tell her."

Nissa stared at him. "Tell me what?"

Neither Danny nor Bear answered her. They left in silence and Nissa went with them to lock the front door. Returning to the attic she looked at me squarely. "As soon as I saw your face in the slaughterhouse, I knew something had happened."

So I told her about the photograph of Lallie, and Mr. Sharone's revelations. And lastly, as concisely and unemotionally as I could, in empty words, I told Nissa about The Tod.

I felt as if a ball of ice had formed around my heart and the cold bit into my bones. As I talked, I saw with renewed despair how easy I had made it for them.

"Oh, God," Nissa breathed. "Oh, Nat. That poor little thing."

And that was all it took to reopen the floodgates.

There was a bitter sweetness in the tears that came, because Nissa put her arms around me and held me tight. Her heart beat strongly against my cheek, and hurting for The Tod was somehow muddled up with how I felt for her.

I cried until the ice in me had melted, washing away the

black killing fury and leaving only a desolate emptiness.

At last the tears stopped and I sat quietly, oddly calm. Nissa sat back, her eyes searching my face. Her own eyes were dry, and I thought bleakly that I had never seen her cry, and maybe her way was better. Never loving so that nothing could hurt you.

But as I looked at her in the glowing lantern flame, I understood that maybe love wasn't something tame that could be controlled. It was a wild thing that might kill you with its claws as easily as its beauty. And it came when it chose, so that sometimes you could as soon choose not to love as not to breathe.

Nissa's eyes were so blue; as deep and beautiful as the sky on the most perfect summer day as she leaned forward slowly and pressed her lips on mine.

They felt soft and cool, and my heart stopped beating altogether.

Then the kettle started bubbling and bubbling, spilling into the jet. Nissa jerked away from me, as if she had been burned, and sprang up to switch it off. She made us both a drink without turning to look at me once. When she brought the mugs back, her face was cool, her eyes shuttered.

"Nissa . . ." I began, but she cut me off deliberately in a hard voice.

"I'm sorry about The Tod, Nat."

"Nissa . . ."

She shook her head with a finality that stung me. "You better go home when you finish that."

When she locked the library door between us, we stared at one another for a moment through the glass. It was freezing cold out, and my breath came in tiny frost-puffs of air.

It was almost winter, I thought distantly as I turned away, the summer as unreachable as Nissa.

It was dark. The wind was blowing hard and smelled of the sea as I walked home, but I was numb to the cold. There were garbage bins out in front of some of the houses, even though the garbage truck didn't come until Friday. I remembered a notice had come in the mail saying the garbage would be picked up a day early that week. Then I thought how stupid it was to be thinking about the garbage.

As I opened the gate, I opened my mouth automatically to call The Tod, half imagined him barking in the laundry to be let out.

Then I remembered with a dull little shock that he was dead.

I had never felt so sad as when I came into the empty house.

Except it wasn't empty. The light was on and my mother was sitting on the couch with a face like stone, staring accusingly at me.

29

I stared at my mother, stunned. Her car must have been in the driveway, but I had been too overwrought to notice.

"Where have you been?" she asked. There were black rings around her eyes, as if she hadn't slept for days.

"I . . . I was walking."

"Walking where?"

"Just walking," I said, striving for normality.

"I've been into your bedroom."

The Tod, I thought bleakly. I had no words to give her.

"I had a call from the school at work this afternoon. They said you were missing this morning. So I come home and I find that." She pointed toward my bedroom door. "But no Nathaniel. What have you been doing all night?"

I shook my head. What could I say? That some of my schoolmates had torched my dog; that I had been to the slaughterhouse fighting the hound of the Baskervilles; that I had been kissed by Nissa Jerome?

Sure.

"I suppose it was the same place you went last Friday, when you were supposed to be home sick. The school said you were seen by police wandering the streets when, as far as I knew, you were in bed!"

Her voice was like a wall pressing down on me.

"I wasn't doing anything wrong," I said at last. Then something she had said struck me. "Who told you all this?"

"Mr. Karle. He said the school was worried about you and they were afraid you had gotten mixed up with a gang of . . ." She shook her head. "I don't know why I brought us here. I thought it might lay some ghosts to rest. You see, it was when we lived in this district that we . . . your father and I, separated. I should never have come back, but there was something about this area that . . . drew me. Even all those years back with your father—he felt the same way." She laughed, a broken sound with tears in it. "You know, he actually wanted to live in Cheshunt."

I felt a cold finger down my spine at the thought that the calling power of Cheshunt had reached even my father and mother.

She gave me a hard, weary look. "Mr. Karle called me because he was concerned about you."

I bit back the fierce desire to tell her Mr. Karle had arranged to have my dog killed, knowing she would not believe me.

Again I saw Buddha smile and strike the match.

I swallowed dryly. "He was lying to you. There's no gang." Somehow we had come the full circle and the end was the beginning. Like Lallie had said.

My mother laughed harshly. "And you haven't been lying to me?"

I bit my lip. "I haven't told you a lot of things, but I swear I haven't been doing anything bad. Not the things he told you."

"Nathaniel, it's not just Mr. Karle. I had a call from the police not half an hour ago looking for you. A house was burned down in Willington. There were witnesses and one of them described you."

"I wasn't even in Willington!" I told her, dazed. "The police are lying."

She groaned. "Nathaniel, listen to yourself. Listen to how

crazy that sounds." She pointed to my hands. "I can see your hands are burned. Are you trying to tell me that happened while you were walking?"

"I wasn't in Willington. I swear it."

"Then where were you?"

I couldn't tell her. I knew that. If she thought I was crazy now, what would she think if I told her the truth? "If you could just . . ."

She cut me off and now there was a flatness to her voice. "Nathaniel, I also received a report on you from the school counselor in today's mail. She recommends psychiatric counseling."

I resisted the urge to say the school counselor was in on the conspiracy. "What does she say is supposed to be wrong with me?"

She shook her head tiredly. "It doesn't matter what she said. I know what the matter is."

The conversation had turned into unknown waters. I felt confused, out of my depth.

"It's my fault for not dealing with it sooner; my fault for coming to this district and raking up the past."

"The past?" An abyss seemed to be opening at my feet and I started to shake.

She came closer. "Nathaniel, I'm not blaming you for what you did. I understand that you couldn't fight what was born in you. But why did you take The Tod with you? How could you let that happen to him?"

I recoiled in disgust and incredulity. She thought I had burned a house down and let The Tod die in the fire!

"I should have told you sooner, like your grandmother said. Maybe this wouldn't have happened."

"You think I killed my own dog?" I whispered. I felt on the verge of overload. Too much had happened too fast.

"We're going to get through this together. I promise you.

Mr. Karle is going to help. He said there is a place you can be sent . . ."

My head snapped up. "What sort of place?"

"Not an institution. A private place where there are people to help you."

I felt like I was on a roller coaster. She wanted to send me to Mr. Karle to be cured? I started to laugh.

She held her hand up, as if she was trying to ward off the evil eye.

I was laughing and then I was crying. I opened my mouth to say what happened to The Tod wasn't my fault, but then I saw him pushing himself against the gate and howling mournfully. And I heard Lallie telling me there would be payment exacted for saving me.

A tidal wave of exhaustion rolled over me, and with it a terrible lonely longing for The Tod. The tears spilled, blinding me, blurring my mother's expression.

"I can't talk about this," she said, rising suddenly, her own voice thick with tears. "I'm . . . I'm going to work. We'll talk when I come home, but I don't want you to leave the house. Not for anything."

"Mom . . ." I called.

She turned slowly to look at me.

"Mom . . . I'm not crazy. However it looks. If you loved me, you'd believe that."

She stared for a moment longer, and I couldn't tell what was going through her mind. Then she left without saying anything.

The Tod was no longer on my bed, and I felt a fresh surge of grief because there had been no chance to say good-bye. I didn't even know where she had buried him. If she had buried him. I couldn't bear to go down to the yard and look.

I felt as if I had been beaten up. I just lay on the bed, curled up, staring at the wall, my hands throbbing. I felt as empty as a dead tree. I couldn't imagine getting up ever again. Even the thought of Nissa didn't help.

I slept.

And I dreamed.

I was back in the overgrown hillside garden, the bloated red moon hovering like a malevolent eye.

Anna was alone, sitting on a swing suspended from a thick tree branch. The rope creaked, though she was still.

"Anna?"

It was Zeb and he pushed through the bushes. His face was haggard; blue-black hair hanging lankly over his forehead, eyes filled with bewildered sorrow.

"Anna, you're smarter than I am. I know that. I guess you're smarter than all of us," he said humbly. "I don't understand any of it. How he could make Sam do that to himself just by talking to him."

"They want a scapegoat," Anna said in a hard voice. "He's made them want that. It's all of us, or one. You're the eldest."

"He was my friend," Zeb said dully.

"What else can we do?" Anna demanded angrily. "Some of us have to stay to stand against him."

He nodded again. "All right, Annie." I was astounded to see the mute adoration in Zeb's eyes as he looked at her. But she would not look up; would not see that Mrs. Heathcote had been wrong about him not loving her.

After a long minute Zeb nodded twice, as if it were a required countersign. When he turned to make his way slowly back up the hill, his shoulders were bowed low as if under a terrific weight.

Only then did Anna Galway look up at him, and her face was wet with tears.

And then I was alone, the swing empty. I heard something running through the trees toward me. Terror filled me and I started to run too, crashing through the tangled undergrowth.

"You can't run away from me!" the monster howled.

FOUR

The Binding

30

I woke to a dark, still day filled with fleeting images of the previous day, as clear and disconnected as snapshots.

Lallie's still body in the hospital bed and then her face, older, in the library photo.

The Tod writhing in flames.

Seth leaning over Nissa in the slaughterhouse.

The feral dog charging at me.

Nissa kissing me in the attic.

I thought with fresh incredulity of my mother believing I had killed The Tod. My mind replayed fragments of her words, but they made no more sense to me than they had the night before.

I had been perilously close to a total shutdown, I realized now.

The whole time, from The Tod's murder to my arrival home again, seemed like some dark, nightmarish roller-coaster ride. Even now I felt battered by what had happened, and strangely lethargic. It seemed to me I had somehow compressed my lifetime into a day and though I had slept more than twelve hours, I still felt exhausted, emptied out. But under all of that a slow hate burned.

My heart began to beat faster even thinking about what they had done to The Tod.

"The way to get revenge is to beat him," Danny said in my memory.

I sat up abruptly, thinking about my idea that Anna and Zeb

had been part of a previous Chain. That notion had been superseded by The Tod's death and Nissa's rescue, but now I thought of it again and wondered if I could possibly be right.

And if I was, then how had the previous Chain failed? I thought of Anna's diary and sat up, certain the answer would be there.

My hands were painful and swollen, but using wrists, elbows and teeth, I managed to extract the notebooks from my backpack.

Clumsily I turned the pages, skimming and searching for proof that I was right about Anna being part of an earlier Chain.

In minutes I had what I needed.

"I brought Lallindra the token she desired," Anna wrote. "It was a perfectly round stone from my father's collection. She told me it meant I was the circle bearer."

I felt the blood drain out of my face.

Anna Galway had been the circle bearer of the last Chain! I thought of the bitter, raving old woman in the garden with a shiver of fear, wondering if that was what lay in my own future.

I read on, piecing it together like a jigsaw.

Anna had been drawn to the school after hours, as we had, meeting Zeb and three others. Lallie—Lallindra—had told them how to get their symbols.

I couldn't find anything about the Forging, but the next thing she wrote about was trying to figure out the Healing ritual, just as we had done. Apparently they had worked it out because she then wrote that they were unable to complete the ritual because Sam McLainie had killed himself. According to Anna's diaries he had not died in the library after all, but outside. He had stumbled against the wall setting it alight by accident.

Anna wrote after this: "We know we shall not be believed if we speak the truth about what happened to Sam. That is his power of course—distorting the truth. Lies and illusion to distract us from seeing the true battle. Yet we must remain to complete the Healing and to stand against Koster Laine. Zeb will take the blame and I will be a witness so that he alone is charged. One must be sacrificed so the rest of the Chain may remain."

She wrote then of Zeb being taken away and the rest of them waiting to fight their Kraken while Cheshunt darkened around them, the whole place drawn into a dark waltz by the school dance master, promoted soon after the fire to headmaster.

There was no way of telling at what point they had failed. It could not have been their failure to complete the Healing, since Anna wrote that they had completed the Healing after Zeb had gone. Somehow, without knowing why or how or when, they had lost their battle to the dark. I felt a cold fist tighten around my heart at the realization that we could fail as easily and unknowingly.

I jumped as the phone rang.

It was Nissa calling from a phone booth a few streets from the school. My heart started to pound as I pictured her leaning toward me last night and kissing me on the lips.

"Nissa . . ."

She cut me off sharply. "Nathaniel, have you looked outside yet?"

"I just woke up. I'll have a look now."

"Wait," she said. "Just listen. There were a whole lot of kids at school early this morning. Dozens of them. Now they've disappeared and no one's turned up for school. The whole place is deserted."

"*What?*"

"I don't know what's happening, but I have the feeling time is running out for us. I think we should do the Healing now. Can you come?"

"I'll be right there."

"I'll call the others. I'll wait here for you." She hung up.

I raced into my bedroom and dragged on my clothes and shoes. It felt cold, so I jerked on a parka and pulled a hat over my ears. I scrawled a note to my mother saying I was sorry but I had to go out, then I ran out to the back door to get my bike.

I stopped.

The whole sky was blotted out by dark congested clouds in fantastic shapes. The air seemed as thick as syrup and smelled like some kind of fetid animal's den.

I decided against the bike after all, realizing it would probably hamper me. I hiked around the side of the house and out the front gate. Then I ran. Not jogged, but ran.

Almost at once I had a stitch, but I didn't stop. I didn't even slow down when the stitch turned into a jagged spike twisting in my side. The pain barrier rose up in front of me, insurmountable. I ran harder and after a long minute of pain, the suffocating feeling disappeared.

I ran around the corner to the street where the phone was. The dark, yellowish light made it oddly hard to see, and I didn't see the phone booth until I was practically on top of it. My heart plummeted because it was empty.

Nissa was gone.

I froze as two sleek black dogs emerged from a house and slunk along the street toward the school.

Then a hand touched my arm lightly.

"Ahhh!" I gasped, spinning round.

It was Danny. "Hell, you scared me," I breathed.

"Come on, we're in the bus shelter back there."

Nissa and Bear were there, but there was no sign of Seth.

"It's been like this since about five," Nissa said.

"What do you think it is?" I asked.

"The darkness growing," Bear murmured. "Where's Seth?"

Nissa scowled unhappily. "I don't know, but if he doesn't come in the next few minutes, we'll have to go ahead without him."

"We don't need him," Danny pointed out. "His bit is over. We know where we have to do the Healing now. Besides, he knows where to come if he turns up late."

"Did you bring your symbol?" Nissa asked me, the sword cradled on her knee.

I pulled the circle out from under my shirt and she nodded approvingly.

"Let's go then," Danny said impatiently.

Nissa looked up and down the dark street, but there was no sign of Seth. She shrugged. "Okay."

Retracing our steps of the night before, we crossed Cheshunt without seeing a single soul.

"This is really weird," Bear murmured uneasily. "Where are all the people? He couldn't just make them disappear. What about the other teachers?"

None of us had an answer for him.

By the time we reached the end of the streets, it had grown darker and a chill wind had risen. Our clothes flapped and our hair whipped back and forth under its force. We stopped, looking across the field at the slaughterhouse. Instead of appearing less fearsome in the daylight, it was oddly malevolent in the sepia-toned light, surrounded by a sea of hissing grass.

"Come on," Nissa said resolutely, and climbed over the fence into the field.

The rest of us followed, and as we walked up the slope, the wind increased in strength until we were almost bent in half.

Nissa turned to say something, but the wind had grown so strong, her words were whipped away. I pointed to my ears and shook my head.

By the time we reached the trees, the wind howled around us and it was darker still; a bleary twilight. Nissa tried again to talk, but it was impossible. Danny shook his head and pointed to the slaughterhouse. She nodded and we struggled the final few yards, battling the force of the unnatural wind for each step. Just moving forward required such effort that there was no energy left over to be afraid. It was enough to put one foot in front of the other.

Once we were partly sheltered from the wind by the wall,

Nissa climbed up to the window, putting her own coat over the sill to pad it against the glass. She climbed in carefully. The coat flapped wildly in the breeze as the rest of us followed. Above, the tin roof rattled and quivered, as if it would take off.

Once inside on the ground we looked at one another, wild-haired and wild-eyed.

"That wind." Even inside, Bear's voice was barely audible above the noise outside.

"It's him," Danny shouted.

"It's the dark," Nissa corrected. "It knows we're trying to get rid of it. Let's not waste any time."

She held up her sword decisively and for a moment the howling winds seemed to falter. She took a deep breath. "I cleave the sorrowing earth to let out the darkness."

The blade flashed in the dull light as she heaved it forward. It clove the damp ground at her feet.

I gasped to see the tip of the blade come away stained red.

"It's from the cattle that they slaughter here," Danny yelled, but he looked shocked too.

Collecting himself, he stuck the torch in the ground to free his hands, lit a match, and set it to the top.

It flared brightly, a ragged flame in the cross draft, and the orange glow lit his pale face and blond hair as he stood over it.

"I burn this earth to cleanse the wound," he said, and bent to take up the torch.

Outside the wind had reached a shrill crescendo and the sound of it actually hurt my ears.

"The whole place could go up in this wind," Danny said, looking up at the rippling tin. "If the wind doesn't tear it apart first."

"Finish it," Nissa yelled, pointing to the torch stuck in the ground.

Again Danny bent down, but at the same time we heard the slow, deliberate sound of someone clapping.

We all swung around.

Mr. Karle walked forward out of the shadows, still clapping
mockingly, his eyes as cold as a shark's.

"The game is over. Welcome to the Gathering at last."

31

He wasn't alone. The bad guys never are.

Before we could react, the doors opened and kids poured in with the wind, sending Danny's torch flame into a wild fluttering dance. There must have been more than a hundred, mostly from the older grades and the school patrol. They were all wearing dark clothes, and their faces were painted in garish red and black markings, like some bizarre cult.

But the chilling thing was that each of them carried some kind of weapon. An ax or a knife or a hammer. And a couple of them had guns.

Fear evaporated when I spotted Buddha. I began to shake, not with fear but with instant rage at the indelible memory of him smiling as he lit the match that destroyed The Tod.

"I would not think of it, Nathaniel," Mr. Karle said smoothly. "There would be a price to pay, and as before, it would not be you who paid it, but one of your friends."

I glared at him with hatred, wanting more than anything in the world to smash the mocking smile from his face. Dimly, I remembered Bunny saying thinkers rarely acted, but when they were pushed to it, as Hamlet was, they were capable of dreadful carnage.

At that second I would have given my life to make carnage of Mr. Karle and Buddha. But there was the cost. I did not think I could survive another price like the last one.

"How do you like my army?" Mr. Karle inquired. He didn't

raise his voice, yet it was clearly audible above the noise of the wind and the rattling of corrugated iron.

"They are about to go out and teach Willington and Saltridge an object lesson in the need for control and order." He leaned closer and his lips stretched over white teeth as his smile broadened. "They will administer this lesson to the good citizens of those suburbs in my name."

"You won't get away with this!" Nissa shouted, her voice barely audible above the incredible wind. "No matter what you do to us, they'll get you."

A wave of wind swept around us as another group of kids came in from the outer door, swelling the crowd. They had lanterns and lit them, and the light played strangely over their painted faces, making them look oddly demonic. The dense, foul air seemed to slide against my skin with a greasy intimacy, like some kind of hellish cat wanting to be petted.

A boy came over and whispered something in Buddha's ear, then the two of them went out.

"What are you going to do with us?" Danny demanded.

Mr. Karle's brows lifted playfully. "Do? I will do nothing to you. I will leave you to the authorities. They are the proper agency to deal with delinquents. I daresay you will be put into reform schools, or perhaps in your case some other institution for disturbed children."

"We'll tell them," Bear said. "We'll tell them you're behind the gangs."

"And you really imagine they would take your word against mine?" He laughed. "I think you underestimate me. And you certainly overestimate yourselves."

"I couldn't go low enough to underestimate you," Nissa said scathingly.

He only smiled. "You misunderstand the nature of this society. The strong are believed because they can defend their truth."

"Truth doesn't need defending."

"You are wrong, girl. If you spoke against me, I would defend myself and I would be believed because I am a reputable figure and an adult, and after this day you will be amazed at how persuasive I shall be."

"Only here," Nissa said bitterly. "They'd only believe you in Cheshunt because the whole place is poisoned with evil."

Mr. Karle laughed. "Oh, my dear child. Wrong again and again. With as many witnesses as I will produce, I should be believed anywhere. And the same voices that will defend me will bear witness against you."

Nissa laughed at him with fearless scorn, but he was unmoved. "I have all the time in the world to conquer. But your time is very limited indeed. Your interference sets a bad example. You must learn to obey your betters."

"We'll never do what you say," Danny yelled defiantly. "Not even if you torture us."

Mr. Karle chuckled. "Torture? Where do you get such foolish, melodramatic notions, boy? I think you must truly have damaged your brain in that field. The dog must have bitten into it."

His eyes flicked sideways at Bear. "Or perhaps he simply hit his head and damaged it. What do you think, my stolid friend? You would know, wouldn't you? You would recognize the signs of concussive brain damage."

Bear said nothing.

"You bastard," I said.

Mr. Karle turned his pale blue-green eyes to me. "Nathaniel! My poor boy. Such a violent temper. Just what your mother fears most. How it distresses her to know her only begotten son is going the way of the father. So terribly sad. So ironic."

"What are you talking about?"

His brows lifted in mock horror. "Oh, dear. She hasn't told you yet? Tsk tsk. How remiss of her. How cowardly. But then, life has made her a coward. She became a coward to survive."

"Don't listen to him!" Nissa shouted.

Her voice sounded distant, flat. Bile rose in my throat and I thought I might vomit at a sudden vision of my mother crying, blood leaking out from the edges of her lips.

"Are you beginning to understand? Do you see yet?" Mr. Karle asked eagerly.

Nissa kicked me hard in the ankle. "Nathaniel, don't look at him. Don't listen. He's trying to get inside your head. He's trying to poison you."

"Not at all, my dear girl. Nathaniel does not need me to poison him. He carries his own poisons; he was born with the seeds of violence and murder."

I was dizzy. Disoriented. I felt that I had lost my grip on the world and it was sliding away from me, out of my reach.

"Think, Nathaniel," the Kraken invited. "Think hard enough and you will break through the walls your mind has erected. Think of the zoo. . . ."

Obediently my mind threw up a picture of the small monkey lying passively while the gorilla punched and kicked it. I heard my mother murmur, "It's too frightened to run."

"Leave him alone, you bastard!" Nissa shouted.

Mr. Karle's smile only deepened. "My, my. What a crude little girl you are, Nissa. How unfeminine and unattractive you are. How rough. No one could ever love such a creature, except out of pity."

The stricken look on her face was like a bucket of cold water, and abruptly the world stopped shifting under my feet. "That's a lie," I said, but the wind ate my words.

"Imagine how surprised I was when my students told me there was no Nissa Jerome at your address," Mr. Karle was saying to her. "And where do you live, I wonder? Where is your burrow, little rabbit? Where do you go after dark?"

He looked around at the four of us. "Do you see now? No one would ever believe your word against mine. To begin with, you are not children of good character. But more importantly I am an adult and you are children. And children should be seen and not heard."

I jumped and he saw it. "Does that strike a chord, Nathaniel? Does it ring a bell?"

I was shaken at his use of the words from my dream. What did it mean? Could he look into my sleep?

Nissa tried to kick out at me again, but the boy behind her wrenched her viciously sideways.

"Such bad manners, Nissa," Mr. Karle smiled. "Let him have his memories in peace." He looked at me. "Let them come. They will, Nathaniel, if you let them. They want to come."

And as if called up by the Kraken, I did remember.

As if in a dream, I saw it all.

I was very young and going to the zoo for a picnic with my mother and father. The leaves were brown and yellow, and my father shouted at the ticket lady for something. I was too excited by the sound and smell of animals flowing out to care, and I didn't like listening to the sound of his voice when he was angry. I had learned how to stop hearing when he shouted and my mother screamed and cried in the night.

We went inside and my mother laid out a blanket and unpacked the picnic basket. I was thirsty and my mother gave me a drink. The cup was big and it slipped out of my hand. Milk lay in pale beads on the blanket like a mermaid's necklace.

My father's mouth opened and closed. He reached out and slapped me hard. He had never done that before. It frightened me and I screamed. Told him he was a bad daddy. His face reddened and his eyes darkened, and I screamed in terror because he was turning into a monster like in the movies. His hands reached out for me, but my mother flung herself across him and cried out to me to run.

I ran as fast as I could into the trees. I heard a scream from my mother, and then I heard footsteps and the crashing and cracking of branches. *I was terrified because I knew he was after me. My father. The monster.*

He caught me. His fingers bit into my arms like teeth.

"Children should be seen and not heard," he said, and his big hand closed around my neck. And squeezed.

I blinked in horror and Mr. Karle was smiling into my face. "You see? There is no fighting the dark. It is in all of us. All of you."

"Nat?" Nissa called, but I couldn't look at her.

The Kraken grinned triumphantly, showing his teeth. They were very white. *All the better to eat you with,* I thought. Crazily.

Another group of kids came in, darkly dressed and painted. The last wrestled the door shut, and I suddenly remembered the cold ghost wind that had blown through the car the first day my mother and I came to Cheshunt. "It's an ill wind that blows nobody any good," my grandmother would often say. Now I wondered if there were winds like that; winds that blew ill, and more than ill.

I looked around at the others. They seemed to be a long way away from me. Nissa's sword lay at her feet. No one had bothered moving it. Maybe it was true they couldn't see the symbols. Or maybe they just didn't care about them. Bear's bowl lay on its side in the dirt and Danny's torch flickered, still stuck in the ground by his side. They looked like they were posing for some sort of offbeat publicity shot for the war at the end of the world. They looked like the losers.

As I watched, the torch drooped slowly sideways, the flaming end coming to rest on a timber roof support. Flames licked up along the support beam.

By now the place was packed, and Mr. Karle turned to address them. "Let the Gathering come to order."

Instantly they fell silent. The wind outside shrieked and wailed, but Mr. Karle's voice rose above it.

"We have made Cheshunt into a place to be proud of. Here, there is control and order. There is unity and obedience," Mr. Karle said in an exalted voice. Then his expression became somber. "But the outside world refuses to understand. They are constantly bleating about human rights and freedom of choice while chaos reigns. And so we have a mission. Our mission is to save them and teach them the way."

There was a murmur of agreement from the crowd. They were starting to come to life. The Kraken was pouring energy into them.

"We must allow them to see where the road they are on will lead. We must demonstrate to them in clear lessons what will become of them if they do not learn. We must teach them. *You* must teach them, for shall not the young teach their elders?"

"Yes!"

"Yesss," the Kraken said. "Yes. Tonight you will show them the error of their ways. You will teach them with pain and sorrow and suffering, and they will never forget, because that is the best way."

"Yes!" Louder still.

"You are my instruments," he cried, lifting his hands.

His audience roared in unison.

Nissa drew herself up, gazing around with contempt. "I'm not afraid of you. Of any of you."

"No," Mr. Karle sneered. "You are afraid of yourself. But you will be afraid of me, you can be sure of that."

"Listen to me, all of you," Nissa cried, ignoring him. "You don't have to do this. You can stop right now and go home. If you do that, there's nothing he can do. Alone he's just one man! You make him powerful by doing what he tells you. You can take his power away."

There was a stillness among those arrayed around us, as if for a moment they were really listening.

Then the Kraken stepped forward and slapped her across the face. A trickle of dark blood ran from the corner of her mouth, but her smile didn't falter.

"You won't win."

The flash of anger in his eyes penetrated the strange, distant calm that had enveloped me—because if he was so sure of himself, why would he become angry?

"I *have* won, or are you so stupid you fail to perceive it?"

The flame from the torch had begun to lick along the beam, but I couldn't cry out or even whisper a warning to the others. My mind was filled up with the realization that my father had tried to kill me, had beaten up my mother. I kept hearing the Kraken saying: *There's no fighting the dark; it's in all of us.* And I knew we had lost.

The Kraken leaned over to Nissa. "You don't see, do you? You still have hope. How touching." He smiled, a bright corrupt glee in his eyes. "And why do you hope? What possible reason could you have for hope? Could it be that you have something hidden from me? Some resource?"

Nissa said nothing.

The Kraken nodded a curt signal to Buddha, who flung the door open again. The black death wind swirled around us, bitter cold.

As if their entrance had been timed to have the most impact, Seth Paul's father entered, and behind him Seth.

Nissa gave an anguished cry. "Oh, God! They got him too."

But Mr. Karle gave Nissa a radiant smile. "Got him? But you misunderstand, Nissa. I didn't *get* Seth. He came to us."

"You filthy liar," she snarled.

He laughed. "Do you really think that, Nissa? Do you imagine his love for you would make him a hero? Do you imagine anyone of worth could love you?"

Nissa recoiled, as if he had struck her again.

Without warning Danny leaned forward and spat full in the Kraken's face.

There was a hiatus—a complete, shocking absence of sound, as if the whole world had been disintegrated. A violent rage showed fleetingly in the Kraken's eyes. For a second he looked as if he would kill Danny with his bare hands.

Then he visibly controlled himself, taking a clean white handkerchief from his pocket and carefully wiping the dribble of saliva from his cheek.

"I can punish him for that," Buddha offered eagerly, and a spike of hot anger pierced the numbness surrounding me like a mist.

"Oh, he shall be punished. It will give me exquisite pleasure to see that you are sent to one of those places where your manners can be adjusted permanently."

"Seth, where did he catch you?" Bear called.

But Seth seemed not to hear. The Kraken signaled Seth's father to bring him nearer.

"These kids have to pay for leading my boy into trouble," the policeman said. There was a dull red rage in his eyes, and he seemed oblivious to the fact that he was surrounded by a horde of teenagers about to go on a rampage of destruction.

The Kraken grinned rapaciously. "Seth has been very confused, but fortunately he came to his senses in time, and like a good, obedient son, he confessed everything to his father."

"Seth, you weak bastard," Danny cried. "I knew we shouldn't have let you in."

Seth's head jerked up, as if someone had pulled the strings of a puppet, his eyes dark holes burned into white chalk. "I'm sorry . . . I couldn't be what you wanted. I tried, but I . . ."

The Kraken patted Seth's shoulder consolingly. "You did the right thing, the only thing you could have done under the circumstances."

But Seth had eyes only for Nissa.

She was staring at him, her face like stone; as unforgiving and proud as a goddess. There was no sign of the hurt that had flamed in her eyes at his betrayal, no anger—only a dark, contemptuous courage without weakness, without compassion.

A thread of fear ran through me somehow linked to Nissa's face; a premonition of disaster that overrode even the shock of remembering the truth about my father. Abruptly I wondered what on earth I was doing, letting myself worry about something that had happened so long ago. Hadn't Lallie warned me to seek beyond the shadows of the past for the truth? I forced myself to concentrate and the feeling of danger increased.

"Nissa . . ." I began.

Mr. Karle whirled, his pale eyes narrowed to slits in the lantern flame. "Nathaniel, I should mention that it was Seth who told me about your dog. Now, what was his name? Oh, yes. The Tod."

Hatred bubbled into my brain, but before I could react, I found myself wondering why the Kraken had chosen that moment to tell me that Seth had marked The Tod for death. And for the first time I wondered why he had forced me to remember about my father.

To anger me? Shock me? Frighten me? *Or to distract me?*

I thought of Anna's diary, and of her saying their Kraken had tried to distract them. To stop them from seeing the true battle. He *wanted* me to think about the past, to stop me from thinking about what was happening.

Why?

It had to have something to do with being in the Chain. With beating the Chain. Anna's Chain had lost. So had we.

Or had we?

Most of the kids were crowded down at one end of the slaughterhouse, facing us in a bizarre parody of a theater audience. Mr. Karle stood to one side, like some hellish director. It occurred to me suddenly that Seth could not have arrived at exactly that moment, unless it had been arranged in advance.

265

But why would the Kraken have set up such an elaborate drama?

He had caught us, and what he said about the authorities believing him was true. Especially with Seth's father to back him up. He had won.

So why was he wasting time gloating over his victory?

Unless he hadn't won yet.

I looked again at the torch and was startled to see the flames climbing up the beam toward the roof. I could smell smoke now too, but no one else had noticed.

Lallie's words came into my mind: *See the true battle, Nathaniel.*

Mr. Karle was staring at Nissa, his pale eyes, deep stagnant pools; the kind little kids are drowned in.

Danny was struggling in the grip of two older boys and raging at Seth. "You bastard. You shit! You're just like your stinking pig of a father. Like father, like son."

I shivered, thinking of Mr. Karle's hints about my father.

Seth's father snarled and took a step toward Danny, but Mr. Karle held them apart.

Why?

Seth had eyes for no one but Nissa. "Please . . ." His lips shaped the word, but the shrieking wind blotted out the sound of it.

And she, as cold and beautiful as a princess who discovered the prince who woke her was a leper. "I was wrong about you."

Mr. Karle leaned forward, his eyes running hungrily from Nissa to Seth.

"You're a coward and a traitor."

Seth bowed his head like a prisoner preparing for the death sentence. His shoulders slumped and I shivered at a surge of déjà vu. Words and phrases flew in my thoughts as if driven by the screaming winds battering on the roof and walls outside, but instead of suppressing them I concentrated, trying to follow my thoughts to their conclusion.

"That is his power . . . the power of lies and illusion to distract us from seeing the true battle . . ." Anna Galway had written of the Kraken. But Anna's Chain had been beaten. Did that mean the illusions had won?

And what was the true battle?

Lallie had told me the sign of the circle meant I had to find the answers to the future in the past. Beyond the past.

Yet may a greater Chain be forged between you . . . to bind the dark. Lallie's words rang in my thoughts, but I couldn't think what they meant; how they could be applied. Lallie had warned us the dark would win if the Chain was broken. That meant the object was to keep the Chain safe and intact.

Did it mean the symbols had to be kept safe or together?

You are the symbols . . . the symbols must be forged into a greater Chain to bind the dark . . . the Chain must not be broken.

I looked at Seth's bowed shoulders and the sense of déjà vu strengthened, solidified into a memory.

Time froze as a memory exploded in my mind, of Zeb Sikorsky walking away with his shoulders bowed, isolated from the others, cut off, a link in the Chain broken.

And that last Chain had lost.

In a flashing realization I saw.

The Chain was about to be broken.

"You're not one of us," Nissa was saying to Seth. "You—"

"No!" I cried, but the wind howled, eating up the sound. Only the Kraken heard. He swung around, his pale eyes flaring.

Remember: The circle completes the Chain. It will suffer no obstacle to the linking. . . . Lallie's words. A warning. A promise.

And then I understood what had to be done. A great surge of exhilaration pounded in my heart as I fished the circle on its thong from under my shirt.

Nissa's lips moved stiffly. ". . . no longer of the Cha—"

"Don't, Nissa. *Don't say it!*" I screamed.

This time she heard. Her head snapped around, and she stared at me in astonishment. The wind began to batter at the walls and doors, and the ground to vibrate under my feet, but I ignored it. The smoke was swirling and billowing around us, and at last some of the kids began to cough and notice the flames.

"Nissa, we're the Chain," I bellowed, coughing because of the smoke. "The five of us make up the Chain and he's trying to break Seth away from us!"

"What are you talking about?" snarled Danny. "He betrayed us."

I shook my head, struggling to escape the guy holding onto me. "We almost betrayed him!"

Seth lifted his head slowly, and I held out my spare hand toward him. "Seth, you're one of us. You're part of the Chain forever, Lallie said. No matter what. Till death do us part. . . ." I laughed at the incongruous phrase, and the Kraken *cringed*!

I laughed again and felt the power flow through me. "Seth!"

He moved forward, but his father caught him by the arm. "Don't worry, Son, soon we'll be home and we can get you straightened out. You're just like your mother. You need a firm hand."

Incredibly I realized his father hadn't heard what I was saying.

"Seth! Listen to me—you are what you are," I yelled. "Lallie chose you because we need you. The Chain needs you. Not as perfect golden-boy Seth who can do no wrong, but as Seth as he really is. As Seth who knows the dark. Who can fight it because he knows what it looks like! We need you to help us chain the dark."

But he just stood there in his father's grip. Behind them more kids had noticed the fire and a hum of trepidation rose.

Desperate now, I swung to face the others, coughing hard. "Tell him!"

Danny nodded and elbowed his own captor in the stomach, wriggling free. "Seth, you silly bastard. What would we do without you?"

"Come on, Seth," Bear rumbled.

"Link hands," I shouted. I reached over and grabbed Nissa's hand on one side and Bear's on the other.

"Seth, link with us!" I cried.

But he was staring at Nissa in disbelief.

I looked at her too, and my mouth fell open. Tears were pouring down her cheeks. She made no move to hide them or wipe them away. And she was smiling as she held out her hand to Seth. He moved forward, as if she were a magnet, his feelings for her shining in his eyes. I felt no jealousy or envy, only an incredulous gladness.

The Kraken screamed at Seth's father to hold him, but Seth pulled free of his father's hands. At the same time the Kraken leaped forward to bar his way.

"Get back!" he snarled.

Seth faltered.

The smoke made it hard to see, and stung my eyes and throat. Dimly I was aware of running feet. Someone cried out in fright as a piece of timber fell in a shower of sparks.

"Fire!"

"Seth!" I cried. "Hurry, before it's too late!"

The Kraken howled like a wounded animal and swung around to smash his fist into my face. Pain exploded in my nose and the salty taste of blood filled my mouth. I could hardly see for blood and tears of pain, but I laughed because I had no other way to defend myself and laughter is one of the weapons against the darkness.

He recoiled violently, his face a mask of fear and revulsion. Buddha and the other big boys who had been holding us let go and grabbed hold of Seth, dragging him over to Mr. Karle.

Nissa reached for her sword but one of the kids running out the door kicked it, and it spun off into the clouds of smoke.

"Nathaniel! Do something!" she cried.

The circle will suffer no obstacle to the Forging . . . Lallie said in my mind, her voice light with laughter and triumph.

I looked at Bear squinting and coughing. "Sometimes you have to fight."

He began to shake his head, then he stopped, and a broad smile spread over his face as he turned to face Buddha and two other boys holding a struggling Seth.

"Piss off, wimp," Buddha sneered.

Without a word, Bear swatted him aside. He dropped like a stone, and the other boys let go and backed away fearfully. Now we were all free and I yelled to them to hurry.

There was a scream of terrible rage and pain, of fury and thwarted hatred, of evil vanquished then as Seth took Nissa's hand.

"Kill them! Kill them all!" the Kraken shrieked, almost dancing in fury.

The smoke was so bad now, I felt dizzy and disoriented.

For a fleeting second I thought I saw a group of people huddled around a campfire. They all wore long white robes.

Then I thought I was in the hillside wilderness, with the monster stalking me.

"Children should be seen and not heard," it growled.

"Nathaniel!" I reached for Nissa's free hand and closed the circle, and there was a flash of blinding, painful light as the Chain was forged anew, and Lallie's voice rang out, strong and incredibly powerful: *May the Chain prevail long!*

32

By the time the fire brigade arrived, the flames were spreading rapidly, running through the long, dry grass in a searing tide toward Cheshunt. Firemen and State Emergency Service volunteers unraveling hoses and unloading equipment shouted to make themselves heard over the howling winds as they fought to contain the blaze and prevent it from reaching the houses.

Miraculously none of us were hurt, though we had been last to leave the building as the roof collapsed. Bear had singed his ponytail, turning back to grab the bowl.

"Look," Seth said suddenly.

He was pointing to Mr. Karle who stood on the footpath, gazing over the sea of flame to the burning slaughterhouse. Great billowing clouds of smoke coiled above it into the dark sky, lit by showers of orange sparks. But his face registered neither fear nor anger. It was completely devoid of expression, his eyes empty but for twin reflections of flame.

"We beat him," Nissa murmured.

"Now, why doesn't it surprise me to find you here?" said a familiar voice.

I turned to see Mr. Sharone from the *Examiner*.

"I was listening to the police radio band for an update on the hurricane when I heard there was trouble over here," he said, looking across at the burning field.

"Hurricane?" I echoed. I looked up. In the last few minutes

the wind had dropped, but it was still dark, the clouds stirred into ragged spirals.

"You're telling me you didn't know about it?" Mr. Sharone asked incredulously. "It was on the radio all morning, and people were being asked to stay inside and batten down the hatches. For a while there it looked as if it would go right through Cheshunt, but about twenty minutes ago it sheered off and went back out to sea."

We exchanged shocked looks.

"So how come you're not wearing war paint? The police call said a group of kids in dark clothes and war paint had set the slaughterhouse on fire," Mr. Sharone probed.

"We're from a different group," Danny said with a quick grin.

Mr. Sharone smiled appreciatively. "Well, do you know how the fire started?"

Before we could think of what to say, a policeman came over.

"We can't make any sense of this. The kids in paint don't deny they are members of the gang that has been causing trouble in Willington and Saltridge, or that they were meeting in the slaughterhouse, but they claim they didn't light the fire."

"It was—" Danny began.

"It was a hurricane lamp. Someone knocked it over," Nissa said smoothly.

The policeman frowned at his notes. "What part did you play in this affair, miss?"

"My friends and I came on the whole thing by accident. We took refuge from the storm in the slaughterhouse, and there was a meeting going on. They saw us and chased us. In the struggle a lantern was broken."

The rest of us were silent with astonishment.

The policeman wrote for a bit in his notepad, then flipped back a couple of pages to read. He nodded. "There have been reports that adults were behind the gang, directing it, so to speak. We have been unable to get a name. None of the members seem able to tell us. Did you see anyone?"

I held my breath unconsciously, waiting to see what Nissa would answer.

"I didn't see anyone. Did any of you?" She looked around at us.

In turn we shook our heads, obeying the message in Nissa's eyes.

"In the past this gang has been involved in petty theft and minor violences on property and person, but they have not used weapons. Several illegal handguns were found tonight, but again, no one is prepared to say what they had been intended for."

"The storm was so loud and we were only there a second before they spotted us," Nissa said apologetically.

"Then you have no idea what was planned for tonight?"

"Today Cheshunt, tomorrow the world," Danny said.

The policeman gave him a hard look, then he wrote down Bear's address, which Nissa gave as her own, saying he might need to get a formal statement from her. He nodded to Mr. Sharone, then went away.

The journalist looked at Danny. "I'd watch my tongue, son. Police don't have much of a sense of humor."

"That's what's wrong with them," Danny said. "People who take themselves too seriously get in the habit of thinking they know everything. That makes it easy for them to miss the truth."

Mr. Sharone gave him a level look. Then he turned to me. "So, you're making like the monkeys?"

I stared at him blankly.

"See no evil, hear no evil, speak no evil," Danny explained.

The journalist gave him a respectful look. "You're a sharp kid. Ever think of journalism as a career?"

"Look," Nissa murmured, and we turned to see the policeman

who had questioned her approaching Mr. Karle. The policeman took out his notebook and spoke. The Kraken stared past him, blank-faced as an empty page. Finally the policeman took him by the arm and began to lead him away.

On the far side of the field there was a yell, and two policemen started to run. It was hard to tell because of the smoke, but I thought they were chasing Seth's father, and was glad the policeman hadn't taken Seth's name and address. It would be too much of a coincidence for a son to stumble on his father involved in a criminal conspiracy.

Seth hadn't noticed, but Nissa had. She gave me a pointed look.

"Let's get out of here," I said.

"Good idea," Nissa said ironically. "We don't want to get mixed up in any of this legal stuff. Too much we can't explain. We'll meet back here tomorrow."

"You and Seth better come to my place," Bear offered, but Nissa shook her head.

"Not me. I've got my own place."

"I better go home too," Seth said. "I'll be okay."

And so we parted.

The *Examiner* the following morning reported the arrest of the gang members, the fire, and the storm. It said a man believed to have worked with the gang had evaded police at the scene of the crime, and had not yet been located. It gave a description of Seth's father, but did not mention that he was a policeman. It also said a teacher from Three North Cheshunt High School, believed to have been involved in the incident, had been transferred to an asylum, having suffered catatonic retreat.

Mr. Sharone's byline was under the story.

"Catatonic defeat, I'd call it," Danny said when we met at the edge of the still-smoking field to finish what the fire had interrupted. It was a cold, windy afternoon, but the sky was clear and the sun shining. Danny and I had arrived first.

"It doesn't seem enough," he added, leaning on the fence. "Seth's father disappears and the Kraken goes to an asylum."

"I don't think it matters anymore," I said. "The Kraken was a vessel, and now he's empty. He can't do anything else now that the dark has gone."

"Let's go across. I want to see if I can find the torch," Danny said.

We picked our way across the field, charred underbrush crackling beneath our feet. We had just reached the blackened ruin of the slaughterhouse when Nissa came running across the field. Like Danny she wanted to find her symbol and began sifting through the mess. A moment later Bear arrived, carrying his bowl.

He said he had finally told his mother the truth about the day his little sister had fallen from the monkey bars.

"She said she knew." His voice was subdued. "Someone who had been there told her, but she had never blamed me. All these years she knew." He blinked hard and was silent for a while.

Danny yelped in delight and pounced on the torch fused into a blackened club by the heat of the fire. He held it up and looked around triumphantly.

"You think that hurricane was part of it? It was pretty odd, the way it just turned around in the nick of time."

"Hurricanes can do that," Nissa said, still poking through the debris. "You can't predict." She grunted in satisfaction and withdrew the sword from a heap of rubble, blackened but unharmed. She spat on the blade and began to polish it with her sweater.

"Where's Seth?"

"He called my place," Bear said. "His father didn't come home and the police are after him. They reckon he won't be back. Seth called his mother and she's driving over to pick him up tonight. He's going to live with her."

"But where is he now?"

Bear shrugged. "He said he had something to do, but he's going to meet us at the school." He knelt and scraped some of the powdery earth into the bowl.

"I take this healed earth to the sacred place to complete the Healing," he said softly.

Seth was waiting for us out in front of the library.

"Lallie's gone," he said without preamble.

"Gone!" Danny cried. "You mean she died?"

Seth shook his head. "I mean gone. I went to the hospital because I thought maybe she would have woken. I wanted to tell her we won, but the nurse said she had disappeared. The police have her registered as a missing person."

We stared at one another wonderingly, but strangely no one said anything. Maybe we were all thinking the same thing. Whatever Lallie was, she was not like us. She had come to heal an old wrong, and now that it was done, she was gone.

"Let's finish it," Bear said. "For Lallie."

And so we climbed into the attic, all of us for the last time together, not even worrying about whether anyone would see us. Nissa lit the lanterns and we set all of the things on the crate table together around the bowl containing the dirt. Without a word we linked hands.

"You do it," Bear said.

I took a deep breath. "We have healed the sorrowing earth. We have bound the dark. May the Chain prevail long."

And a faint breeze blew from nowhere, lifting the ash from the bowl and whirling it away.

"It's over," Nissa whispered.

But she was wrong.

That night my mother told me the whole story of my father.

"He was insanely jealous. Unstable. Violent. I learned it was better not to speak to anyone or smile . . . for their sake as well as mine. Silence was safest."

Then she had discovered herself pregnant.

"More than anything else I was scared. I thought he would kill me. He liked to have complete control of everything that happened to me. But he was happy. Ecstatic. Those nine months were the happiest days of my marriage." Her eyes shone with tears. "I really thought things might be all right."

She had sat silently a long time, holding my hand tightly. "But as soon as you were born, I realized what I had done. He was jealous of you too. Jealous of the time I spent with you. He hated it when you were dirty or fretful. I had to sometimes hold your mouth to stop your crying."

Her eyes met mine, dark with pain. "Then one day when you were about seven, we went to the zoo."

I shivered.

"The three of us were together. It was a lovely autumn day and we had a picnic lunch. He seemed in a good mood. But when we got there, things started going wrong. Little things, but it never took much. The lady at the ticket box was rude to him and a woman jostled him in the crowd."

I seemed to see the words as she spoke them. The sun pricking through the leaves as I looked up into the trees. People crowding past, laughing and joking. The quiet murmur of my mother's voice above. The exotic croaks of a peacock.

"We were sitting on a blanket and you were eating a sandwich. I was pouring a drink and you spilled some on the blanket. He reached out and slapped you. He had never hit you before.

You shouted at him. 'Bad Daddy.' I was terrified when he lunged at you, and I grabbed him and screamed for you to run. Then he punched me and knocked me unconscious. . . ."

"He tried to strangle me," I whispered hoarsely. "He tried to kill me."

She hugged me and told me the zoo authorities had managed to knock my father out and pull him off me. Finally she had given into my grandmother's urgings and divorced him. She had also charged him with assault, but this had only put him in jail for a few years. After that she had moved often so that he would not be able to find us.

"So that's why we moved so much," I murmured.

I wanted to ask why she hadn't left him sooner, but I knew the answer to that. Like the little monkey in the zoo she had simply been too frightened. I even knew why she had taken me to see his body. Not for me to get over him, as I had imagined, but so that she could be sure he was dead; that the nightmare was really over.

She hadn't told me any of this earlier because I had wakened after the incident with no memory of what had happened. She had thought it better to let the memories stay buried. Better to let sleeping dogs lie.

"I was wrong." She hesitated. "Nathaniel, I'm sorry I believed that you . . . hurt The Tod."

"It's all right," I murmured, hugging her, because I knew it hadn't been her. It had been Cheshunt, working on the darkness in her.

"It's over now," she whispered into my neck.

But she was wrong too.

Epilogue

• • •

I buried the circle where The Tod was buried in the garden.

Nissa left the sword in the attic when she moved in with Bear's family, and Seth returned his telescope before he left Cheshunt with his mother.

Bear took the bowl back to the Maritime Museum, where he goes to look at it sometimes. He told me he thought he would be a doctor or maybe a nurse when he left school. Something to do with healing.

Danny still has the torch suspended above his bed on wire. I keep telling him to take it down before it falls on his head and brains him. To which Nissa says that he hasn't got a brain, so why worry. He punches her affectionately and calls her maggot.

And me? I still dream about kissing Nissa, and one day soon I will, because I think this time she might not push me away.

Lallie said the dark would be bound until the Chain was gone and forgotten. And we are the Chain, each of us a link in it. We'll die one day—a long way off, I hope—but the dark won't be free until our names are forgotten.

That's why I decided to write this whole thing down. Because books can live forever, and as long as this book lives with my name on it, the dark will sleep.

May the Chain prevail long!

Isobelle Carmody

grew up helping to care for seven brothers and sisters, whom she kept in line by telling horror stories. Already a well-known, critically acclaimed novelist in her native Australia, Carmody has three previous books to her credit—including one that was shortlisted for the Children's Book Council of Australia Book of the Year Awards. *The Gathering* marks the U.S. publication debut of this brilliant young adult novelist who has already received a warm welcome from some of the most notable young adult authors working today.

Author Robert Cormier calls *The Gathering* "a triumph of Y.A. storytelling," while Lois Duncan says, "Isobelle Carmody may unseat Stephen King as Grand Master of the Macabre for teenage horror lovers." Author Joan Aiken also gives Carmody high marks: "I was impressed by the strong control Ms. Carmody has over her style and the way that, like Susan Cooper, she combines actuality with a sense of mysterious threat and impending catastrophe." And according to Joan Lowery Nixon, "Isobelle Carmody's strong, sympathetic characters and chilling suspense blend to create a novel so intense and horrific that the spell of evil lingers after the last page has been read."